UNDER THE SYCAMORE TREE

TIM CONNOLLY

Under the Sycamore Tree
Copyright Year: 2024

Copyright Notice: by Tim Connolly, all rights reserved.

This book or any portion thereof may not be reproduced or used in any manner whatsoever without express written permission from the author.

This is a work of fiction. All of the characters, names, incidents, organizations, and dialogue in this novel are either the products of the author's imagination or are used fictitiously.

Front Cover Art Credit: Dan Connolly

Dedicated to Detectives Everywhere

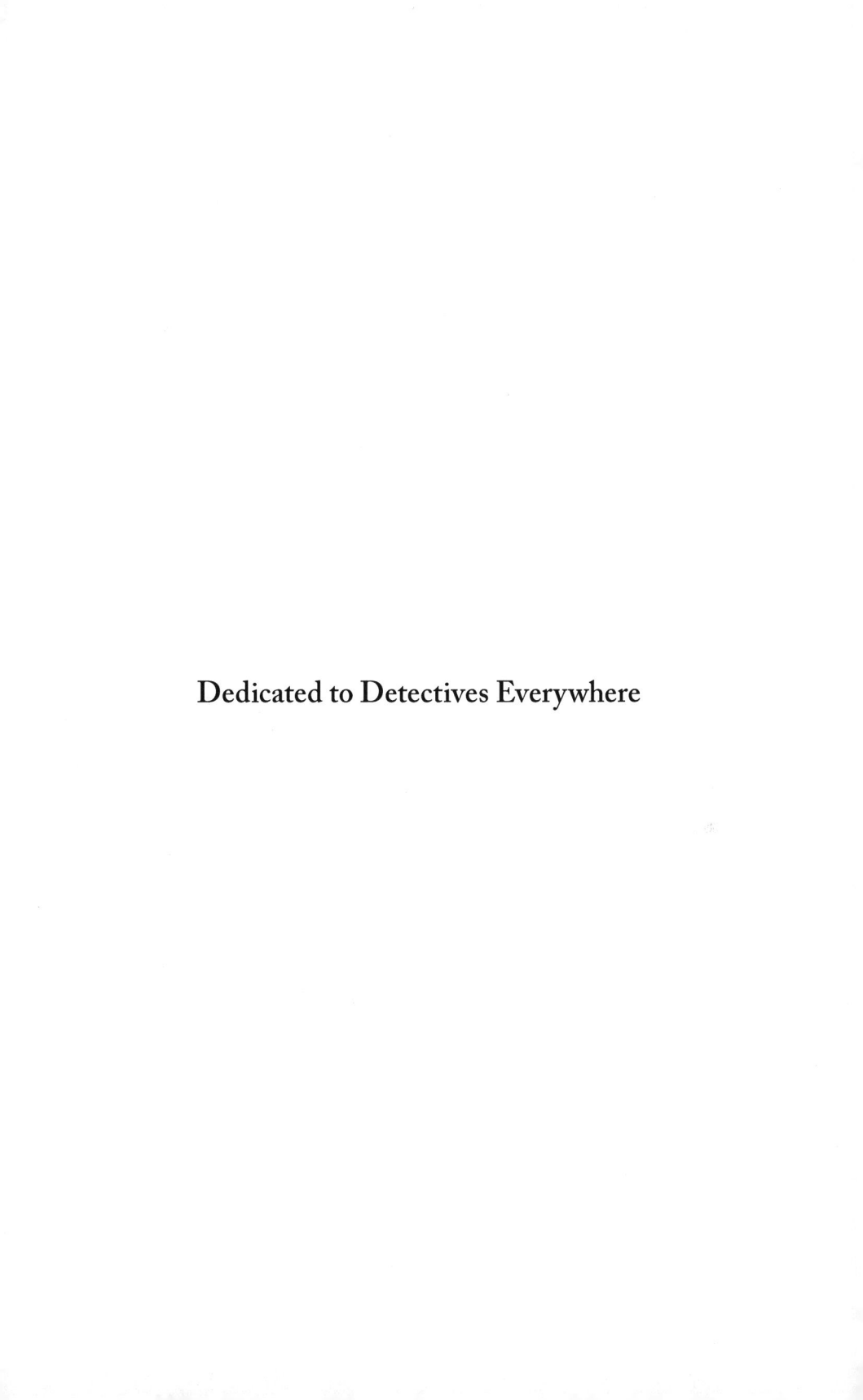

PROLOGUE

"Mr. Jackson, what can I get you? I was just about to close."

"Sorry, but do I know you?"

"No, I guess not. I'm Allison Breckinridge. As a kid, my family liked going to your ranch when the calves debut."

"Glad you enjoyed the visits. Always a special time for us. I'll have a black and white shake."

On his way home after entertaining some prospective bison meat distributors, Jackson detoured into Dairy Queen to satisfy his sweet tooth. It was 9:50 p.m. No one else was being served.

"You alone."

"Yes, my co-worker just left. Had a date. I'm left to clean up but it shouldn't take long."

With the shake in hand, as she began to wipe down the counter, he looked outside and didn't see any other vehicles. Engaging with her, he found that she was in no particular rush, even asking if he hired part-timers, as she had an interest in becoming a veterinarian. About to leave, he was surprised when she asked if he could drive her home since her house was in the same direction as the ranch, saving her dad a trip.

"He's probably out on the sofa."

"No problem." As he heard her on her cell tell her mother that she had a ride and not mentioning him by name, he thought his time had come.

"Mr. Jackson, where are you going?" Allison asked, nervously, when he had detoured in another direction.

"There's something I have to pick up, only minutes away."

With his truck going down a narrow single lane she was unfamiliar with and now into woods, she panicked. "Please turn around! My parents will be worried."

Eyeing his stone-cold, hardened face, she pulled out her iPhone. But in a flash, he grabbed it and tossed it out the driver's side window, into thick shrubs hugging the lane.

CHAPTER 1

For Julie and boyfriend Justin, they had to pretend to be satisfied with sleeping on the high-riser in the cottage's main room. The adults had two of the four bedrooms upstairs and their siblings, his brother and her sister, had the two downstairs. But Julie was okay with the arrangements. Had to be. It was all a charade anyway. Her mother wouldn't permit her to sleep with Justin in her company, but yet allowed her to come to the cottage alone with him at times. But with Justin's parents here this weekend, she considered it a win that she wasn't forced to sleep with her sister. With curtains for bedroom doors, every sound could be heard by all. For Julie, even fooling around under the blanket risked setting off the squeaking high-riser.

Determined to lose her virginity to Justin before leaving for Quinnipiac University in two weeks, Julie had considered making an excuse to remain at home. But, as she mulled options, she figured she could have it all - an enjoyable final cottage weekend and alone time with Justin.

Once the golfers – her father, Mr. Edwards, and Justin's brother - departed for golf, she admired the face of her high school sweetheart. She recalled when she had made a play for the good-looking guy in art class who was hailed as the second-coming of Pablo Picasso for his unique ability to weave dramatic colors into unimaginable creations. But as much as art faculty pushed him to attend the Rhode Island School of Design, the math instructors won out in promoting engineering at

Rensselaer Polytechnic Institute. For her, the six-hour distance between colleges meant swimming against the tide to maintain a relationship.

Staring at his perfect nose and thick eyebrows, she got out of bed, put on her bathing suit, retrieved her towel, and went down to the lake. With the next-door neighbors away, she soaked up the quiet before diving in, swimming out to the raft and back, before washing. Her skin tingled. She didn't know if this was the result of the cool morning breeze or what was to come.

Drying off, she wrapped the towel around, laid her bathing suit on the deck railing, and climbed back into bed. Reaching over, she touched Justin's cheek and took his hand to her breast.

"What are you doing?" he said, trying his best to whisper. He jerked her hand away.

"How about a kayak ride?" she whispered back, pushing close. "The golfers left and the rest will be stirring soon."

"Put your clothes on."

Extending her hand down to his groin, she felt him respond but he moved her hand away and got up.

"Let's go kayaking," she said.

"I'd prefer hopping in the car for breakfast."

When she flipped the sheet to the side, breakfast was no longer the priority.

"Are you going to paddle this time?" he asked. "I can't do all the work on an empty stomach."

"Look, get the kayak ready. I'll mix up some Muesli."

Before he exited, she whispered, "Get all of the spiders out." Justin smirked, recalling their kayak ride last summer when she jumped up, shouting madly upon seeing a spider, causing the kayak to flip. While she managed to hold her cell above water, his found the bottom of the pond.

Justin devoured the Muesli and glass of chocolate milk. "What about the beds?"

"Collapsing them will make too much noise."

"What else do I need to carry?" He held the life jackets.

"Here, take the water bottles."

She put towels into a beach bag, along with a few protein bars, suntan lotion, and an airline pillow.

Excited, Justin recalled last summer when Julie guided him under the small bridge passageway under Route 165 to the Rhode Island side of Beach Pond, where no motor boats were permitted and only a few houses existed. The entire back end was uninhabited, composed of tall, stately pines. He had enjoyed steering the kayak to the serene far end, where Julie directed him to a small inlet. According to her, she was sent to find her missing older sister Danielle who had gone off with her boyfriend and future husband. Julie had seen them venture under the bridge and spotted the yellow kayak along the water's edge. Pulling hers up alongside, she said she spotted her sister's naked behind up in the air and had to cough to get her attention.

In that same spot last summer, Justin first saw Julie naked. However, before removing her bathing suit, she expressed that intercourse was a "no-no," that she wasn't ready. He respected her decision and, especially so, after she satisfied him. But recent, near misses marked their alone time. Only last week, with her parents and sister out, Julie asked Justin to make love to her in her bedroom. Later, he kicked himself for spurning the offer, fearing her parents return.

What he didn't know was Julie's determination not to go to Quinnipiac a virgin. And with her flashing herself in the cottage, he got what this kayak ride was all about. Arriving in the same deserted location, he pulled the kayak up and out of view and followed her to the fallen brown, soft pine needles. Laying two towels on them and the soft airline pillow under her head, she held out her arms. Nervous, he surveyed the surrounding area one last time.

"We're alone," she said. "Think of this as the Garden of Eden and you and me as Adam and Eve." She removed her top to get his full attention.

Kneeling, Justin couldn't care less about anything, focusing on Julie's great body. With her breasts heaving with every breath, he pulled her bottoms off.

"Justin, look at me." When he did, she implored, "Be slow."

She didn't know how much this may hurt. But she had built in that it might but would do her best not to let that interfere. With the moment she had been dreaming about moments away, her body trembled, even more when he removed his t-shirt and bathing suit and she saw how aroused he was. She held out her arms. "Hold me."

Lowering himself on top of her, he wrapped his arms around her upper torso, uniting them behind her, allowing her breasts to affix to his chest. Freeing his arms, he kissed her passionately and ran his fingers through her hair before kissing her nipples. As he reached down between her legs, not only didn't she object but she spread them. Reaching for his bathing suit, he took hold of the condom.

They had gone far enough. Alfie Doolittle and Goobie Crenshaw had waited patiently for more than a year. Last year one of their hunting cameras caught the young couple embracing and kissing, minus clothes. Also, within the camera's range, they spotted a yellow kayak. On a scouting mission for the kayak, they traced it to a red cottage not far from the Rhode Island border. Every summer weekend since that time, they pulled into the closed Rhode Island Beach across from the red cottage and aimed a telescope to see if the young lovers were spending the weekend. Last evening, they caught sight of them. While the kids didn't have sex the first time around, they expected full blown action on their next voyage. Waiting in camouflage, in a blind some 50 yards away, their patience now paid off.

Justin was the first to see the two men with shotguns rushing toward them. As he and Julie attempted to put their bathing suits on, they heard, "leave them be."

Covering his groin, Justin asked, "What do you want?"

They laughed. "Why, the same as you. Young lady, let that bikini be and lie back down. Sonny, you stay right where you are if you know what's good for you."

With the larger of the two leaving toward the water, Julie considered screaming. But just as she entertained that thought, they were told to put their bathing suits on and wasted no time doing so.

With the formidable guy able to hoist the kayak alone, he dropped it near them and was told by the other, "Go back and scratch out the footprints as best you can." As he did, the other secured masking tape.

"Leave us alone!" Justin implored, before his mouth was taped over.

"Just be a good boy."

With the life jackets firmly tied around the kayak seats, Justin was ordered to pick up the back end. He considered running. He figured that he could make it to the woods and scoot around to the road, with these two in no shape to catch him. But he couldn't leave Julie.

As he carried the kayak down a narrow path leading away from Beach Pond, he peered behind. Julie was sobbing with a pistol aimed at her back.

CHAPTER 2

When Anne Stapleton came downstairs at 8:12 a.m., she saw that the high riser wasn't made and figured that Julie and Justin had gone swimming or maybe took the speed boat out to watch the sunrise and/or water ski. But she nixed that in seeing the speedboat moored.

Pouring coffee that the golfers brewed, set up the night before, she saw that Julie and Justin left cereal bowls in the sink. Typical Julie, she thought. She didn't know where she had gone wrong. Her other daughters always chipped in but Julie was on to the next thing without ever considering that others had to pick up after her. The delivery of numerous 'citizen of the household' messages didn't sink in and Julie only made faces when advised to marry rich.

Taking her coffee out to the deck, Anne sat at the picnic table and reviewed a text from her oldest daughter Danielle that her grandson had settled into kindergarten, accompanied by photos of him smiling and interacting with his teachers and playmates. Motherhood had turned Danielle into a worrier. In college, she studied hard and played hard, dating a handful of boyfriends, before settling on one much like her dad, a good provider, husband, and father.

Taking an iPhone photo of the sparkling pond, she sent it to Danielle with the message, 'hope you'll join us soon.' At the edge of the deck, she noticed the kayak missing and now knew where Julie and Justin had gone. She scanned what little she could see of the pond but couldn't spot them.

After checking Google News headlines, she heard movement inside.

"Get a good night's sleep?" she asked, as Joan came through the sliding door.

"I did. Slept like a log until the sun shone in. But I did fall back into a sound sleep."

"Those are the best kind."

With a coffee mug in hand, Joan walked to the edge of the deck. "You're so fortunate to have this place."

"This palace?" Anne said, kidding, knowing that she had to forewarn visitors of simple cottage living.

"I'd never change a thing. So charming. How long did John's parents have it?"

"His great grandfather built it so he enjoyed summers here with his mother and brother, while his dad joined on weekends. When his brother got killed by a drunk driver, the place was his. We almost sold it when he got reassigned to Cleveland."

"That would have been a mistake."

"Yes, I'm glad we didn't pull the plug." A pause. "Julie and Justin are out kayaking. Or I should say that Justin is kayaking for likely Julie is being chauffeured like Queen Cleopatra on the Nile."

Joan smiled. "That's the way it should be. I'm sure Justin is loving every minute."

Neither said anything about what was top of mind: whether their children would maintain a relationship after going off to college. They both hoped if there was a break-up, that it would be amicable because they had become good friends.

Back inside, Anne smoothed the beds and lowered the high riser, as Joan washed the dishes.

"I'm going for a jog. Wish to come?" Anne asked.

"No, you go. These legs require more caffeine."

An hour later the house was abuzz. April finally rose, the golfers had returned after their typical nine holes and diner breakfast stop, and Anne got back from her run.

"What did you have to eat?" Anne asked her husband.

"A Soho omelet. You wouldn't believe how good it was. The goat cheese is amazing."

A new diner, Hannah's, had opened on the route back from the golf course. Discovering it two weeks ago, they continued to rave about it. She would have to check it out.

"April, up for eggs?" she asked.

"I'll pass. In the mood for a kayak ride."

"Afraid you'll have to wait."

April walked to the end of the deck and back. "What time did they head off?"

"Not here at eight."

John eyed the clock. "Shouldn't be long. They've been out a while."

A half hour later, concerned, Anne text her daughter, 'where are you guys?' before expressing her concern to John.

"Could be she doesn't have service. Let's give it another half hour and, if they're not back, I'll look for them in the speedboat."

With that half hour passing, John and Dave whisked off. They proceeded to go around the pond, in various inlets to ensure that they didn't miss the kayak. After circling, they returned.

"No luck," John shouted up to anxious wives.

"Leaves only the Rhode Island side," Anne said to Joan, staring in that direction. "Let's drive over and have a look."

After parking her SUV at an entry point for boats, Anne led Joan over the causeway, where they could see a great distance. Only sign of life was a fisherman.

Anne yelled to get his attention. Pulling in his line, he rowed over.

"Our children are missing. Have you seen two teens in a yellow kayak?"

"Sorry, I haven't."

"How long have you been out?"

"Since about eight."

"So sorry to have troubled you."

It was now 11:30 a.m. Still no message from Julie.

Back at the cottage, Anne was beside herself. "John, I'm worried."

Telling Anne to take the speed boat out for another ride, in case they missed them, he and Dave loaded the row boat to check the Rhode Island end of the pond, as he knew you could only see so far from the causeway. Still without success on either end, Anne called their good friend Pete Lewinski who lived year-round two houses down. Long divorced, with a lot of time on his hands, the Navy veteran served as an unofficial caretaker for their cottage and a knower of everything Beach Pond. He tested the water for years, knew everything about its wildlife. Handy, he helped neighbors fix their walls and properties when the pond was lowered every few years.

Hearing Anne out, Pete had no answers. He had gone out for his Dunkin' run but didn't see the kids or anything unusual. The only thing he could think of is that they went off somewhere to fool around and fell asleep. But he wasn't going to float that.

"Give them another half hour and then let's contact officials." A pause. "I'll have a look."

In his speed boat and exploring spots that lovers frequented, Pete came up dry. He stalled the boat and shrugged to John and Anne, after which John rang the constable who promptly notified the state police. An hour later a helicopter hovered and an hour after that, a missing person's alert was issued. About 4:30 p.m., Anne presented Julie's sweats and Joan served up Justin's tee shirt to four police officers who had come with search dogs.

Before dark, the Stapletons and Edwards received a text: 'dogs found scent at far end of RI side of Beach Pond. Scent ended on dirt road.'

CHAPTER 3

Benny Fidalgo set his alarm for a 6 a.m. Blacksburg Police Chief Thompson had called for a 7 a.m. meeting with he and fellow detective Trish McGlucas, more than an hour before Town Hall sprung to life. Diagnosed with insomnia in college, there was little chance of needing the alarm. He watched several episodes of Peaky Blinders until he heard Charlotte stir upstairs and started the coffee before heading up to shower and change.

It had been a week since the four Apache gang members were taken to prison for gang-raping Deidre Esposito. Her leap from her third-floor dorm window no longer a mystery. And while Benny received volleys of compliments, including a more formal salute at a New York City mayoral event, he continued to kick himself for not unravelling the case sooner. In particular, he would have placed Deidre's uncle, Gus Esposito, under surveillance. That would have saved Juan Gutierrez's life. He couldn't get the image of Juan in that electrical substation, tortured, with his neck snapped.

Kissing Charlotte goodbye and leaving with his favorite New York Giants mug of coffee, he tried to guess Thompson's big reveal. He didn't think any of the other detectives were working on anything major. And, Dennis "Murph" Murphy, his detective colleague and hub of every piece of gossip and buzz, couldn't even venture a guess.

Waiting for Trish in the detective room, he headed to Thompson's office at two minutes to 7 a.m. figuring maybe she was calling in.

Finding Thompson with his head down, engrossed in paperwork, he was told to take a seat.

Doing so, Thompson fiddled with a budget spreadsheet and ignored him. He was used to it. In his three years serving the Blacksburg PD, he had his ups and downs with Thompson, more downs. Reminded often by Trish that it was the chief's nature to be surly, he felt he suffered more abuse than the others and often pondered whether Thompson regretted hiring him. Yet, no matter what, he remained loyal, his Navy Seal days ingrained into him.

Thompson, he felt, at 64, was becoming more and more isolated. It didn't help that he had to use a cane to support his arthritic knee. He was actually surprised to being summoned, in that Thompson didn't go with Trish alone to tackle whatever was being served up.

"Remind me," Thompson said, "when are you leaving for vacation?"

"Embark for Portugal in three weeks."

Expecting Thompson to elaborate, he didn't. And now he feared that whatever this was might interfere. While he longed to return to Portugal, it was Charlotte who needed the break from the stresses of ER nursing. Yesterday, she cried in telling him about their inability to save a six-year-old who had fallen from a second-floor window onto a spiked metal fence. She rarely took her job home but as he held her, sobbing, she relayed that "the hole above his eye was so deep and gross that my knees wobbled." Also, he had his excited mother to think of. Yesterday, she texted that relatives in Funchal had arranged for a special Madeira Botanical Garden tour.

As Trish entered, Thompson asked her to close the door. "Anything wrong at home?"

She looked at her watch. "Shoot me for being three minutes late."

He shoved the spreadsheets to the side. "What I'm about to disclose is highly confidential. Do I have your word you'll keep this private?"

Both nodded.

"We believe some of our officers are on the take."

As they sat a bit stunned, absorbing what he said, Trish spoke first. "I assume you have solid evidence?"

"That I do. Hold on." He lifted his cell. "I have to take this."

"Want us to leave."

"No, will only be a minute."

Being the daughter of a NYC Police Captain, Trish understood the terrain they were about to enter. Her father described takers as "dead to me." "It's a cancer," he said. "Needs to be excised quickly to prevent good cops from following bad." Yet, while her father took a hard line, she knew it ate him up, for many accepting payments were friends, family men, some whose fathers and grandfathers served the department. "High achieving guys, many I respected, begged for their jobs," he had related, "and there was nothing I could or would do about it."

Trish couldn't imagine deep scale corruption in Blacksburg, for she had been a town cop for several years before being promoted to detective. She felt she would have gotten wind of something pervasive, though she also knew she wouldn't have been approached. In fact, stopped for driving 43 miles per hour in a 25-mile-an-hour zone, she forced the rookie town cop to give her the ticket. When word got around, even her close colleagues thought she was nuts. Nonetheless, it served as a telltale signal that she wouldn't cross the line.

"Why do you need us?" she asked, once Thompson disengaged. "Isn't it easier to assign a special investigator."

"Don't you think I've considered that? Due to our size, the investigator would be outed as soon as he or she entered the building."

Benny doubled up on Trish's initial question. "How reliable is this?"

"Hold that. I need to know if you two are in."

Thompson's eyes darted from Trish to Benny and back again.

Trish broke the ice. "Don't exactly feel comfortable with it."

"That's to be expected."

Thompson anticipated Trish's uneasiness. He didn't even consider Murph for he was familiar with just about everyone in the department, would be anguished in getting involved, and might be tempted to look the other way. Trish, he knew, wouldn't; and Fidalgo, for sure.

"I'll assist." Trish felt it is what her father would expect, though dreaded the day when the spouse of a fired cop dressed her down at Shop Rite.

"What about you Fidalgo?"

"I'd like to know the full scope, what's expected of us."

"I have an officer who has come forward with evidence. And I'll expect the two of you to dig, wherever it goes."

"Then, I'm in."

"Good. Let's not waste time."

To ensure secrecy, Thompson arranged for a meeting in a student parking lot at Bergen Community College. In pulling in, Trish saw red in eyeing Patrol Officer Sheila Morgan. She regarded Morgan as nothing more than a drama queen who played men to her advantage. And she still stewed over Morgan's inappropriate interference in the Deidre Esposito investigation, when she had approached witnesses without approval. Only six months on the force, Morgan had Thompson and so many others wrapped around her fingers, courtesy of curves that a cop's uniform couldn't hide. Alongside Morgan was Blacksburg DA Cody Barrett.

"Morgan," Thompson began, "tell them what you told me."

Morgan revealed that she was approached by Officer Tom Carney three weeks ago in a pre-arranged, after hours meeting in a Suffern bar. Carney complained that he needed a second job to raise his family. He said, "what's it come to when you can't afford to live in the town you're working." She said that conversation veered to receiving a pay boost without hurting anyone. When she asked him to explain, she was told Russians would pay to have them look the other way on a prostitution and escort enterprise. "Carney labeled it easy hay…no harm, no foul."

"Why would Carney clue you in?" Trish questioned.

Morgan shrugged. "Maybe because I was assigned to him as a rookie, feeling he couldn't hide the activity from me…or maybe he felt I could use the money."

"What money do you need?" Trish snapped, knowing Morgan was single.

Morgan abruptly turned to Thompson. "I don't have to take this shit from her. Here I'm trying to do the right thing and she's got a bug up…"

"Ok, let's get a grip," Thompson replied, before she could complete the sentence. "McGlucas, Morgan isn't part of the problem, she's part of the solution. Morgan, go on."

"Carney knew I moved into a new apartment and needed furnishings."

Trish couldn't help but wonder if Morgan had something else going on with Carney.

"Go on," Thompson said.

"He said I'd receive five hundred a month to start."

"Did he say who else was involved?" Benny asked.

"I asked but he wouldn't disclose."

"How did you leave it with him?"

"I told him I needed to think about it."

"When was this?"

"Three weeks ago. He's approached me twice since. I'm afraid to decline."

DA Barrett hadn't weighed in. He had accepted the meeting to hear this out. Having worked with McGlucas many times before, he was taken back with her harshness toward Morgan and didn't know what he was missing. But in speaking to Morgan for 10 minutes before their arrival, he got the sense that she had her head on straight and obviously Thompson had lined up behind her. And he hadn't heard anything that would deter the County from moving forward.

"You're committed to this?" he asked.

Morgan nodded.

"Are you aware of what this means?"

She frowned. "I'm not following you."

"Let me back up. It's one thing if this turns out to be with Carney. But consider that it extends ten deep in the department, twenty deep? That's a quarter of the force. Significant penetration. Even with a successful conclusion, you'll be vilified and defamed and might find it difficult to continue." A pause. "And let's say this leaks during the investigation and you're exposed…no telling what may happen to you." A pause. "Are you still interested in moving forward?"

Morgan mulled what he said. "But how do I back out?"

"You tell Chief Thompson that you misinterpreted what Carney said. He will be obligated to look into it but without you."

She shook her head. "I can't back out. I might as well turn in my badge."

"Ok, then, accept the five hundred," he said. "Feed Carney that you can use the cash. We'll take our cues from that meeting. We'll not wire you the first time around, in case he suspects something. We'll do so after. Does that sound reasonable to everyone?"

Getting nods, he added, "Morgan needs one point of contact, someone always available.

"Fidalgo's her go-to," Thompson said. He would have preferred Trish but, under the circumstances, that would end poorly.

"Good," Carney said. "Any questions?"

Though upset at not being chosen by Thompson, Trish knew why and had to accept it.

Delighted with the arrangement, Sheila faced Benny. "Can we meet later?"

"Sure."

"Text when you have time and we can pick a secluded place."

With Morgan departing, Trish dwelled on her parting comment and realized that she may soon have Benny eating out of her hand too.

"I'm assuming you believe we ride Morgan as long as possible," she said to DA Carney, "to get her well established on the inside. But I believe relying on her is going to blow up in our faces."

"Where are you going with that?" Thompson said, annoyed.

"Just that we don't know whose she's sleeping with or…"

"McGlucas, you're off base."

"Listen," Carney said, interrupting. "Fidalgo will brief her on what to do and what not to do. She's going to need a lot of guidance. She has no idea what's she's in for and will need our support. There's no telling where this goes. Let's err on the side of caution. If it takes a year or two, so be it."

Driving away, Sheila Morgan was glad she snagged Fidalgo. Since joining the department, she has received only bad vibes from McGlucas. She crossed it off to being 10 years younger and supplanting McGlucas as 'the looker' within the department. What did it matter? She had the war hero, crime solving Fidalgo to mentor her through this and enjoyed that he had so many of her peers twisted up.

She also didn't care that he had paid no attention to her, even though she did her darndest to flash her Miss Oregon frame whenever she passed him in the hall. She also had cleverly brought Fidalgo into the investigation, after Thompson felt it wiser to assign only McGlucas.

Her carefully delivered message to the chief: Fidalgo would take no prisoners. It worked.

Now together, Fidalgo would take notice. They all do, if they had any trace of testosterone. She felt certain it wouldn't be long before Thompson stepped down as chief and she wished to hitch her wagon to the rising star. She knew what worked in Oregon.

As Trish drove off, still steaming, Benny checked his iPhone. Noticing a voicemail from his brother-in-law, he caught the panic: 'Julie's missing. She left kayaking with her boyfriend several hours ago. Police search on.'

CHAPTER 4

Terribly shaken, Julie and Justin did as they were told, keeping quiet and walking in single file away from the pond. When they came upon a pick-up truck, Alfie checked the tape around their mouths and tied their wrists before ordering Justin to lie on the floor and Julie across the back seat. While Alfie sat sideways in the front to keep an eye on them, Goobie went back and retrieved the camouflage blind, two small folding seats, and a cooler, before hoisting the yellow kayak into the cab and covering it with a tarp.

As they neared exiting the woods, Alfie walked to the main road to ensure that no joggers, cyclists, dog walkers or anyone else around to witness their departure. Waved on, Alfie jumped in and they exited. Less than 10 minutes later, they entered another off-road and, before long, were deep in the woods.

Lying prone and unable to see much of anything, except the tops of trees, and after navigating some rough terrain, the truck came to a stop and Julie and Justin found themselves outside and facing what appeared to be a simple, grey-weathered cabin.

"This is your Little House on the Prairie," Alfie said.

Escorted in, Julie and Justin saw that the cabin had but one main room, with a pot belly stove, a card table, several folding chairs, and a mattress covered with deer skins.

To Julie, this had all the makings of a retreat house for men up to no good.

"Don't fret little lady…sit on that mattress and get comfortable and we'll look after ya…at least for a while. I'm going to take off the tape but, if you scream, you'll get a whupping. Goobie there wouldn't mind tanning your hide."

Grinning and oafish, Goobie removed his belt and snapped it into the air.

"That's my boy. We have a whipping tree out back. After a little raw flesh, we always find our bovines very accommodating. Isn't that right Goob?"

"Let me give her a little taste."

"Not yet. She'll be no trouble. We're reasonable folk."

Julie tried to speak.

"Little lady, I'll remove the tape so you can tell us what you feels important."

In pulling off the duct tape, tearing, she said, "I have to pee."

"Oh, so you have to go."

"Let me take her," Goobie offered.

"No. You stay here. She'll not be able to go with a big lug like you staring at her."

Around the back of the cabin, when Julie seemed unsure of where to squat, Alfie voiced, "One place is as good as another."

Julie leaned on a tree for support yet had difficulty. With her hands restrained, she couldn't shift her bathing suit side to side to lower it.

Admiring her, Alfie couldn't wait for later. "You surely had to go."

Struggling to pull the suit up, Goobie said, "Let me help you there, little lady."

Putting the gun inside his pants, Julie moved quickly to do it herself. Returning to the cabin, she sat closer to Justin who was pleased to see her back unharmed.

"I have to go too," he said.

"Goob, take him and don't lower the gun. Missy here was polite but I don't trust him."

Exiting, Justin took in the surrounding area. While some trees existed around the cabin, it was fairly open, except for a few bushes and a fallen tree, until the wood line, some 40 yards away.

"What are you going to do with us?" he asked.

"I don't rightfully know. I has but one vote."

Justin attempted to draw him out. "How many votes are there?"

"Never mind that. That's far enough."

With the wood line now only 20 yards away, it was very tempting to make a run for it but Justin couldn't leave Julie.

Led back inside, he saw that Julie's wrists had been fastened to a loop eight feet up on the wall. Masking tape had been reapplied over her mouth. Justin went along with being taped and affixed, just grateful nothing had been done to them thus far.

"We are going to leave you here for a bit," Alfie said. "But don't worry your little heads off. We will be back shortly for the party is in your honor."

Hearing that, Goobie asked. "Maybe just a taste?"

"Nothing doing. That taste will turn into full blown, heated pleasure and spoil all the fun."

"Let me tell them about the party?"

Alfie seemed to give it thought. "I guess. It doesn't have to be a surprise party."

Goobie hunched lower, between Julie and Justin. "This here party is going to be a continuation of the one you was having, naked as the day you were born. Maybe we'll have ya doing some dancing."

Alfie interjected. "That's enough. Just know little lady that with the grand finale you are going to get lit."

As soon as they exited, Julie lost it. Waiting until he could hear the truck no longer, Justin stretched his mouth up and down and side to side to undo one side of the masking tape. Encouraging Julie to do the same, she dislodged hers.

"Justin, they are going to rape me."

"Don't lose hope. Let me try and pull the loop from the wall."

Yanking furiously, he couldn't dislodge the metal ring and had to give up when the skin tore from his wrists.

Julie had lost all hope. "He wants us to continue with what we were doing…did you hear him?"

Justin heard it all. He also knew they wouldn't be rescued for some time. They had travelled deep in woods, maybe even a few miles. He heard branches thrashing against the side of the truck and the splashing of water as they navigated through many ditches. This suggested that only off-road, heavy-duty vehicles could make their way back here.

"I'll tell them that our families will pay anything," he said, trying to lift her spirits. "One of them has to be reasonable."

Vulnerable, in her bikini, Julie knew their gawking was only a precursor to what was to come. "Justin, I'm afraid of what they're going to do to me."

Futilely tugging again, he quit when he could no longer stand the pain and not having moved the loop at all.

When Julie began screaming, Justin joined in, hoping to connect with someone. After many attempts, they gave up.

"I'm so sorry," Julie said, tearful.

"For what?"

"For getting us into this mess."

"Nonsense. Who knew we'd wind up with these sickos."

"Do you think there's any chance they're after a ransom?" Julie asked.

"Probably calling our parents now."

Hours later Justin and Julie heard truck engines, doors slamming, and elevated voices.

CHAPTER 5

Not wishing to disclose anything to Trish just yet about his niece's disappearance, until he had a chance to better assess what was going on, Benny hurried into Town Hall. There, he secured a small conference room and returned his brother-in-law's call. With Julie missing, Benny worried about the impact to his sister's heart, which had been weakened by Kawasaki disease at age four. The fact that John had outreached was maybe an indication of how distraught she was or a case that she was still mad at him. It turned out to be the latter.

At an anniversary party for his parents at an uncle's home, John and others had had more than their fill of Jamesons when one suggested an arm-wrestling contest. Despite the urging, Benny knew better than to participate. He didn't even want to be a bystander, fully knowing that these affairs often turned ugly, with egos hurt at the very least. Although his nieces and nephews were sent to lure him, he remained content on the patio talking with his dad about the Portuguese national soccer team's prospects in the World Cup.

But in heading to the bathroom, the arm wrestlers spotted him and began cackling. When Benny's mother told them to quiet, one of them declared that she had raised a coward. Hearing that, Benny told Charlotte that they were leaving, only his mother begged them to stay for coffee and Pasteis de Nata, which she had especially made for him. Miguel, his brother, taking it all in, encouraged his older brother to arm wrestle, fully knowing the outcome. But Benny held fast.

In the kitchen saying his goodbyes, he overheard Charlotte say "shut up," followed by trumped up cackling. Springing from the kitchen, he told John to sit. They locked grips. Seven seconds later John was on his way to the hospital with a broken arm. With his sister screaming at him, he and Charlotte exited hastily.

"We are beside ourselves," John expressed, filling Benny in.

Having been to John's family cottage, Benny was familiar with the landscape and had used the yellow kayak himself. Hearing about hounds being deployed, it brought back their successful use in finding the bodies of the deceased boys in the psych center investigation.

"Have the investigators told you of the plan from here?"

"They have helicopters searching for the kayak and have scuba divers in case it had been sunk. And they are speaking to the few homeowners on that side of the pond."

Hearing the extent of the rescue mission, Benny felt it comprehensive enough. With the state police involved, he pondered what value he could add. But he couldn't very well say that.

"How is Anne?" With nothing said, he looked at his watch. "I can be there in five or six hours if you like."

"Benny, I apologize for what…"

"Stop there, John. It's just I've been handed a major assignment. Let me speak to my boss."

In the detective room, Benny let Trish know what happened. "Thompson's going to blow a cork."

"Never mind him. This is family. Your sister needs you. I'll cover here. As Carney said, we could be at this for years. And I know you… you'll be miserable here."

Outside in the hall, Benny reached out to FBI Agent Hank Russo who he worked with and befriended on the serial killings at the Blacksburg

Psychiatric facility. Russo provided the name of Dom Scalia, the Rhode Island FBI lead, and said he would notify him as a way of introduction.

Before ending the call, Russo had to message the bull dog he came to know and respect. "It will be better for you to be the family advocate and not directly involved."

"You know me. How can I sit still?"

Russo couldn't come down harder, for he knew that if it was a member of his family kidnapped, he'd be engaged.

"We're talking rural America in those parts. You have your lake owning crowd and the leave-me-be crowd. With the latter, many are carrying."

"Appreciate it, Hank, as always."

Benny knew what Hank was intimating. At the Beach Pond cottage a year ago, he had been sent to pick up pizza and, while waiting outside, a woman exited and proceeded to throw her screaming young daughter into a rusty Chevy truck. A few minutes later this big redneck comes out with a pizza box. While holding a slice, he reaches in and smacks the child, after which he and the woman eat the pizza on the hood, vape whatever, and drink from brown paper bags. When the kid attempted to join them, the mother flung her into the backseat.

Benny opted not to interfere; almost did when the redneck cast a menacing look his way. After he left, he kept thinking about that little girl's future.

Approaching Thompson, he expected an argument but was surprisingly told to take all the time he needed. He pondered whether Trish had text him to pave the way and offer double-duty on the police corruption matter.

Reaching Charlotte at Jacobi Hospital's ER, in the middle of her shift, he was a little bit taken back, in that she didn't want him to go.

"Listen, I'm upset and feel for John and Anne, but I know you. Let the police handle it. Didn't Gus Simeone get engaged when his niece committed suicide and look what happened there."

"Please don't lump me with that bastard."

Benny filled the silence. "Listen, the first forty-eight hours are crucial. I'm bringing clothes for only a few days. I'll call you tonight."

"Listen. I don't have a good feeling about this. They wheeled a Bronx detective in here last night with a stab wound that punctured his lung and all I could think of is you."

"You know I can handle myself."

"He thought so too."

Benny thought of their Iberian trip and the need for Charlotte to get away.

"Nothing's going to happen to me. I love you. I'll call tonight."

CHAPTER 6

After packing an overnight bag, refilling his water bottle, taking a few protein bars, and stopping at the deli for a roast beef sandwich, it took Benny three hours to drive to Beach Pond. Checking his GPS, he was glad the roads were fairly clear and opted to take Route 95, which was 10 minutes quicker than the Hutchinson and Merritt Parkways through Middletown.

Arriving at dusk, he almost missed the turnoff for Beach Pond Extension and did wind up driving past the cottage, forgetting that it had been newly sided with a brown exterior instead of the striking red and white Candyland version. Parking next to an unmarked vehicle, he left his belongings in the car, not quite sure of the reception from his sister Anne.

Greeted by his brother-in-law John as he entered the cottage, he saw his sister Anne in conversation with a state police representative on a loveseat, with their backs to him, and spotted who he presumed to be the parents of Julie's boyfriend on the high-riser.

"Inspector Falcone, this is Anne's brother Benny who I spoke to you about."

While the crew-cut, imposing Falcone, who had to be at least six-five, with perfectly square shoulders, rose to shake hands, Benny saw that Anne remained seated with her back to him. He had his answer as to whether his sister could get past the arm-wrestling incident.

"Benny, this is Joan and Dave Edwards, Justin's parents." Dave came over to shake hands.

When a moment of awkwardness settling in, Benny attempted to melt into the background saying, "Please, don't let me interrupt," before leaning against a small dining room table just inside the side door.

"Where were we," Falcone voiced, sitting back next to Anne. "I believe you were telling me about your daughter's activities on the pond."

As Anne began to respond, Benny could hardly hear her and, as she continued to speak, he thought maybe she was on anxiety meds as she did so unemotionally. But that all changed after she spoke of the speed boat being used quite a bit for water skiing and sunning and began to address the missing kayak.

"She and Justin left sometime after the golfers, that's after six forty-five, and before I got up a little after eight."

"Wouldn't think teens would be so ambitious early," Falcone raised.

"They wouldn't. But with the high-rise being where it is, you can't sleep for long with people stirring. I guess with the men going off golfing, they must have awakened shortly thereafter."

"Got it. Tell me, why is the Rhode Island side of the pond favored?"

"I guess for its tranquility. It's quiet over there, without speed boats or jet skiers. When you make your away from the road, you feel away from civilization."

"So, they head over there most times?" Falcone asked.

"Not always. You can't access it at times when the water levels are high. Can't make it under the road." She paused. "I sure wish that was the case this time."

When Anne raised up the balled-up tissues to block the tears, Falcone let her be.

"I think I can leave you people be. Just one last question. And forgive me for asking."

As Falcone paused, checking the faces of all of them, John felt he may be seeking permission. "Please, ask. We want to help in any way we can."

"Thank you. Are Julie and Justin sexually active?"

Benny couldn't see his sister's face but he did Joan's. "What does that have to do with anything?" she snapped.

"Honey, please," Dave Edwards said.

"Don't give me that! Don't you think that's a bullshit question?"

Falcone stood and saved them from answering. "I guess it's not that important."

"It's inappropriate," Joan continued. "They're kids."

Benny felt Falcone's question reasonable. With his niece and boyfriend having little privacy in the cottage, he felt they likely left to get some.

"Would you mind if I went over there?" Benny floated, as Falcone reached for the handle of the screen door.

The question turned all heads, Anne's for the first time.

"Best to avoid contaminating the abduction site."

An outsider, Benny hoped to get a different response but had to respect Falcone's decision. After he nodded and Falcone left, he saw his sister perturbed and thought it best to go outside to figure what role he could play. As he proceeded to the end of the large deck, he checked out the pond and its million-dollar view. Tonight's was fairly spectacular as the nearly full moon cast a radiant line toward him. The noise of passing trucks on the causeway that split Rhode Island and Connecticut served to throw cold water on his face. Pulling out his cell, he called Dom Scalia, the Rhode Island FBI lead who Hank Russo had contacted and received clearance for investigating the abduction site in Rhode Island. He learned that whoever took the teens exited through Connecticut and that he would need Falcone's permission to cover that area.

Peering inside the cottage, he was able to John's attention and he came out on the deck. Benny motioned with his head to Rhode Island. "How does one get over there?" Seeing his brother-in-law perplexed, in having heard Falcone, he added, "Don't worry. I got permission." He explained that he spoke to an authority with the Rhode Island state police.

"You mean now?" John asked perplexed as to how his brother-in-law could accomplish anything in the dark.

"Yes, now."

Though he had reached out to his brother-in-law, feeling that Navy Seal credentials and his investigative prowess in Blacksburg cast him as a go-to in desperate times, he now felt he didn't think it through. Benny could be standoffish, testy, and often unpredictable. And Anne would be furious at what he was asking, after hearing Falcone tell her brother to stay away.

But as Benny awaited an answer, he didn't have the heart to spurn his offer to help. "I'll get Pete Lewinski to guide you. You remember him?"

Benny nodded in the direction of Pete's house. He couldn't forget the opinionated Lewinski, unafraid to present his conservative views, especially with a little Woodford Reserve in him. But he felt a kinship to the career Navy man.

Watching as John walked to Lewinski's house and disappear inside, Benny pondered whether he should go in and make amends with his sister. But as much as he felt it might be the right thing to do, he feared it backfiring. He also questioned how he could look into this with a sister in disfavor. About to go inside, he heard voices at Lewinski's and saw John returning and Pete Lewinski headed toward the road.

"Pete will take you over there," John said. "He has no problem with it."

"Do you have a problem with it?"

"If I did, I don't now." A pause, as John's eyes became glassy. "We need all the help we can get."

"John, I only know one way to operate and that's all in. Are you comfortable with that?"

After raising his arm up to wipe the tears with his shirt sleeve, John nodded. "Pete is waiting for you up at the road."

Sitting in an older model Chevy Silverado, Pete poked his head out the driver's side window as Benny opened the trunk of his car.

"What are you in need of?" Pete asked.

"Flashlights."

After Pete held an industrial one out the window, Benny closed the trunk and hopped in.

"Glad you came," Pete said, shaking hands.

"Had to."

"I've been worried sick. Can't imagine what Anne and John are going through. When was the last time you were up?"

"You mean you forgot?"

"Sorry, yes, the Jitterbug." Pete had been summoned to remove the lure's imbedded hook from Benny's thumb.

"Did you ever watch Captain's Courageous?" Benny asked.

"An all-time favorite."

"Well, I have only one thing in common with Manuel."

Pete chuckled, knowing that Benny was referring to the character's Portuguese heritage and not his fishing ability. While Pete had low regard for local law enforcement, who subscribed "to the over-the-top, knee-jerk you're wrong and I'm right theory," he appreciated confident and accomplished people who could poke fun at themselves.

Pete had only driven a few hundred yards before turning off onto a dirt road. A mile into woods, the truck's headlights illuminated strips of yellow police tape extended between two pine trees.

"I guess this is the end of the line," Pete said, reaching into his back seat and retrieving the flashlights. Handing Benny one, they walked slowly until yellow cautionary tape seemed everywhere. They shined their lights around to get the lay of the land.

"You take it from here," Pete said. "I'll follow alongside to double up on light."

Benny advanced slowly to where the police tape was the heaviest. "I guess this is where the kids ran into trouble," he said, training his light on soft brown pine needles. He hesitated before going under the tape, until he saw the area disturbed. "I assume the pond is below?"

"That's right. Not far."

Lowering himself back under the tape, Benny followed Pete to the water's edge. "Appears they were careful in extracting the kayak," Benny observed. "Not an indentation line along here. Had to weigh fifty pounds, wouldn't you say?"

"Probably more. Those older LL Bean models run sixty, seventy pounds. That's a two-man job or possibly with a strong lady. Don't think Julie could manage."

Benny thought the same. Considering what had gone down, he envisioned possibly as many as three men involved. It wasn't impossible that one man could lift the two-person kayak but it had to be a bitch to evenly distribute the weight.

Viewing the water, and understanding that divers had been deployed, he didn't think the kidnappers had the time to submerge it and risk being seen.

Satisfied, Benny led Pete back to the other prominent area marked by yellow cautionary tape, maybe 40 to 50 yards away from the pine needles. It featured a heavy concentration of what Pete said were Mountain Laurels. "Some hacked off." He pointed. "Not by storm, I'll tell you that." Shining his light inside one bush, he bent over and picked up a cigarette butt. "Homemade."

Before Benny could warn Pete not to touch it, it was too late. And it occurred to Pete. "I'm sorry."

Benny took hold of the smoked end and smelled it. "What makes you sure it's homemade?"

"No filter, the paper, and smell."

Before putting it into his pocket, Benny quipped, "Don't see how the troopers could miss it."

"Maybe they found others."

"Should have taken them all."

"You see these," Pete said, pointing his finger to rather small indentations in the earth. "Likely from portable chairs. Those a bit deeper from someone with a larger frame. Wouldn't surprise me if a few fellas were hunting in here."

It hit Benny as to what they may have been hunting and he asked.

"In summer, only small game, squirrels, rabbits. But that doesn't stop the locals from taking whatever they want. I know a guy whose freezer is stocked with venison year-round." Pete cast his light wider. "Awful spot to set up, with all these bushes."

Finished and walking back to the truck, Pete asked, "Do you mind?" He held a pack of Marlboros.

"Please, go ahead. Smoked back in the day, rather enjoyed it after a roll in the Afghanistan mountains."

Floating Benny's name to a former Navy friend and officer, who also served in Afghanistan, Pete had learned that Benny Fidalgo was a legend in the Seal community, nicknamed The Assassin. At first, Pete couldn't believe he was that, in speaking to someone 5'8", maybe 170-pounds and a little squeamish in removing the Jitterbug.

"How'd you quit?" Pete asked, as they walked to his Silverado.

Benny smiled. "A fiancé, now my significant other, said either they go or I go."

"A smart woman."

"Yeah, she is."

As they continued on, Pete had to ask. "What do you make of it?"

Benny stopped walking. "What puzzles me is if those kids were taken by those guys in the bushes, as it now seems…how the hell did they know the kids would be in there? The odds are that it couldn't be by happenstance, but who knows." With Pete quiet, Benny continued walking before stopping abruptly.

"Seems to me this being a perfect spot for lovers, these guys waited for their prey to show. They could have easily gratified themselves sexually and headed off, but didn't. They went to the trouble of removing the kayak…which means, they had an end game in mind but not here."

A long pause. "I'm going on the premise that this was done by locals, someone around who knew the lay of the land and that they could come in and out of here as often as they liked, without being seen or bothered…all of which tells me that my niece and boyfriend may not be far off."

Pete listened, impressed.

"Odds are against strangers settling in here," Benny continued, "coming from afar and investing time in an abduction plan, though you first have to cross off anyone occupying the few houses on this end of the pond. No, I'm thinking locals."

As his mind whirled, in taking it all in and contemplating what might have gone down, Benny tried not to think of his niece. The only upside, he felt, is that kidnappers going through all of this effort wouldn't finish what they intended in one night. Maybe they'd demand a ransom, which should be delivered soon enough.

Also, the thought crossed his mind that his niece may have been kidnapped for human trafficking purposes. But Justin in the mix complicates that a bit, though he could be sold too. Just the same, the abused girls in the movie "Taken" fed with narcotics and raped repeatedly until they had no more left to give, served as an eye-opener.

"Pete, can you give me a read on this area?"

"Can do. Are you intending to confer with the police?"

Benny wasn't surprised by the question and owed him an answer. "These kids have a short leash, maybe forty-eight hours at most." A pause. "It is obvious that the lead Connecticut investigator doesn't want me involved. Can't say that I blame him. But I won't stand on the sidelines if I don't feel the right attention is being paid."

"I hear you…you've got to do what you've got to do."

As Pete went to start the engine, Benny asked him to hold up. "Pete, I've plowed through many stop signs. If you don't want anything to do with me from this point on, I won't think any less of you."

Pete turned toward Benny. "Consider me forewarned."

CHAPTER 7

Recognizing Alfie Doolittle's cell number, Blake Masterson glanced around his office to ensure that the three other insurance salesmen were preoccupied. He answered, "Hold on," and headed toward the parking lot.

"We snared us some real good ones," Doolittle proclaimed.

"What do you mean ones?"

"We got the prettiest girl you ever laid eyes on and carted off her boyfriend to boot."

Masterson's blood began to boil at the stupidity in taking such risk.

"Got some video," Doolittle said, excited, "right before he was about to do her. Want to see it?"

With the deed already done, Masterson began to recognize the possibilities. "You notify Dupree and Jarvis and I'll get hold of Jackson and Whitey. Let's meet at ten. Tell them to bring five hundred."

Doolittle couldn't wait to learn what special betting games Masterson had in mind. "You'll be pleased," he said. "She's got some class and a nice ass."

CHAPTER 8

Exiting the woods with Pete, Benny considered what he might be able to accomplish at this late hour. He asked where they might find a tobacco shop open, knowing that most have late hours with clients interested in THC and CBD.

Thrown momentarily for he thought they were calling it a night, Pete said there's a popular one near Jewett City.

"Drive me to my car and I'll find it," Benny said.

"Nothing doing. This is more interesting than bedside book reading."

At Fred's Smoke Shop, they waited for someone to get into the lone car directly outside.

"Pete, I'll need to handle this alone for I don't want whoever in there to think there's something afoot."

"Got it and good luck."

Entering, a long-haired salesman, wearing a red bandana around his neck, stood behind the counter puffing a solid wood pipe. Approaching, Benny instinctively breathed shallowly for gale force winds couldn't clear the smoke.

"What can I do you for?" the salesman asked.

"That's a nice e-pipe you got there. Mind if I take a closer look?"

Benny held it long enough to demonstrate an interest.

"We have several, including that one. The e-puffer is hot. Set ya back though."

"No, not at the moment. But maybe after the next poker game. I came to see if you carry a special blend that my brother-in-law smokes.

Only trouble is, I'm not familiar with it." Benny removed the butt from his pocket and extended it. "I was able to swipe this from his ashtray."

Securing a tweezer, the salesman sniffed the butt. "With that tiny a sample, I'd need to be Sherlock Holmes."

"Can you make an educated guess?"

He smelled the butt again. "Possibly Pueblo."

"Is that a common brand?"

He shook his head. "If it's Pueblo, it's German."

"Sell much of it?"

Benny kicked himself for asking too eagerly, for the salesman now sensed that the person before him had another agenda. He placed the e-puffer down. "Your brother-in-law is out of luck. We don't carry it any longer."

"Did you carry it at one time?"

"Used to. Expensive stuff to keep around."

"Where might my brother-in-law go to buy it around here?"

"Not sure. Maybe he buys directly from the company."

Thanking the clerk, Benny rejoined Pete. "We may have stumbled on to something. That tobacco is German made and expensive. So, there can't be too many people around here able to afford it."

Considering next steps, Benny took out his cell and turned to one he could count on. "Trish, need a favor."

"I was just thinking about you."

"I'm sitting next to Anne's neighbor, Pete Lewinski, who should have been an investigator."

"Put him on for a second."

Benny handed Pete his cell.

"Keep an eye on him," Trish warned. "His only course is full speed ahead and his Portuguese temper rubs people the wrong way."

"Anything on the plus side?"

"Well, yes. He's quick to pick up the tab so eat out as much as possible." A pause. "And this: If his niece can be found, he's the guy to do it."

Handed back the cell, Benny filled her in. "Can you call the manufacturer of Pueblo and see if they can identify where it might be sold around here or if you squeeze out individual buyers. Pete, what county are we in?"

"New London."

"In New London, Connecticut."

"I'll give it a shot, though I don't have to tell you that foreign-based companies have stronger privacy protection laws than us."

"Thanks much."

"You got it. Can I deliver my oft repeated message?"

"Don't."

"But are you getting the impression the investigators there are on it?"

His lack of a response told her that it was a waste of time to caution him about going it alone. She just wished whatever agencies were involved would include him. "I'll get back to you on the Pueblo."

On the drive back to the cottage, from the way Benny talked up Trish, it was obvious to Pete the mutual respect they had for each other.

"Mind if I stop and grab a coffee?" Pete asked.

"Please do."

Pete pulled into a Dunkin', alongside a gas station.

"Pete, order me an egg and turkey sausage on an all-everything bagel and get whatever you'd like." As he reached for his wallet, Pete said, "Put that away."

"You heard what Trish said," Benny reminded.

"You can get the next one."

Waiting in line at the drive-thru, Pete had to ask. "How do you know the guy in Fred's isn't misleading you?"

"About the butt being Pueblo?"

"Well, that. And not carrying it. They are the largest and most popular store around."

Benny exhibited a broad smile, so glad to have Pete by his side. "As to it being Pueblo, I believe he was honest. At that stage in our conversation, there was no reason to be playing games. However, if Trish finds out that Fred's carries Pueblo, I'll be back there strangling a certain salesman with his own bandana."

CHAPTER 9

Goobie and Alfie arrived at the cabin first. It had taken them considerable time to offload the kayak due to bickering over what to do with it. While Alfie lobbied for cutting it into pieces, burning it, and burying the remains, Goobie insisted on cutting a hole in its bottom and sinking it in a lake a few towns away. Not settling it, they left it under a tarp at Goobie's.

Entering the cabin and shining his light on their catch, Alfie saw that the tape covering their mouths had come loose.

"Geez, Goob, can't you do anything right?" He scolded Julie and Justin, in a playful manner, as if reprimanding a puppy. "I'm so disappointed. Bet you two howled your little heads off."

"Yeah, too bad no one came a calling," Goobie added. "You could set off a cannon back here and no one would hear."

With a truck door slamming, Alfie rubbed his hands together. "Time to greet our brothers in sin. We'll be back before you can say 'give it to me babe.'"

As other trucks pulled in, their drivers exited holding flashlights, Some with six packs and snacks.

"How'd you snooker them?" Jackson asked.

"You'll hear soon enough," Alfie replied.

Masterson checked his watch. "What's holding up Whitey?"

"His loss," Dupree said. "I'm for checking them out. Time's a wasting."

Masterson thought better. "He'll get all pissed off. In the meantime, give me the card and let's check the video."

Securing his laptop from his vehicle, Masterson walked over to a wooden picnic table missing two top boards and inserted the SIM card. Everyone huddled close. But in his haste, he fast forwarded past Julie removing her top, eliciting catcalls.

"Hold your shirts. I got it." Masterson rewound to where Julie had done so. "Appears Goobie and Alfie have set the bar high. I'd say that gal is eager."

Hearing voices outside, Julie and Justin couldn't make out what anyone was saying. Seeing the flashlight beams, Justin told Julie, "Let me try and reason with them." However, as he eyed several determined men placing metal folding chairs in a semi-circle, he couldn't summon the courage to do so, more so as LED lights were positioned to shine directly on them.

"Enough fiddling with the lights," Dupree shouted at Masterson. "Sit down."

After peering at the gawking men, who all had their eyes trained on her, Julie closed hers.

"Leave us alone," Justin implored. "My dad will give you all the money you want."

"How much money does your daddy have?" Dupree asked. Taking the toothpick from his mouth, he held it between his index finger and thumb. "All I need is a stack of hundreds this size. Don't have to be a greedy motherfucker."

"Let's table any designs on a ransom," Masterton said.

"Wait. We can at least hear what the daddy has."

Justin had no idea of his dad's net worth. "I don't know. But I'm sure he can give you each tens of thousands."

"Now we're talking," Dupree said. "Never turn my back on hay."

Whitey burst in. "Were you bastards going without me?"

He swept right past those seated and pointed his index finger menacingly at Julie. "Are you a virgin?"

The others quieted, eagerly interested.

"Whitey, take a seat," Masterson said. "We're just getting started, and you're annoying her unnecessarily."

"Needs settling. Hey, boy, what's your name?"

"Justin."

"Well, Justin, have you been sticking it to her?" When Justin bowed his head, he followed up, demanding, "It's a simple yes or no." He stared at Julie, until she turned her head away. "Seeing that fine body, how you could hold out? Did she deny you the pleasure?"

Julie began to sob.

"See what you've done," Alfie voiced. "Don't you get all fussed up, little lady. Masterson, a little order."

Annoyed that Whitey hadn't yet sat, Masterson said, "You'll spoil everything, like before."

"Shut your damn mouth," Whitey snapped. "Dupree told me to stop her bitching."

Dupree had captured a 23-year-old hitchhiker and notified Whitey first, though protocol called for him to contact Masterson. On their way to the cabin and with the hitchhiker cursing and kicking, Whitey convinced Dupree that they shouldn't be taking any shit from her. Climbing into the back seat, he slapped her a few times before yanking off her jeans. Pulling over, Dupree joined in. While she begged for them to stop, it was too late. They didn't make it to the cabin.

After Whitey finally backed away, grabbing a Heineken from the cooler Goobie carried in, Masterton asked Goobie and Alfie to explain how they trapped the teens.

Disgusted, Whitey voiced, "Let's just get on it with it."

"We might have had this out of the way, only for you being late."

With some of the others supporting Whitey's bid to start the entertainment, Masterson reminded all that they elected him and one of the rules they enacted was for the capturer to disclose the trappings. He deemed it important for two reasons. One, that they could learn from it; and two, more importantly, to detail how they avoided being seen and covered their tracks.

"Alfie, you got the floor," Masterson stated.

"Why thank you." Alfie proceeded to explain how he and Goobie set up a blind on the Rhode Island side of Beach Pond, aware that lovers liked to engage on "a mattress of pine needles." He shared that they affixed hunting trail cameras to a few of the pines and caught three couples having sex."

"Why the fuck didn't you show us?" Whitey charged.

"If you'd let me explain. We had the cameras wrongly positioned on the first and the other couple was so fat, they weren't worth looking at. The last one we got was good alright, only we messed up the recording."

"Figures," Whitey said.

With that, Goobie stepped in front of Whitey. "Shut up, before I do something!"

Masterson rose and took him by the arm. "Goobie, let's not get all lathered. "Alfie continue. Get to the two before us."

With calm restored, Alfie said they observed the two teens last summer and banked on them returning to the pine needles. From the video clip, he said they were able to match their yellow kayak to a cottage on the Connecticut side of Beach Pond, not far from the road.

"While the girl was up often," he explained, "the boyfriend hadn't been back before this weekend. Knowing that, we set up the blind this morning and lo and behold...wasn't he about to do her before we got there in the nick of time."

With Alfie stopping, Masterson prodded, "go on."

Alfie seemed puzzled.

"Tell us how you cleaned up."

Whitey heard enough. "I'm sure they did an absolutely perfect job. Let's get it on. Even those two are getting bored."

As all eyes turned to Julie and Justin, Julie tried to hide behind Justin's shoulder.

Paying Whitey no mind, Alfie shared how Goobie managed to haul the kayak before Whitey shouted, "This has gone on long enough."

When Goobie angrily rushed Whitey, it took three of them to hold him back. An unstable and unpredictable Goobie, of considerable size and strength, is not what they needed right now. Two years ago, during hunting season, they watched him kill a doe, remove the heart, and begin biting into it viciously with the blood dripping from his jaw. For the most part, they left him alone.

As they once again regained their seats, Jackson was the first to speak, addressing Alfie. "Are you sure the law won't be up our ass?"

"We was careful."

Masterson followed up. "You did extract the cameras?"

Displaying a face of alarm, Alfie slapped the side of his head. After a second or two, he rose up smiling. "Got you, didn't I?"

"Get serious," Masterson said, annoyed. "It's our necks on the line."

"Of course, we did. Do you think me and the Goob are that stupid."

"I don't know about the rest of you," Masterson said, leaning in to see each of their faces, "but I'm sold. Alfie and Goobie, congrats. You move up the leader board."

"It will take some doing to unseat me," Whitey boasted.

During a severe blizzard, tow-truck operator Whitey had spotted a car in a ditch and a young woman desperate for help. She had already spent hours alone, with a dead car battery and cell. Unable to pull her car out, without putting his truck in jeopardy, Whitey felt he needed his "monster" tow truck.

Taking the woman along to retrieve it, she continued to gush, revealing that she was headed to Rhode Island University after a short Christmas break, to perform with her dance team during a New Year's college basketball tournament. But caught in the blizzard, she lost sight of the road and veered off. Afraid to leave the car, she feared freezing to death.

As she kept talking, Whitey couldn't believe his good fortune. With not a chance of anyone out in these conditions, he felt this was an ideal situation to convene the hunting group and called Masterson when he got back to the garage. While Masterson agreed, the worry was in getting to the cabin in this storm, to which Whitey guaranteed that he could round up everyone in his monster. But right after speaking to Masterson, he kicked himself for calling him as he watched the shapely dancer remove her coat and head to the bathroom. That's when he decided he wasn't following the rules. Ordering her to take off her clothes, she refused and when he advanced, she picked up a hammer, which he had no trouble wresting from her. Tossing her into the backseat of his Monster, he raped her. It turned out to be a long night as he had to drive all of the hunting club members to the cabin. At times, making his way, he almost got lost in a forest of white. But the effort turned out to be worth it. At the cabin, Masterson ordered the college senior to perform dance routines in the nude while they played poker. He declared that the winner of the poker game could do with her as he so pleased, with runner-up to follow. According to the rules, the winner had to dispose of the body. Jackson won the poker game, and had kept her at the cabin for two days until he could make his way back in.

"Wasn't my college dance girl the best piece of ass we've ever had?" Whitey reminded them.

"She was…" Alfie posited. "But this little lady takes a back seat to no one."

"Yeah, bullshit."

Trying not to listen, Julie leaned in to Justin even more, especially when the leader came over. "Look at me," Masterson, ordered, "Not him, me. That's right. Now, do you treasure your life?"

Though it was quite warm in the cabin, a result of the sun's rays on the roof all day, Julie couldn't stop shaking.

"Maybe this will help," he continued. "We intend to release you two after having our fun. But that may not be the case, if you don't answer that simple question." He pointed to the others. As if on cue, they held flashlights under their chins to accentuate grotesque faces. "Good looking lot, aren't they. No telling what they'll do if upset."

If on cue, they stomped their feet in unison for the show to begin. Masterson waved his hand behind him for them to stop as he heard Justin begin to say something.

"Repeat that, young fellow. Seems we were making too much noise."

"Are you really going to let us go after…?" Justin asked, holding out for any hope.

"Absolutely. What do you take us for?"

After Julie and Justin locked eyes, Justin bowed his head, defeated, recognizing his question was meaningless. He felt like he had just thrown Julie to the wolves.

Terribly shaken, Julie locked onto an inner, calming voice, 'you can do this. You can do this…'

Separating from Justin and wrapping her arms around her knees, Julie stared up at the leader, admitting, "Yes. I'm a virgin."

CHAPTER 10

Moving his jigsaw puzzle to another table, Pete pulled out his regional maps on his coffee table and waited for Benny who was checking in next door and gathering his belongings. He had invited Benny to stay with him, knowing the cottage had limited quarters and aware of the friction between brother and sister. It was very telling how rough things were between the two when Benny accepted the offer without hesitation.

"All ok?" he asked as Benny entered. Taking in his embittered face, he had his answer, before Benny imparted, "What can I say."

Noticing a map, practically covering the coffee table, Benny moved to it. Pete held his coffee cup. "Want some? Always have coffee brewing."

"Can't turn it down."

Pete called out from the kitchen, "How do you like it?"

"Black's fine."

Sitting together and leaning over the coffee table, Pete pointed to huge swaths of various shades of green on the map. "This is all Pachaug Forest, one of the largest in Connecticut. Much of it state land for hikers, hunters, and campers. My ex and I used to do quite a bit of hiking but only skin deep as the forest goes."

"May I ask how long you've been single?"

"Fourteen years."

Uncomfortable speaking about his personal life, Pete continued Benny's education. "These grounds here attract a fair number of campers." A pause. "Might they be behind it?"

"Everything's on the table, but don't campers congregate? Might be difficult to pull the wool over the eyes of other campers who I'm sure have an interest in who is nearby."

"That's true. Except that there are some who don't stick to the defined campgrounds, play by the rules."

"How so?"

"All need to register but some bypass state officials and do their own thing…like to drift."

Benny sipped his coffee, while reflecting. "They'd have to risk the kids screaming out…though I imagine kidnappers would have considered all of that."

Pete pinpointed the areas designated for campers, on the fringes of the forest, as if to show how insignificant the camp grounds are.

Sensing resignation in Pete's voice, Benny assured him. "This will come together."

"I wish I shared your optimism."

"Like your jigsaw puzzle. Border aside, it gets tougher until it clicks, and then all falls into place."

Pete refilled Benny's cup and let him know that Anne surprised him with a $100 Dunkin' gift card for his birthday. "She's always been kind to me. Have an open invitation to dinner."

"I'm sure she's thankful for all you do for them. Aren't you their de facto watchman?"

"Doesn't require much watching."

"You say that. But while their home, one less worry."

Sitting back, Pete said, "I once couldn't wait for the summer crowd to leave for peace and quiet. Not anymore. Six months of quiet weighs on you." As the words left Pete's lips, it dawned on him that the Stapletons might very well put their cottage up for sale over this.

Gazing at piles of books on the floor, with subjects ranging from astrology, to ancient Greeks and Romans, to politics, Benny understood how Pete survived the lonely winters.

"If the campers are in these areas and these trails are marked for hikers," Benny said, "is hunting permitted through the rest of it?"

"Yes, for the most part. There's also significant private land, in the hands of families through generations, but even they typically lease to hunting clubs to help cover taxes."

"Hunting any good?"

"Better than you might expect, though Connecticut doesn't roll off the tip of your tongue like nearby states."

"Do you know anyone who belongs to a hunting club?"

"I don't. But Clete Markey will. He runs the bait and tackle store in town and is a taxidermist on the side."

Benny made a mental note to speak with Markey and also needed to check in with FBI's Dom Scalia to gauge where his Rhode Island investigatory team is headed. He also hoped to connect with a forest ranger who can enlighten him more on Pachaug Forest.

Surprised by a loud knock, Pete went to the door and found himself facing a huge man, with a ruddy complexion, bellowing, "I'm with the Ancient Order of Hibernians. Bless this house and all in it."

While Pete stood dumbfounded, Benny yelled, "tell him we don't want any!" Seeing Pete bewildered, he added, "You can let the big lug in."

Benny introduced Pete to Detective Dennis Murphy, calling him the resident know-it-all on the Blacksburg Police force.

"What the hell are you doing here?" Benny said, genuinely surprised.

Murph shook Pete's hand.

"Yes, hard for me to leave with all the tough cases on my plate," he said, egging Benny. "But my boss figured I could use a few days in the country to rejuvenate."

"Sure, he did."

"I figure to hole up here and do some fishing. Heard the bass are thirsting for caterpillars."

When Pete countered that caterpillars weren't preferred, Benny added, "he wouldn't know a bass from a catfish."

Murph plopped down on the easy chair, filling it. "Pete, let me tell you about the time I hooked this monster bass."

"Can I get you some coffee?" Pete asked.

Murph looked around. "Might you have something a wee bit stronger?"

Opening his liquor cabinet, Pete held up bottles of Jameson and Woodford Reserve.

"My ancestors would be rolling in their graves if I didn't choose the whiskey."

"How did you know I was here?" Benny asked.

"Trish told me, thank you. And your brother-in-law pointed the way."

"Add comforting the Stapletons to your to-do list."

Murph smiled. "Pete, already with the orders."

Updating Murph, Benny concluded with his belief that Julie and Justin were being held locally and of Trish's outreach to the German tobacco conglomerate.

"By the way, her head's down. Seems on a secret mission."

"Leave her be. You are the nosiest person I know."

With that response, Murph knew Benny was familiar with whatever Trish was working on. "Not going to tell your good pal?"

To Benny, he wondered if word hadn't already leaked of an investigation into officers on the take. He pondered Murph's real reason for coming, but quickly nixed that notion. Murph was the most righteous person he had ever come across. Keeping the investigation from him, however, was going to take resolve.

"When was I ever given a seat at the table," Benny said.

"Sure, you are."

Benny hated to be evasive, especially to someone he had the utmost regard for, but felt he had no choice.

"Listen, whatever you think I've got going on in Blacksburg, I'm here now. Pete, do you have a bed big enough for him?"

"I do. But that means you'll have the couch."

"So be it. I don't sleep much anyway."

With Murph insisting on going to a hotel, Benny cut him short. "I need you close and searching local records for anything that gives you pause…maybe missing persons. Need to rule out that this isn't connected to others."

Murph smiled. "You did say investigators from two states are on this?"

"Did I?"

"The last thing Trish said was to keep you out of trouble."

"Let's just say I'm running a parallel investigation."

"Official or unofficial?"

"Stop being a pain in the ass." A pause. "Murph, time is not on our side."

CHAPTER 11

Up at 5:55 a.m., hardly sleeping at all, Benny considered scrambling eggs, until he realized that the noise would have everybody up. With Pete pre-loading his coffee machine, Benny hit the brew button.

With coffee in hand, he re-examined the map of Pachaug Forest. It was clear that it would take significant manpower to put a dent in surveying it, which he didn't have. He pondered whether he could make use of small aircraft but that would be overstepping his bounds. Maybe the investigators were on to it or drones. Yet, he really didn't know if they would go along with his theory that the kids were being held locally and, if so, that they were being held in the forest, as he had nothing tangible to go on. They might just as well be captive in any one of the isolated homes set back from the road, ideal for anyone with devious intent. What he knew about Voluntown, like any rural community, is that residents don't take too kindly to nosy strangers.

"You're up?" Pete said, emerging from the master bedroom and heading right for coffee.

In being shown the house, Benny saw Pete's master bedroom as nothing to write home about. In it was a family-sized bed, a narrow chest of drawers, no closet, and a small area rug on a hardwood floor badly in need of refinishing. It made him ponder whether Pete's divorce had anything to do with a bottled-up wife feeling the walls closing in, and an inability to add the feminine touch to someone set in his ways.

As Pete took the easy chair, cradling his coffee, he asked, "Did you sleep?"

"Closed my eyes for a bit."

"I guess that sofa has seen its days."

"No, it was fine. Just something I'm saddled with."

Pete pondered whether it was related to PTSD from his military days. "How about some eggs or should we wait for Murph?"

"Let's not, or there won't be anything left for us."

As Pete served up scrambled eggs and English Muffins, out came Murph stretching in shorts and t-shirt.

"Something smells really good."

"Yeah, well, you're not included in round one."

"Pete, I'm surprised he didn't ask you to build him one of those fancy omelets, you know the ones with the spinach and goat cheese."

Pete smiled. "I guess we're more the barebones type. Murph, whatever I have is yours."

"Don't give him that license or you'll be food shopping twice a day."

"Well, for your information," Murph said, "I'll be getting my breakfast on way to the library."

"I want you to go back several years?"

Helping himself to coffee, Murph couldn't let that comment go. "Pete, I've been a detective for a lot longer than know-it-all."

Leaving Murph, with the library closed until 9:30 a.m., Pete drove Benny to Markey's Bait & Tackle. He had explained to Benny that the proprietor had his ear to all goings on in town. "In some towns, it's the barber. In ours, it's the guy with the nightcrawlers."

As Pete parked out front, Benny was delighted in seeing no other vehicles. "How well does he know you?"

"A bit. I've come in for bait, typically when the nephews visit. I was asked to help judge a fishing contest he sponsored but won't make that same mistake."

"Why?"

"No fun in dealing with a bunch of sore losers."

Although Pete played down his interactions with the store owner, he was greeted like a long-lost buddy. In coming from behind the counter to shake hands, Markey turned to Benny, "This man here won't share his secret fishing spot. I wouldn't call that neighborly, would you?"

"I guess that's considered top secret."

Quickly moving to a large cork board, filled with beaming fishermen and their catches, Markey said, "See here. That's him, with one of the largest landlocked salmon ever caught in Beach Pond."

At a VFW meeting, Pete learned that a Vietnam vet, suffering from an inoperable brain tumor, desired to spend his last days fishing. When Pete offering to take him out on Beach Pond, the vet was thrilled and brought along his wife and son. Anchoring near the deepest part of the pond, and using live shiners, Pete saw the vet's pole bend and did all he could to grab it before the pole vanished. Together, they netted the salmon, which became a subject of discussion at Markey's for months. As the vet retold the story at a subsequent VFW meeting, all tuned in. One even produced a map of Beach Pond for the Vet to identify the exact location, which he did eagerly. With all mentally making note of it, Pete saw that he had pointed to a spot nowhere near where they had fished. As the vet was being wheeled out, he shook hands with Pete and leaned in, "That secret belongs with you." The vet died 16 days later.

"This is Benny Fidalgo, a friend from New York," Pete said. "He's the uncle of the missing young woman."

"I'm so sorry. What's the latest?"

"Like they disappeared into quick sand," Benny said. "The family hasn't received too much information, and I was hoping you could help."

Clete gazed at Pete, perplexed. "Don't rightly know how I could?"

"Well, Pete said that your store is quite popular. Whatever you're hearing would be helpful to me, even rumor."

Clete Markey didn't know what to make of the request. He would be more suspicious if Pete wasn't involved.

Pete could see that Markey wasn't readily signing on and attempted to engage him and win him over. "What do you think happened to the teens?"

"What do I know? Would only be a guess."

"We'll take it."

"One believed they likely drank too much and drowned. More think they're just wild kids who ran off."

Hearing a car door slam, Benny and Pete stepped behind a circular display of fishing poles as if they were interested in purchasing one. A heavyset man in camouflage overalls and a sun hat with various lures attached to it approached the counter and ordered two dozen nightcrawlers.

As they chatted, Benny felt more comfortable that Markey was someone he could trust. Being in a town foreign to him, he needed to line up sources that could help in gaining information.

When the fisherman left, Benny got right to the point. "Can I speak to you in confidence?"

As Clete nervously fiddled with fishing licenses, Benny thought the visit was for naught, until Clete declared, "I'll tell you what. If Pete shares his secret fishing spot, I'll be receptive to what you got going on."

Pete reached out to shake hands. "That's a deal."

To be sure, Benny also shook Clete's hand and confided that he was a New York detective who had taken leave to find his niece. He also relayed that in his gut, he felt the kids were being held locally, but withheld the discovery of the hunting blind, afraid that if Markey shared that, it might have the kidnappers moving too quickly. He was also sensitive about disclosing information privy to only the state police. With Clete a taxidermist, with several impressive bucks displayed at the other end of the store, Benny also didn't wish to infer that the kidnappers could be customers, which may have been the real reason why Markey had been reluctant to get involved.

Pete unfolded his map. "You familiar with Pachaug Forest?"

"Why are you asking?"

"Because if you step back and look at this region, Pachaug dominates. As you know, that's twenty-five thousand acres we're talking. If the kids are anywhere, they might be deep on here."

Benny could see that Markey didn't dismiss what Pete was saying as Pete continued, "If you consider entry points, to get deep, what one or two come to mind?"

Focusing on the map, Clete pointed. "Probably here. They lead to some remote hunting cabins. That's where the guys' bag the trophies."

"You've been back in there?" Benny asked.

"Not in a dozen years. A buddy took me in. Won't go back."

"Can I ask why?"

A pause. "Really difficult getting in and out, easy to get turned around. Nothing as frightening as finding your ass in the middle of nowhere."

Surprised that an avid hunter, with compasses and other tech equipment, would make such a statement, Benny had to dig. "Wouldn't think experienced hunters would have face such difficulty, especially if trophy bucks were to be had?"

With Clete not responding, instead straightening a pile of fishing licenses, Pete said, "Let's see now...where is that fishing spot?"

Stopping what he was doing, Clete eyed them both. "You saw the movie Deliverance?"

They nodded.

"I had a bad feeling, that's all."

"Was that due to the guy who brought you in there?"

"No, not him."

"Others with you?"

"We were alone."

"Can I speak to the friend who took you there?"

"Impossible. He's dead. Liver cancer. Drank himself to death."

Though wishing to probe further, Benny backtracked. "Will you help me?"

He saw that he had Clete's attention though he didn't commit. "I want you to make the abductions a main topic with everyone coming in."

Not only did Clete appear puzzled, but Pete was also at a loss.

"Tell them a New York detective had been in asking a ton of questions. But don't reveal that the girl is my niece. Just tell them that this detective is crazy and said that when he catches up with the two assholes who took his niece, he intends to skin them alive."

Clete appeared dumbfounded, Pete even more.

"Why would you have me do that?" Clete asked.

"To flush them out. Anyone overly interested, make note of it. A clear signal is if they ask to describe me. Possibly get the license plate or make of vehicle and call Pete."

After writing down his cell number, Pete held out the pocket map of Beach Pond. "Tomorrow I'll bring this in with a certain spot circled." He winked.

"One other thing really important," Benny added. "Don't mention me to anyone in law enforcement. Can you do this?"

Clete had been listening. "What makes you so sure two guys are involved?"

"I'm certain of it. And I want you to definitely make a point of sharing that."

As they were leaving, Clete said to Pete, "You owe me, big time."

Outside the bait and tackle shop, Pete lit a Marlboro. "Do you think enlisting him is a good move?"

"I don't know. But need to stir things up. These assholes need to feel threatened, when they're apt to make mistakes."

"But won't that push them to…"

Benny got what Pete was implying. "Taking a gamble, for sure. But I figure it will take time for Clete to make a connection to the right interested party. And by the time, things will be bleak anyway."

Benny, noticing Pete dejected, couldn't leave it that way. "Thanks in there for going along on the fly. Didn't think a fishing spot could be so enticing."

"Big stakes in bass tourneys." Enjoying coffee each morning at his bay window, Pete particularly liked the days of fishing tournaments as hard-core fishermen took turns swinging by.

"Like what?"

"Upwards of a hundred thousand nationally. Around here depends on the level of sponsors. The more prominent ones, like Napa or Bay liner, maybe see prizes in the five-to-ten thousand range."

"Wow, that much."

"Nice chunk of change."

"Then, with your knowledge, why don't you enter?"

From behind the wheel, Pete drew on his Marlboro and blew the smoke out his window. "I'd only win once. While these guys fish, they keep one eye on the competition. And besides, while I know one or two prime spots, it isn't an exact science."

Aware that Pete was being modest, Benny took a moment to consider next steps. On the top of the list was checking in with the Rhode Island investigatory team and identifying a conservation officer familiar with the Forest…in particular, where those hunting cabins might be.

As Pete reached to start the engine, he stopped. "Weird his mention of Deliverance?"

"Surprised me as well."

"Do you think he knows more than he's letting on?"

"Possibly," Benny responded. "He's smart enough not to casually drop names of his customers or it could mean curtains for his business. He'll help to a point."

CHAPTER 12

After hearing from her own lips that she was a virgin, Masterson nodded in the direction of the door and they filed out, over to the picnic table and far enough away so that their voices couldn't carry.

"Let me restate the plan," Masterson said. "We'll have her give him a blowjob and we'll time how long it takes. The one getting the closest..."

"That's bullshit!" Whitey interrupted. "Let's put her up to the highest bidder and be done with it."

"Agree," Dupree seconded. "Why piddle around."

As expected, Masterson once again had his hands full in trying to persuade them to his way of thinking. "I ask you where's the entertainment value in that? Goobie and Alfie went to all this trouble and you're suggesting that just one of us partake?" He paused. "We heard Alfie say how they covered their tracks. Why the rush? We have time and let's make good use of it."

"Ok, then," Whitey offered. "Let's bid on who goes first and down the line, and we can all have a piece."

Masterson scanned the faces before him who seemed to be amenable to Whitey's suggestion. "Look, if we play our cards right, we can all have at it. But let's begin with the show I drummed up for tonight."

While the majority of them hated Masterson's pretentious bullshit, they also knew his evil mind had concocted pleasures one could only dream of.

"Here's what I'm thinking," Masterson said, to bring this to closure. "We get on with the oral sex tonight and tomorrow night watch him have at it."

"What the hell are you talking about?" Whitey charged. "She's a damn virgin and you're allowing him to pluck her? And you're asking us to leave tonight without getting some?"

Masterson reminded them that their funds were running low, needed for leasing the cabin and hunting acreage. He played to that. "I'm thinking we can make some real cash selling the video of those two in action. Ought to net us enough to pay taxes for three to four years, at least."

"I'm not for any damn video," Jackson protested. "That's taking unnecessary risk. Need to stay low key and keep our mouths shut."

Masterson couldn't lose Jackson's vote. The owner of a highly successful bison farm was a prominent man around town and one the others listened to. Masterson had been one of the last holdouts in capturing an unsuspecting young female for group pleasure, until be netted the Dairy Queen worker.

They had their fun that night, hiding behind trees in a semi-circle around the cabin. While the night belonged to Whitey, whose tree she ran the closest to, it was a night to remember as she satisfied them all.

"What you're suggesting is that we ante up for both nights," Jackson said, summing up, "and then bid on her...but we're tabling the video."

"Fine with me," Masterson said to placate Jackson. "We ante up five hundred tonight and a thousand tomorrow."

Though Alfie barely could scrape together that kind of money, he said, "Sounds reasonable to me."

Goobie concurred, agreeing with anything coming from Alfie's lips. The two had made enough side money cleaning chimneys, which Alfie hid from his wife.

"Not buying in," Whitey declared. "The rights to a virgin shouldn't be handed over to some kid who hadn't stuck it to her by now."

"I'm with Whitey," Dupree declared, as he removed his knife.

Mesmerized as he proceeded to carve his initials into the picnic table, Jackson was the first to speak. "I'd etch them out if I was you," Jackson said. "Curtains for you if and when they search these grounds."

With Jackson floating something they all thought of but never said openly, all heads turned to him. "I'm etching out nothing," Dupree stated. "Let them come after me." He thrust the knife into the table and left it standing up.

Masterson felt he had to get them refocused, after the distraction. "Jarvis, what are your thoughts?" He observed Jarvis Wingo preferring to remain detached, as always.

"I'll go along with what you said. But my preference is to end this tonight. Who knows how much time we have."

Masterson had considered that. Could never be sure Alfie and Goobie hadn't been as meticulous as stated in leaving the Beach Pond woods. And while he understood why they took the kayak, it still may have been spotted along the road, even though they had it covered. But he loved his plan of a two-night soiree. And he figured they could keep an ear to the ground as to local news and an eye on police doings.

"I don't think we need worry about tomorrow," Alfie piped up, smiling broadly. "She may empty him tonight."

"Yeah, right!" Dupree stated. "That young buck should be firing like a damn roman candle."

They all laughed.

In thinking it through and finding himself in the minority, Whitey had his own plan. It called for coming back tomorrow during the day and having his way with her. "I'll go along with the two nights. But hate jerking off when the real thing is before us."

"What happens if he doesn't come?" Dupree floated. "He may be too embarrassed with all of us waiting for his pecker to stiffen."

"Dupree makes a good point," Masterson said, hating to pay him a compliment. "If he doesn't and quits, I'll stop the clock and threaten to kill him. Maybe we whip him to get his blood flowing."

"At that point, he's finished," Dupree voiced. "Then what do we do?"

"Then we reconvene outside," Masterson said, "and move to plan B."

"If that's bidding on rights to her, I'm in," Whitey expressed.

"Whoa," Masterson countered. "We're getting way ahead of ourselves. He'll be fine. Alfie, wasn't he ready to go earlier?"

"Yes. One hot-blooded American boy we have in there. Got to him in the nick of time."

Masterson was pleased to have things settling out his way. "Two important things to keep in mind when we get in there. No one is to say or do anything while they're at it, which might sway the timing. Second, the time stops when he shot his load and her mouth comes off."

Masterson reached into his pocket. He pulled out five one-hundred-dollar bills, spread them, and put the bills into an envelope. One by one, they did the same. With that settled, Masterson reached into his pocket and pulled out pieces of paper. "Write down the minutes and seconds you think it's going to take and your name. Put it here." He pulled off his Boston Red Sox cap. "Remember, I'll do the directing. You have a beer and enjoy the show."

CHAPTER 13

When Murph pulled up in front of the library, he did a doubletake. He couldn't believe the old, grey-weathered, clapboard building could be functional, with so many off-color replacement shingles appearing like band aids. It was also unadorned, except for a wooden book return box, and a metal bench under an empty window box. If Murph hadn't spotted two cars towards the rear, he would have guessed it was long closed.

In entering, he stopped momentarily and scanned a bulletin board and noticed a colorful flyer touting the Brooklyn Fair, only it had been held five weeks earlier. Inside, he saw who belonged to the cars. An older-gentlemen wearing a white shirt, vest, and bow tie sat at the main receiving desk, while a slightly younger woman with her hair in a bun, and a shawl covering the top of a pleated blue dress, sat in front of a computer.

Nearing the desk, Murph eyed dozens of nine-foot bookcases that dominated the interior. About to ask for help, he noticed that the gentlemen had his eyes closed, so he thought better to ask the woman.

"Good morning. I'm in need of help."

With that, the gentleman sprung to life. "What are you doing over there young man? Do you have a library card?"

"I'm from New York, in town visiting."

"Where in New York?" the woman asked. "My sister Sara lives in Syracuse."

"I live in Rockland County."

The older gentleman shook his head, uttering, "never heard tell of it. Must be way up into that state."

"It isn't," Murph said, feeling that he should back out and find a more modern facility. He explained that Rockland is New York's smallest upstate county by size and is downstate. "Are you familiar with the Tappan Zee Bridge?"

"Gertrude, does he mean the Governor Mario M. Cuomo Bridge?"

"Yes, I think that's what he means."

"Young man, we are very familiar with it, why?"

Murph considered taking out his holstered weapon and shooting himself. He shared that he was interested in missing persons in New London County and the surrounding area. He asked if the library had resources to help him.

"Can I ask why," Gertrude raised, "or do you consider that none of my business?"

"Did you hear about the young kids missing from Beach Pond?"

Dismissing him, they began speculating as to where the teens may be, until Morris posed, "Are you a private eye? You certainly don't look like one."

"Morris, for heaven's sake, private eyes come in all shapes and sizes. Remember Humphrey Bogart in the Maltese Falcone. He was just five-foot-seven."

Morris studied Murph from head to toe. "Never seen one this big. How is he able to sneak around and keep out of sight?"

Though a computer was to her left, Murph saw that Gertrude had begun writing on a blank pad, pausing every so often.

In perfect penmanship, she had written: missing housewife in the Fall of 2012; missing girl from Dairy Queen in Exeter, RI, Spring 2014; and Rhode Island University student in December 2016. She handed it over.

Murph was genuinely impressed. "Wow. You've some recall."

Gertrude beamed. "Not much happening around these parts, except for rising school taxes and corn prices. Morris, did you know that Campbell's charged me six dollars for a half dozen."

"Well, that's what they're all getting."

"If you go, get the Silver Queen, not the butter and sugar."

Murph coughed to get their attention.

"Sorry, we got sidetracked," Gertrude said, apologizing. "The Norwich Bulletin should be a good resource. It's our paper of record."

"Might there be others?"

Catching Morris's reaction, Murph wished he could have retracted the question.

"She doesn't miss a thing, young man. Did you know that she could tell that Mrs. Roberts' blueberry pie didn't contain all fresh blueberries. She mixed in some of those canned ones. She might have won the church contest, if it weren't for Gertrude's keen sense of taste."

Morris again gazed at Murph. "And I bet this big fella can surely eat a few pies."

Murph needed fresh air. "Do you recall anything else about these missing women?"

"I don't. But, in general, we don't get half the attention of investigations in Hartford or downstate in Fairfield County where the wealth is."

"How far back do you have copies of the Bulletin?"

"What do you think we are running around here, sonny, a third-rate operation," Morris said. "We've got the *Bulletin's* first masthead."

Gertrude walked out from behind the desk down a narrow hall to another computer and showed Murph how he could retrieve past articles. "If you need to print, come see me," she whispered. "With Morris, the geese will have arrived in the Carolinas by the time you get what you need."

Thanking her, Murph settled in. He was just grateful he had downed two bacon, egg, and cheese croissants on the way over.

* * *

Unsuccessful in obtaining the names of individual buyers of Pueblo, as expected due to Germany's consumer protection laws, Trish did manage to obtain the names of two stores in New London County that sell the tobacco: Mountain Smokes and Fred's Smoke Shop.

"Get out!" Benny exclaimed.

"I guess I didn't do badly after all."

"I'll say you didn't. The jackass at Fred's claimed they discontinued selling it. That lying bastard. I'm going to ring his neck."

"You are not ringing anyone's neck. Did Murph show?"

"Last night. He's at the library looking into missing persons."

"Let him deal with the guy at Fred's," Trish suggested. "Listen to me. You cause grief up there and they'll throw you in jail…then how are you going to find Julie?"

As Benny switched subjects, asking about Sheila Morgan and the investigation into officers on the take, Trish checked him. "Hold on. Are you working with local investigators?"

"I was just about to call them."

A long pause. "Same old Fidalgo." Trish felt the only way to turn him was to reach Murph and let him talk some sense. She let Benny know that Morgan didn't wear a wire to the first meeting with Carney, as planned, nor did she get patted down.

"Any indication of who else is involved?"

"She was afraid to ask. She did get the five hundred he promised. And I told her to spend it on a high-end Coach bag to signal that she's bought in."

"I imagine she had no trouble with that."

"Not her first choice. She wanted to buy Lululemon leggings."

"What's so wrong with that?"

"Men. That's not the reaction we're interested in. The Coach bag sends the right signal."

To Benny, the Trish-Sheila combo was like oil and water. "Murph asked what you were working on?"

"Why didn't he ask me?"

"Maybe wanted to find out if I was attached as well."

"You didn't say anything?"

"Of course not. It's hard though not bringing him in."

"Hold strong."

"I know that."

"How is Anne and John?" Trish asked, the silence telling her that Benny wasn't into comforting them, a by-product of his investigative tunnel-vision. "It wouldn't hurt for you to spend time with them."

"I'm not good at holding hands."

"She's your sister, for crying out loud, and hurting a great deal."

Promising he would check in shortly, he thanked her and headed straight to Fred's Smoke Shop.

CHAPTER 14

Not finding the lanky, lying bastard behind the counter at Fred's, probably due to the fact that he worked nights, Benny was greeted by a portly man with a handlebar mustache, wearing colorful suspenders and all smiles in greeting him.

"Do you carry Pueblo?" he asked.

"Sure do. Have had it for years. Not very popular right now. A bit pricey. Recession turned many away from the expensive foreign stuff."

Stooping behind the counter, he rose with two tins, each with Pueblo brand letters prominently on the label.

"Burley blend or plain?"

"Plain."

"How much you want?"

Benny acted like he didn't hear the question.

"Do you want a half pound, small pouch, large pouch?"

"Small pouch will do."

As he emptied a portion onto a scale and filled the pouch, Benny engaged. "Last night I was in here with a good friend, Pete Lewinski. You might know him. Lives on Beach Pond, a Marlboro chain smoker?"

"The Navy man?"

"That's him. Bought cigarettes from a tall fellow. Might he be coming in later? We got talking about hiking around these parts and I thought I'd pick his brain a bit more."

The man cocked his head. "Warren Shipley, hiking?" He laughed so hard he had to grip the counter. "That's a good one. Warren needs oxygen walking from here to his truck."

Benny tried to recover. "Maybe a friend or family member hikes. Anyway, he seemed to know a great deal."

The tobacco dealer shook his head. "Maybe hunting and fishing but hiking, no, not Shipley. You've made my day."

Asking again if Shipley would be in this evening, he was told he left for Denver to be with his ill brother.

Benny wasn't a bit surprised. The liar might be headed to Denver alright, probably to get lost in the Rocky Mountains.

He had to try. "Would you happen to know who purchases Pueblo? I'm a New York detective trying to track down an individual who uses it."

"I knew you were up to something. Few people order plain and fewer still go with the small pouch."

"Sorry about that."

"Sorry too. We don't keep that sort of information."

"Can you do me one? I need to speak to Shipley. Do you have a number?"

"Can't go that far."

"Can you go as far as an address?"

"Don't know what good that will do ya either with him being off to Denver."

"Maybe I catch him before he leaves."

The salesman wrote down the address and Benny thanked him.

Outside, he phoned Pete and told him what he found out and that he was on his way to Shipley's.

"Forgive me for raising this," Pete said, "Isn't this a good time to connect with Falcone? Actually, he may be next door."

"I'll get to him after this. Have to move fast."

"What's his address?"

"Lives on Camache Road. Know it?"

"That's about an eight-mile drive from you. You think he could be holding the kids?"

"I should be so lucky."

Pulling up to a large colonial, with black shutters, red door, and three-car garage, Benny moved deliberately so he could size up the house and the property surrounding it. There was an SUV in the driveway. No truck. He had a hard time believing that the tobacco salesman owned a property as nice as this.

He removed his .38 from his calf holster, put it in his pocket, and rang the doorbell. Hearing footsteps, he braced himself but relaxed when a fortyish or so woman, in sweats and headband, as if she had been working out or cleaning.

"I have a package in my car for Warren Shipley. Are you Mrs. Shipley?"

"No. I'm Joyce Peterson. He rents the apartment round back. You can leave it with me. I'll sign."

"Is he home?"

"No, he'll be gone for weeks. Who are you?"

He felt he had to be honest and told her that he was investigating the disappearance of two teenagers at Beach Pond.

"You think he knows something?" she asked, surprised.

"Hard to tell. Can you do me a favor? I'd like to access his apartment."

"Show me your badge."

Benny displayed his shield. "I'm a New York detective."

"Then you have no authority here. Come back with the police."

As he backed up, he was surprised to hear "wait." When she returned, she had a key in hand and led him around the side of her house. As it turned out, she hadn't been in the apartment in two years and wanted to check it out. She said Warren always paid the rent to her husband and that he rarely brought anyone over or stopped for small talk.

Benny retrieved two pairs of gloves, handed one to Joyce, and asked her not to touch anything, anticipating that the Connecticut investigatory team would likely come at some point.

Handed the key before they ascended a flight of stairs, Benny entered and stepped into a kitchen. He noticed an open box of cheerios on the counter and a bowl in the sink. On a small wooden table, with one leaf extended, was an ashtray with several cigarette butts and a few hunting magazines. He checked one of the butts but saw it wasn't Pueblo.

Continuing down a hall, he stopped at the first door, a bathroom, and noticed that Shipley must have just showered, for a damp towel had been left on the toilet seat. Just outside the next room, he put his right hand on the gun, in case. Entering, Shipley wasn't there. Clothes lay strewn on the bed, as if he hurriedly packed and discarded some.

In a closet, Benny spotted a few rifles and some hunting ammo. On the walls were photographs of him with sizeable bass. One had him and seven others in front of a cabin, with what seemed like a coyote dangling from the rafters. He removed it.

"Seems like the happy outdoorsman," Benny floated as Joyce stood in the doorframe.

"Maybe so. But he wasn't supposed to be smoking in here. My husband is going to have a fit."

Before leaving, he thanked her and, curious, asked why she provided him access.

"You didn't appear to be someone with bad intentions. And I did wish to check out the apartment."

"By chance, if he should return sooner than expected, please call my cell." He presented his card.

Heading directly to Beach Pond, he spotted an official Connecticut vehicle parked adjacent to the road. In fact, there were two. Opening the cottage's screen side door, Falcone stood with his back to the kitchen counter engaged with his sister and brother-in-law and the Edwards. Another officer stood in front of the double doors leading to the deck, presumably on hand in case the kidnappers sought a ransom. As all heads turned, Benny quietly shut the screened door as if to indicate for them to go on, which they did.

"We will continue to do everything we can," Falcone said, summing up. "We put out an alert to agencies in several states. With the news out, it often spurs leads. Don't lose hope."

In heading to the door, he turned. "I don't think you need Officer Peterson any longer, unless you feel more comfortable with him around." A pause. "If so, I can have him stay another day."

The two couples looked at each other, before John Stapleton said, "I think we're good."

As they exited, Benny followed him outside. "Can I have a word?"

"Sure."

Disclosing his interactions at Pete's Smoke Shop, Falcone exploded. "What the hell do you think you're doing! You have no authority here!"

With his voice carrying, not only did the Stapletons and Edwards exit the cottage but Benny saw Pete leave his house.

"Give me the name of your chief!" Falcone demanded.

As Benny slowly breathed in and out, he felt nothing he could say would turn things around.

Falcone bristled. "This is a very fluid situation. We don't need renegades at this time or distractions. Got that!"

With Falcone storming off toward his vehicle, followed by his subordinate, Anne screamed: "Can't you do anything right!" She stared angrily at John. "Why did you call him? You let Julie do whatever and look what happened."

"Anne," Pete said. "Easy! Easy!"

With Anne shielding her eyes, Joan took her inside. Earlier, they cried saying their goodbyes to April and Mark, thinking it was best for their children to leave with the situation bleaker by the hour. April begged to stay, but it was better she be home in Blacksburg. Anne arranged for her to stay with a friend whose daughter April played soccer with. The Edwards wanted Mark to leave also. He desired to assist Benny Fidalgo but neither parent felt it was a good idea, for different reasons.

With his sister distraught, Benny felt terrible it had come to this. He and Anne hadn't been terribly close growing up, as he was so engaged in soccer and karate. But he remembered how his big sister stuck up for him when their dad reprimanded him for failing to do chores.

Suddenly, Falcone reappeared, thrusting his cell at Benny. When he didn't accept it, Falcone put it to his ear, "Chief Thompson, I'm sorry, he doesn't want to speak to you." With Falcone off again, Benny shouted after him, "Listen, if it was your niece missing, you couldn't remain on the sidelines."

With awkward silence, Pete felt he had to step in. "Coffee up? I suggest we all chill."

As one-by-one they left to go inside, only Pete remained. "You're taking it on the chin."

"I'm a big boy."

Benny felt his cell vibrating, no doubt Thompson.

Instead, it was a text from Trish: "Got the name of your Pueblo buyer."

CHAPTER 15

Unnerved by the inquisitive customer inquiring about Pueblo, Warren Shipley pondered what to do. He knew the person he was looking for was Alfie Doolittle and that his visit had to do with the missing teens. To him, it would be only a matter of time before the police caught up with Alfie and the others. And he wasn't about to be caught in their net.

Enticed to join the hunting group by Doolittle, lured by all-night poker and prostitutes, he grew anxious when talk bridged "to more exhilarating entertainment" with women who wouldn't be "so obliging." That night when one of them suggested kidnapping "a bovine that wasn't turning tricks," he couldn't believe that others latched onto the idea.

And he was shocked when Whitey abducted a college student and had her dance in the nude. He couldn't shake the memory of them resuming playing poker outside while one by one the others left the game to abuse her inside as well as the screams begging for her life. And while he didn't really know what happened to her and cared not to ask, it became obvious when her photo appeared on local TV and her disappearance reported on. As a result, he changed his shift at Fred's to late nights, to avoid any goings-on at the cabin.

As he left his apartment for Denver, he felt obligated to give Alfie Doolittle a heads up.

"Did you give him my name?" Alfie said, alarmed.

"Of course not. But I'm getting clear."

"What for? You're clean?"

"Clean? I was there for that college student." What Shipley remembered was being the last to leave the poker game and finding the girl inside and semi-conscious. He acted out, for the benefit of the others, that he had satisfied himself but had actually left her right where he found her.

"That's ancient history," Alfie said.

"Well, what isn't ancient history is that I've lied about the Pueblo because I didn't want to give you up."

"Don't get all twisted. They'll never get to us. Masterson will come up with a solution. Was this guy a cop?"

"Didn't say. But he wreaked cop."

Ending the call, Alfie kicked himself for failing to extract all the cigarette butts. He had to report what Shipley had confided and braced for Masterson's tirade.

"Damn," Masterson said, leaving his office to have the conversation in the parking lot. "How can you be so stupid?"

"What can I say? We had a lot to clean up while keeping watch over those kids."

"I can't believe what you're dumping on me. And to boot, numb nuts Shipley panics and tells this guy that they don't sell Pueblo. I can't believe the assholes I've surrounded myself with."

By his car, Masterson told Alfie that he needed a few minutes to think this over. As he did, it wasn't lost on him that a sudden departure by Shipley would backfire. He had to quickly get to him and tell him to take his regular shift, to say he forgot about the store having Pueblo in stock. Furthermore, to convey that there's no urgency to get to Denver, that his brother had called and all is good. Above all, he had to message to Shipley to project calm.

As he thought it through, what equally troubled him was Alfie's blunder in leaving the tobacco butts behind for the investigators to find, which was sure to be traced to him.

He reconnected with Alfie Doolittle. "Sure as shit, they'll link the Pueblo to you. Listen to me...when you're approached, say you were hunting raccoons."

"Rabbits, season always open."

"Whatever. Stick with that. Tell them you've been in there more than a few times, the latest being a week ago."

"What if they ask if I was hunting with someone?"

"Tell them you were hunting alone. Bringing Goobie up only complicates matters. I'll get to him. Key is to not appear rattled. Can we trust Shipley? His exit would have been bad for all of us."

"He's solid. Are we still on for this evening?"

"Of course. As much as you fucked up, this doesn't change anything."

As Masterson continued to give it all some thought, sitting in his car, he felt tossed. While it may be better to dispatch of the teens this evening, if Shipley and Alfie perform up to task, they had ample time to have their fun before pulling the plug.

He wasted no time reaching Shipley. He knew how to neuter him but wished to do so in person. Having not spoken to him in years, he caught up with him in the back parking lot of Odd Lot.

"Go home, forget Denver," he advised, "and take your shift tonight. Leaving would send the wrong signal."

He could tell that Shipley was nervous, hiding behind sunglasses yet constantly looking off to see if anyone was approaching.

"What do you know about us since you left?" he asked.

"Very little."

"Alfie hasn't kept you up?"

"Hardly see him."

"That's good." Masterson caught Shipley's brief hesitation, meaning he knew more.

"Listen to me," he said, sternly. "If we hear that you caved, shared anything about us, and I'll have the boys hoist up your carcass at the cabin and gut you. You know how Dupree likes to work that blade of his. Got it?"

"Why would I say anything? Ain't I the one who tipped off Alfie?"

Masterson liked that he had Shipley all twisted up and thought better of continuing to do so, fearing that he would leave town.

"That's the boy. Continue to remain detached from us and plead ignorance to anyone asking about us. That should be easy. But if you happen to glean other intelligence, connect with Alfie, preferably in person, so that there's no record of it."

With Masterson reaching out to shake hands, he asked, "we good?"

Shipley nodded and reciprocated. But as he left to return to his apartment, he kept thinking about Masterson's warning of being gutted by Dupree. He was familiar with that crazy, bastard Dupree and recalled him catching squirrels at the cabin, cutting of their hind legs, and using them to bait bobcats and coyotes.

Arriving at his apartment, he packed a bag and planned to keep it by his door for a quick exit. He also figured that there would be no going to Denver, for that's where they'd look for him first. He began searching the Internet for low-key destinations in Mexico.

CHAPTER 16

After the Connecticut investigators had left, Benny remained on the deck talking to Pete who urged him to go inside and make amends. But as much as he wanted to do so, also to fully know what Falcone had delivered in terms of information, he couldn't take that first step. He anticipated his sister lowering the boom and also having to cave to her wishes to leave. That he couldn't so.

Listening to a voicemail from homeowner and landlord Joyce Peterson, informing him that Shipley had returned, he apologized to Pete. "Duty calling."

"Need company?"

Benny considered it. "Better for me to go it alone on this one but thanks for asking."

On the way to Shipley's apartment, he checked his watch. It was 10:46 a.m. Attempting to reach Murph, he got voicemail.

"What do you want?" Shipley shouted from behind closed doors.

"Are you going to open it or am I going to put my foot through."

Shipley obliged.

"Not going to Denver? I guess you had second thoughts."

"Yes, my brother rebounded."

"Amazing recovery. Let's stop the bullshit. Last night you said Fred's didn't sell Pueblo, and a more knowledgeable salesman informed me that Fred's never stopped carrying it."

"I guess I got it confused with something else."

"You'd better stop drawing the weed. It's messing with your head. Who's the Pueblo buyer? Who are you protecting?"

"I'm protecting nobody."

Benny grinned. "What do you take me for? Did you think you'd never see me again? I'm the girl's uncle." He paused to let that sink in. "And, I make my living as a detective."

Both revelations, he could see, landed like one-two punches. If Shipley had cancelled his Denver trip, he might be rebooking.

"Are you behind the kidnapping?"

"I've done nothing wrong."

"Then why did you lie to me?"

"I told you I forgot."

With Shipley not making eye contact, it was clear to Benny that he had much to hide. "You can continue to lie. That's your choice. But when I catch up with those bastards who took the teens, they'll be pointing fingers. And I'd expect they won't hesitate in throwing your ass under the bus. You'll fry as an accomplice, unless of course, you're directly involved. In that case, you'll go down with them."

As Shipley made a bid to close the door, Benny's foot prevented it.

"You know where this is headed? One of three ways. A long prison term. And, for sure, a scrawny, weakling like you won't do well with crazed, muscle-bound lunatics seeking new meat. Two, you can choose to hang yourself after I leave and save us all the trouble. Or three, you can fess up, admit what you know. DA's go lenient on those acknowledging their sinful ways."

He added, before taking his foot away, "Better to call me before those two kids are found dead."

On the way back to Pete's, Benny connected with Murph. "Are you still at the library or are you filling your face?"

"Wasn't thinking food until you brought it up. Actually, just had the most pleasant library experience…a real blood pressure tester."

"What have you come up with?"

Instead of getting into it over the phone, Murph suggested meeting at Hannah's, which caught his eye on the way to the library.

When Benny arrived, Murph was seated. "Did you order yet?" he asked.

"For the two of us, in fact."

"What am I having?"

"Trust me."

"Whatever. Tell me what you found or are you going to keep that a secret too."

Murph shared about learning of three missing women happening years apart– one abducted from Dairy Queen, a Rhode Island student, and a housewife.

"You were right to have me look into it," he said. "They were never found."

Hungry, Benny hoped that the bell he heard was their breakfast order. "Only thing different, I guess, is the taking of Justin. Your findings support being focused here."

Surprised that Murph was able to gain that information in just a few hours, he asked if he had been able to dig into any of the disappearances.

His sharing: A housewife went missing in 2012, after she had brought her daughter to the bus stop. There was some suspicion that she was having an affair. But the police checked into it and the man she had been rendezvousing with had a solid alibi. Another person they interviewed was an accountant she worked part-time who showed an interest in her. He also checked out. She had filed a spousal abuse complaint but withdrew it. The thinking was maybe the husband had threatened her again but he also checked out. It was a head-scratcher for no one believed she would take off and leave her daughter.

"You got that from a newspaper account?"

"I have my ways…or I could attribute it to a librarian with a solid memory."

With the Soho omelet placed in front of him, Benny was impressed at how well formed it was, perfectly blended.

"Didn't I do right by you?" Murph asked.

"If it tastes the way it looks, I'll compliment you."

Murph left his pancakes alone, watching Benny lift a forkful of goat cheese, mushrooms, and tomatoes.

"Ok," he acknowledged. "You don't have to make a big deal of it."

As Murph provided details on the other two missing persons, he put a major dent into the four pancakes that completely filled his plate.

Benny tried to make sense of Murph's findings. He told Murph that with the abductions spaced out over that many years, it could mean they're disconnected. On the other hand, he said, they could point to operators who are expert at staying under the radar. "Except for the cigarette butts, not much to go on."

As the waitress leaned in to fill their coffee cups, Murph quipped, "That chef of yours is top notch. Take that from one who knows." He patted his stomach.

"I'll tell him. Glad you enjoyed them."

"What's your dinner specialty?"

"You're kidding, right?" Benny interjected. "You just devoured a mountain of pancakes and you're thinking food?"

Laughing, the waitress brought over a dinner menu. "Short ribs are quite popular."

"Then call the butcher."

Sharing his interactions with Shipley, Benny asked Murph if he was up to tailing him.

"I still have work at the library."

"I know. But he's rattled. May lead us to the guy who bought the Pueblo."

Murph continued eating but had to deliver the bad news. "This might be my last meal with you. Thompson wants my big, fat, wide ass, as he described it, back in Blacksburg. And you're to blame for hanging up on him."

"For your information, I didn't hang up on him." A pause. "But with my niece in the hands of…has me not thinking straight."

With Benny rarely ever showing emotion, Murph couldn't leave him in a lurch. "I got Shipley. And where may I ask are you off to?"

"Trish locked on to a Pueblo smoker, and I'm about to pay that poor, unfortunate soul a visit."

Murph snapped his head back, puzzled. "Then why pursue Shipley, if you have your smoker?"

"Because there may be more than one and because Shipley knows something." Benny rose, taking the check. "I've spooked him to where he's either rebooking a plane out of here or on his way to warn the kidnappers."

CHAPTER 17

Entering the cabin, they placed folding chairs in a semi-circle, about eight feet from the dear-skin mattress on which Justin and Julie sat. Masterson claimed the center chair where he could keep an eye on all of them. He recalled the time Dupree raced over to one woman who refused to go along and started spanking her. He had a difficult time restoring order, with some cheering wildly and others preventing him from interfering.

Removing the wrist restraints, he asked Julie and Justin to stand but they remained sitting. "You had better get used to following instructions or things will get a whole lot worse for you."

After Alfie directed the LED lights on them, Justin squinted but could barely make out the forms in front of him.

"Here's what's going down," Masterson said. "You two are the principals in a little wagering game beginning in a minute. Here's what's going down. When I say "go," Justin, you are to remove your shorts and t-shirt and then slowly – and I do stress slowly - take off the little lady's bikini top and bottom. Once that happens the action turns to you, little lady. You are to perform oral sex on your boyfriend there. Don't stop until he's tapped out. And this is important. Always remain sideways to us, so that we don't have an obstructed view. Do you understand?"

Receiving no reaction, Masterson said, "Maybe you'd like to ask what happens if you refuse?"

"I'll tan their hides," a seated spectator snapped.

Annoyed, Masterson raised his index finger to his lips.

"If that happens, you'll do all of us, little lady."

Although Julie had convinced herself to go along, with whatever, afraid of what may be done to them, she now cringed. It wasn't just getting naked in front of them or fulfilling what they desired. It was what would occur afterward.

Masterson didn't need to further threaten but did so anyway. "And we'll strap that boyfriend of yours to a tree outside and whip him real good."

"Go ahead!" Justin shouted.

From the darkness, Whitey menacingly stepped forward while removing his belt.

"Sit down!" Masterson snapped. "You heard what I said outside."

"Yeah, sit down," Alfie seconded.

"Shut up, you little shit!" Whitey said. "I should be whipping you for leaving the butts."

When Goobie jumped up to defend Alfie, Masterson stepped between them. "Fellas, fellas, if you really wish to square off, wait until later. It's time for the show."

After they sat, Masterson knelt in front of Justin. "Young fellow, we don't care the least about you. The pretty one is who we want. These guys would rather tie you up outside, paste your carcass with bacon grease, and watch the coyotes come in and feast. If you aren't aware, the coyotes are a frightening lot. They tear bit by bit until the pack descends in mass. So, if I were you, I'd just calm myself. Anyway, why bitch? You're the one in for a treat. Yours prayers are about to be answered."

As Masterson took his seat, Julie whispered to Justin, "Do as he said."

Taking an alarm clock with a second hand from a paper bag, that now contained their gambling money, grouped in $100s, $50s and $20s, Masterson declared. "Ready. Go!"

Shaking, Justin removed his t-shirt and shorts, before removing Julie's bathing suit. Kneeling, she went along with the instructions but, after doing so, Justin wasn't getting excited. She thought maybe she wasn't doing it right and tried differently. At one point, in holding his outer thighs for support, it occurred why. Justin legs trembled so much she wondered how he could stay upright. After telling him to lie down, it was soon over. Masterson hit the clock at eight minutes, 12 seconds to shouts from several of them, either excited about the entertainment or because they lost the bet, or both.

Amidst the hoopla, Julie and Justin rushed to put on their bathing suits.

"I'm not too excited," Whitey declared. "She was too willing and steady. Seems like she's been at this before."

"Wait until tomorrow night," Dupree said. "She aint been at that before."

"Keep quiet," Masterson hollered. But he could see that Julie and Justin heard the comment. "Whitey, you're not being honest. Tell me you didn't like the show?"

He shrugged. "It was ok. If she didn't get him to relax and lie down, I would have won the damn thing."

Pulling out the slips of paper, in view of all, Masterson declared Jackson the winner at eight minutes, twenty-four seconds. As he went to hand over the money, Alfie shouted, "Not so fast. I had seven minutes, thirty-five seconds. He went over."

"Doesn't matter," Masterson said. "I said who came the closest."

"Not by Price Is Right rules. If you go over by a dollar, you're out."

"Well, those aren't the rules we were following."

"Masterson's right," Whitey said. "Just get over it."

"Who put you in charge?" Alfie said.

Alfie quit arguing when the others concurred with Masterson.

"Don't be such a sore loser," Jackson said. "Besides, you'll get another crack tomorrow."

"Listen," Masterson warned. "Don't be congregating in any taverns or anywhere else in public. I'll fill the cooler tomorrow night."

"Don't bring any of that IPA shit," Whitey chirped. "Heinekens or Coronas."

"I don't want any of that Mexican piss," Goobie said. "Buds for me."

Annoyed, Masterson shook his head. "I'll bring an assortment. Listen, when you exit onto to the main road, do so minutes apart. You know the drill. Let's not get sloppy." Shaking his head, he glanced at Alfie, still annoyed at him leaving the cigarette butts.

Before leaving, Masterson knelt before Julie. "I'm hearing an uncle of yours has been asking about you." Julie's eyes widened. "What does he do for a living?"

"He's an electrician." It was the first occupation that popped into her head.

"You wouldn't be fooling me?"

"No, he's a master electrician, wired our house."

"He'd better pay more attention to that, if he knows what's good for him."

With Julie asking to pee, Masterson asked Alfie to take her.

Noticing how accommodating they were and hearing a few vehicle engines turn over, Justin also said he had to go. And Masterson told Whitey to take him.

As Justin walked around the side of the cabin, he spotted where Julie was. It was his aim to go past her, closer to the forest.

"That's good right here," Whitey declared. "Notice anything unique about that tree to your left?" Justin shook his head. "See the grooves in it? That right there is one of our whipping trees. Many lashed for behaving badly."

Justin feigned interest while seizing the opportunity. He heard the comment that he wasn't the one they wanted. He didn't know what they ultimately had in mind but felt dispensable, like the walking dead. He knew he could outrun the out-of-shape, middle-aged guy behind him, though he couldn't tell if the guy had a concealed gun.

Seizing the opportunity, he darted for the wood line and made it but had to slow down in trying to navigate around brush and trees. He couldn't tell if he was being followed but knew for sure he wasn't when he heard raised voices in the distance. Proceeding another two hundred yards or so, the only thing he heard was his own labored breathing. As scared as he was in the cabin, the darkness was equally terrifying. He had no choice but to keep moving. He thought if he could survive until the morning's light, he might stumble onto a road, a utility or pipe line, anything to lead to safety.

From being thrashed by bushes and tree limbs, he could feel his body, especially his legs, stinging. Slowing down, the mosquitoes feasted on his legs and neck, drawn to his sweat. With the mention of coyotes, he wondered about them or what other creatures existed, even snakes.

And, as he got farther away from the cabin, he felt guilt for leaving Julie and imagined what they might be doing to her.

Contemplating whether to return, he picked up voices, which meant they were pursuing him. That had him continuing into the unknown, though holding out hope that by looking for him, they weren't harming Julie.

CHAPTER 18

Benny checked the address on the street mail box, which matched GPS. About to knock, the door swung open.

"Oh, you scared me," said a woman in jeans, wearing a tee-shirt with the words 'Wallys Diner' in front, and holding keys. "Can I help you?"

"Does Alfie Doolittle live here?"

"He does but he's at work."

"Are you Mrs. Doolittle?"

"I am. And you are?"

"I'm conducting research on a tobacco product called Pueblo and understand that your husband may favor it."

She rolled her eyes. "Unfortunately, he does from time to time. Costs us dearly."

"I'd like to survey him. Will take no more than fifteen minutes. Do you think he'd mind if I bothered him at work?"

Suspicious, she hesitated. After all, who comes unannounced and aggressive over a damn survey that could very well be done via the phone or on-line.

"Leave your number and I'll have him contact you."

Benny searched his pockets. "Sorry, out of business cards at the moment." Taking a pen from his sports jacket, he wrote his name on a Dollar Tree receipt, while struggling to come up with a way to extract Doolittle's work address. Telling her that he had to head to Massachusetts to interview three other Pueblo smokers today, he hoped that would explain the urgency. It fell on deaf ears. However, he cleverly moved to a fallback.

"There's a hundred dollars for his time." He could tell that got her attention. "I can see you're off to work. Are you a waitress?"

"Yes. At Wally's diner as you can see."

"You've got competition. I was at Hannah's this morning and they sure do make a great omelet."

She laughed and then smirked. "Wally's has been operating for fifty years. Do you know how many fly-by-nights have come and gone? As I said, leave your number. If he's interested, he'll call you."

As soon as the Pueblo salesman left, she called her husband, telling him about the visitor and the $100 offer.

"That so?" Goobie knew who the visitor was and wrote down the number.

"Are you going to call?" she asked.

"Maybe. What did he look like?"

"Kind of short, maybe five-seven, five-eight. Black hair. Sports jacket. What does that matter?"

"I don't know. Matters."

"Well, bring home milk and eggs. We're out."

"I'm going to be late, I'm afraid."

"Not again."

"We're still finishing Goobie's deck." He heard the sigh. "We can use the extra money."

"I haven't seen any of it yet."

"Don't worry. He's good for it."

After disconnecting, Alfie thought long and hard about placing a call to who he knew to be the girl's uncle, matching the description Shipley had given. But he felt if the uncle had managed to get his name, he'd wouldn't quit until satisfied that he had nothing to do with the kidnapping.

In reaching out, he listened to the so-called survey taker weave a story about travelling through the northeast, asking if he could accommodate him. Accepting, Alfie suggested meeting at the Brook Ridge Golf Course, where he worked in maintenance.

When a bearded guy with an Australian outback hat pulled up at the course's front entrance, Benny matched his face to one in the hunting photo.

"I really appreciate you meeting me on such short notice," he said. "Is there somewhere we can sit?"

"Jump in." Alfie took him around the side of the clubhouse to an unoccupied picnic table.

Holding a clipboard and note pad he bought on the fly at Dollar Tree, Benny reached into his pants pocket. "Here's your hundred dollars, and Pueblo thanks you."

"Must be an important survey if you're doling out hundreds like that?"

"My company considers this a landmark study, to better understand brand loyalty. Have you been smoking our product for long?"

Pulling a cigarette packet from his shirt pocket, Alfie lit up. "Hope you don't mind?"

"Did you think I'd prevent a customer from imbibing?"

Alfie grinned. "I guess not. The answer to your question is twenty years."

"I'd call that loyalty. Do you try other brands?"

"Did years ago, but find this quite satisfying."

Benny explained that he had several questions to cover, such as how many cigarettes he smokes in a day; when he craves Pueblo; where he buys the tobacco; and cost.

As Benny jotted his responses, he deftly moved to questions close to the heart of the matter.

"Do you tend to smoke during recreational activities?"

"Like bowling?"

"Yes, or hunting and fishing."

"Fishing maybe. With hunting, spooks the game."

"Yes, of course. Can I ask, where is good hunting and fishing around here?"

Alfie checked a smile, thinking back to the girl stating that her uncle was an electrician.

"All over. If you're into small mouth, you could take your fill at any of the lakes around here."

"Is the area around Beach Pond any good? Someone earlier labeled it the best, even mentioned that it had land-locked salmon."

"It's been said. But why waste your time chasing after fish rarely seen when there's small mouth to be had for dinner."

Benny didn't know how much time he had because another golf course maintenance worker stopped to tell Doolittle that he'd meet him on the 14th green.

"Shame what happened to the missing teens," Benny said, focusing on Doolittle's face. "Everybody's speculating. What do you suppose happened to them?"

Benny didn't notice any outward sign that Doolittle had something to hide, though he delayed responding by taking a long draw.

"My guess is that they've probably eloped and are half way across the country."

Remaining calm, Alfie flicked his cigarette butt out onto the grass and latched on to another. "What do you think happened to them?"

As to whether Doolittle was involved, Benny wasn't sure. He didn't seem nervous.

"My take," he said. "Two jackasses have them holed up around here."

Doolittle couldn't help but smile. "Wow. For a survey taker on his way to Massachusetts, you sure seem to have a view. The news didn't seem to indicate that. Did I miss something?"

Benny observed Doolittle's casualness and pondered whether he was barking up the wrong tree. That said, he had to press.

"Well, I'm told these guys were complete assholes. They left cigarette butts behind, in fact, our brand, and indentations from two portable chairs. One guy is a bigger asshole because he left larger indentations."

"Is that right? Where are you coming by this information?"

Benny figured it was time to come clean and said calmly, "I'm a detective."

With that, Doolittle flicked the half-finished cigarette and stood. "If you'll excuse me, I'm needed on the fourteenth green. I guess we're finished?"

"Not by a long shot."

As Doolittle whisked off, Benny sensed he was involved. Anyone innocent would have at least challenged him. He didn't get a 'you're not accusing me of anything' come back. He had to know for certain and drove to Wally's diner, where he spotted Mrs. Doolittle behind the counter. He sat in front of her.

"Did you meet up with him?" she asked.

"I did and he was very helpful."

"What can I get you? Want to compare our corn beef hash and eggs to that goat cheese concoction?"

Benny enjoyed her sense of humor. "No, maybe tomorrow. I'd like to keep heart healthy. I'll have coffee."

After she delivered it, Benny told her he could guess what's most often on the Doolittle dinner menu.

She smiled. "What's that?"

"Small mouth bass.

"Not tonight. He's off again helping a friend build a deck."

"Does this friend smoke Pueblo?"

She reflected for a moment. "Don't really know."

"Do you think I can go to the friend's house and find out?"

"I guess Goobie can use a hundred, if he smokes it." She wrote down his name and address.

With Julie and Justin unlikely at the Doolittle's, with this woman unlikely to be part of any kidnapping, and with the teens not captive at Shipley's apartment, maybe they were being held at this friend's house. With Murph tailing Shipley, he'd ask Pete to keep an eye on Doolittle while he caught up with this Goobie Crenshaw.

CHAPTER 19

Benny's vehicle display screen lit up with an incoming call. It was Thompson. He debated whether or not to answer it, fully expecting The Chief to be presenting a loaded question and then chastising him on his response.

He answered: "Sammy's whorehouse, Sammy speaking."

A friend once told him that his father always picked up the phone using either that opener or "Joe's bar and grill, Joe speaking," infuriating his friend's mother who scolded his father, saying 'what if it's the school principal calling about one of the children?'

"Who is this?" Thompson asked, bewildered.

"Your dedicated Blacksburg detective and loyal servant."

"Stop the bullshit. Have you conferred with Falcone?" To Benny, that was the predicted loaded question, and he opted to remain mum. "Well, if you had, you'd know that they're following a strong lead."

"And what is that?"

"Why am I here one hundred fifty miles away and your there without a clue?"

Benny had assumed Falcone's irate call to Thompson, about his interfering, was their one hook up but obviously not. "Tell me what they're sitting on."

"Find out yourself. And I want Murph back here ASAP."

"I thought he's here on his time."

"His time or not, he's needed here. If you'd put yourself in my shoes for a moment, you'd know I have limited detective resources, with Trish on urgent matters and you doing the usual end run."

"Chief, it's my niece we're talking about."

A pause.

After calming, Thompson revealed that the Connecticut state police are in pursuit of a 2013 Winnebago that was reported hurriedly leaving a Beach Pond area campsite the night of the kidnapping. A camper, going to a port-o-potty, saw the Winnebago occupants scurrying around and thought it highly unusual, as it is difficult in the dark to collect your belongings, which is why most campers prefer morning departures. In addition, other campers shared that the two men and a woman attached to the Winnebago in question seldom ventured outside, unlike others sucking up the great outdoors or commingling over coffee or beer and swapping intelligence about favored campsites.

"I'd suggest you speak to Falcone," Thompson said, summing up.

Considering whether it wise to just end the call, he couldn't. "I believe they're barking up the wrong tree."

"Figured you say that. In speaking with Murph, he said you are locked in on a tobacco angle. I told him and I'm telling you that Falcone is all over that and has spoken to a Doolittle, who has alibis."

Benny now understood why Alfie Doolittle was unrattled. It was his second go-around. Being released by proper authorities, he didn't fear being questioned by others.

"Mess around if you'd like, but I want Murph's ass here tomorrow."

"Did they share who else they've interviewed?" As soon as the question left his lips, he braced for the onslaught.

"I'm no damn go-between! Speak to Falcone!"

Changing the subject, he sheepishly asked Thompson about the internal affairs investigation.

"It's moving along. Thank God for Sheila Morgan. She's putting her neck out there. Anyway, why are you asking me? Figured McGlucas is filling you in."

"She has been." He lied. "Just haven't spoken with her since yesterday."

"Well, Pete Williams is another name besides Carney. No telling how deep this goes."

Benny knew Murph had groomed Pete Williams but, then again, Murph has ties with half the force serving Blacksburg.

Delighted when Thompson said he had another call, Benny connected with Murph to tell him that Chief Thompson wanted him back.

"Why didn't he call me?"

"How should I know? But you need to leave."

"What else did you two cover?"

Benny sensed it was another bid by Murph to find out what he and Trish were working on, but he stuck to the case at hand and divulged that Falcone had spoken to Shipley and Doolittle and was tracking the Pueblo and that campers had been seen suspiciously leaving the evening his niece and boyfriend went missing.

"Might be truth to that," Murph volunteered.

"Let them. I'll pursue my own track. It can't hurt."

"In that case, I think I'll stick it out with you and the ribs awaiting at Hannah's."

A long pause. Though Murph knew it was a mistake to remain detached from the Connecticut state trooper investigation, he couldn't leave his colleague fighting the good fight alone. And Benny didn't insist that Murph return, for he needed him.

"If you insist on staying and filling your face with ribs, can you stick with Shipley?" Benny asked.

"You got it."

Before heading towards Goobie Crenshaw's, Benny swung back around to Beach Pond to check in with Anne and John and attempt to discover if they had been updated by Falcone. Driving through the town, he spotted his sister and brother-in-law in front of St. Thomas and St. Anne Church speaking to a priest.

After detouring into the church parking lot, Benny saw that their conversation ended as he neared.

"Father Arias, meet my brother Benedito. He's such a great comfort to us during this troubling time."

Shaking hands, Benny caught his sister's dig.

"Call me Benny. Only my parents, sister, and brother call me by my formal name, and it's usually when I'm in the doghouse."

"Benedito," she emphasized again, "Father said he will say a mass for Julie's safe return at 10 a.m. tomorrow."

"The least I can do. I will keep your niece and her friend in my prayers." The priest left for the rectory.

"Are you looking for the camper?" Anne asked.

By her tone, Benny knew she was interested in a fight. "How are the Edwards?"

"How do you think they are? Do you really care?"

"Anne," John said, "I'm sure he's doing all he can."

"Well, obviously, not enough. Have you called mom?"

Benny looked away.

"Of course not. Don't you realize how upset she and dad are. You probably haven't given them a thought."

Benny couldn't disagree. He hardly had time to speak with Charlotte.

"They wished to come here but I told them not to," she continued. "I lied to them. Told them that you were a crutch for us. I should have told them the truth…that you should have stayed home."

Anne's anger rose. "Do you know what they're doing to my daughter right now!" As she sobbed, John put his hand around her shoulder and led her toward the parking lot.

Anne's barbs and emotion tore into him. Before leaving, he went into the church, which had only about 20 pews. As he knelt to pray, he was struck by the eerie silence of the empty church. Remaining far longer than expected, he prayed to God to give him the wisdom and strength to persevere.

Getting into his car, Google Maps provided the route to Goobie Crenshaw's. Entering a long dirt, lumpy driveway, he could tell right away that Crenshaw lived alone, for a woman wouldn't put up with a junkyard, with all kinds of old farming equipment strewn around.

As he climbed the wooden steps leading to the house, the hand railing lay broken below, alongside a rusty barbeque grill. But what he didn't see was any work being done on the deck. At the door, he was greeted by an agitated dog, no Pekinese. Obviously, no one was at home. Trying the door handle, to his surprise, it was unlocked. He went back downstairs and found two old towels, lying next to the barbeque grill, he wrapped them around his hands and forearms.

Back upstairs, he pushed the door open and lurched back. As the Shepard leaped, in one quick move, he forearmed it down the stairs. Moving quickly inside, he slammed the door. With the dog barking madly outside, he unwrapped the rags.

Not surprising, the mess inside equaled that outside. Open beer bottles were all over and the garbage overflowing. He searched room to room. In one closet, he came across a locked firearms' safe, verifying that Crenshaw likely hunted. Backtracking, he found stairs leading to the basement, where animal skins of all kinds were nailed to the walls. Two oversized easy chairs faced a massive flat screened TV. Noticing a few 8X10 photos on the wall, he studied the principals. While Shipley wasn't among them, Doolittle was. And one other principal, likely the owner of this house, Goobie Crenshaw, the same bearded guy who had told Doolittle to meet him on the 14th hole. Behind those photographed was the same dwelling in the photo he had taken from Shipley's. Convinced that the teens weren't here, he climbed the stairs.

With the Shepard still agitated outside, he rewrapped his hands and forearms. Opening the door slowly, he jammed it closed just after the Shepard's head was in. A dog lover, he hated hearing the Shepard whines but had to take the fight out of him. When he opened the door fully, the Shepard paid no attention to him.

It was all becoming clearer now. Falcone could have the Winnebago. He had the hunting cabin.

CHAPTER 20

Leaping to reach a clump of swamp grass, Justin fell short and found his left leg deep in mud. Able to extricate it, he sat exhausted and listened for any sounds that they were closing in.

Scared, he remembered his cousin talking about being lost in the woods and defining it as the most terrifying moment in his life. He could now identify. He figured maybe he had gone two miles. Taking stock, his feet throbbed, so cut up and sore that he didn't know how much farther he could go. His arms and legs had several gashes from working his way through dense brush.

When he set out, he figured that he would eventually come across lit property, anything that would signify civilization, for Connecticut wasn't known for vast stretches of forest. But now, he was quickly losing confidence. He didn't even know if he had proceeded in a straight line and feared that he might be looping back to the cabin. Looking skyward, the stars seemed locked in the heavens, offering no guidance. The quarter moon worked against him.

At the cabin, Julie heard the shouting and stressed voices, aware that Justin had run off. As much as they had taunted him about being weak, he was anything but. In middle school, he scored the highest in tests of agility and did the most pull-ups. Asked to play multiple sports by coaches, he respectfully declined, intent on after school activities such as art and design.

Hearing another engine start and drive off, she figured at least half of her captors were still around.

"Your boyfriend has run off," Masterson said, stepping into the cabin. "But he's going to wish he hadn't."

Julie knew enough to keep quiet. She didn't want to say anything that may draw attention to her. Hearing a vehicle drive up, she didn't know what to make of it until she saw Goobie handing out rifles.

"We've gathered a little hunting party to catch up with your playmate," Alfie said, smiling broadly. "That's if the coyotes don't get to him first. Even so, he leaving this earth one happy guy. You did him nicely."

"I hope he finds help and they…" Her voice trailed off.

"Well, our young lady's a little feisty, isn't she?" Alfie said to Goobie. "We like a little feistiness in our women. You know, a woman too willing doesn't give much of a rush."

"You are a bunch of dirty old men."

"Can't argue there. How did you feel with all of us gawking? You weren't doing much talking then."

When they exited, Julie's hopes lay in Justin succeeding. She also held out hope that Uncle Benny would arrive. Hearing the reference to him brought such joy, yet she couldn't show it. As a freshman in high school, she felt like the queen of the ball with her classmates asking about the detective who captured the serial killer. While she knew her mother and father weren't on speaking terms with him due to the arm-wrestling incident, she also heard the cackling and knew it wasn't his fault. She overheard her mother's derogatory remarks to her dad more than once, "my brother marches to the beat of his own drummer" and "there's no telling what's going on in that head of his."

It was difficult for her to be in the anti-Uncle Benny club. As a child, she recalled his tickling and snuggling, and tossing her around like a rag doll on their sofa. And she loved Aunt Charlotte's teasing of him, saying that he couldn't find a car thief "if the thief hollered, we're over here." She could visualize his face so lovingly gazing at his wife as she playfully tore into him. She overheard someone categorize him as a "man's man" and didn't know at the time what that meant. She came to understand that it had to do with peer respect for someone who faced up to tough challenges and persevered.

Hearing them outside, she tried to listen.

"Jarvis, how do you propose we conduct the search?" Masterson asked, considering Jarvis Wingo the resident expert on all things Pachaug Forest.

There was good reason he deferred to him. For year after year Jarvis bagged the largest buck after countless hours of pre-planning and checking for signs of trophy deer. And he was the go-to tracker for wounded game hit by others. Jarvis's woodsmanship and acquired skills he gained from his dad and grandfather, and Masterson made every effort to stroke him in striking up conversations about Wingo family doings.

Yet, Masterson sought to get close to Jarvis for other reasons. While he needed Jarvis to look after the cabin, keep the rest in line, and vote according to his wishes, he didn't like that Jarvis didn't partake in their sexual exploits. He passed on all the whores they brought to the cabin and hadn't yet absconded with any woman for cabin pleasure and doubted the loving husband ever would.

As the men gathered, Masterson liked how Jarvis had their attention, propositioning that they stay 50 yards apart in the woods to cover a wider swarth of ground. "If you find sign he's been through, wave your flashlight. In this way we can redirect from that point."

"Got it fellows?" Masterson said.

"Never mind," Dupree said. "Just don't be helping yourself while we're gone. I have my own ideas on what should be done to her."

A half hour later, Dupree fired a shot and waved his flashlight. He stood above Justin as the others gathered. "He was trying to skirt around me."

"Get scared, you little pussy," Whitey said.

"Look at him," Dupree added. "City boy thinking he could find his way out."

"Let's get him back to the cabin," Jarvis said.

"Not so fast," Whitey countered. "Let's have a little fun first."

Dupree agreed. "Yes, let's do."

"Let's not." Jarvis was well aware that it never ended with a little fun.

"Don't need another Masterson," Whitey said. "Anyway, he didn't say that we couldn't teach him a lesson."

On the ground, Justin had his arms wrapped around his knees, thoroughly defeated.

"Take off your shorts," Whitey ordered.

Justin didn't move.

"Didn't you hear me boy?" As Whitey put his rifle on the ground, Jarvis raised his. "Whitey, I'll blow a hole clear through you if I have to."

Whitey stood, belt in hand. "I'm only going to thrash him a few. Has it coming after embarrassing me like that."

"If Masterson thinks he should get whipped, then we'll do it at the cabin."

When they arrived back, Masterson beamed. "Leave it to my merry men."

"Shut that mouth of yours!" Whitey said. "You're no Robin Hood. This leader thing has gotten to your head. Maybe we should vote again."

"Go ahead," Masterson said, calling his bluff. "See where that gets you."

Dupree wasted no time making his case that the boy ought to be whipped for running off.

Masterson didn't disagree. "Tie him up."

When Justin fell to the ground, two of them lifted him up, pushed him against the tree, and secured his arms.

"Five strokes," Masterson said. "Whitey, you can do the honors."

Dupree told him to wait. "Why should our Juliet miss out on her Romeo getting his ass whipped."

"Yeah, get her out here," Whitey said.

Outside, seeing Justin naked against the tree, Julie tried to break Alfie's grasp. "Leave him alone!"

"This is what you get when you disobey orders," Masterson said.

As the whip lashed his back, Justin cried out. Hit four more times, each more powerful, he screamed louder.

"That's enough!" Masterson shouted.

But Whitey, in a stupor, wound up again.

CHAPTER 21

While Benny relished having Murph on hand, he missed his interactions with Trish in working investigations. With the clock against him, he needed a sounding board and made the call.

"Trish, what's the temperature like down there?"

"Haven't seen the chief yet. Why are you asking?"

"He called me yesterday after the lead investigator up here spoke to him…and I got the usual."

Trish read between the lines. "Why don't you have Murph bridge between you and the Connecticut investigators?"

"Have him all out right now. If you don't mind, I need an independent view. Do you have time?"

"Fire away."

Presenting an overview, keying in on the three individuals surfacing as a result of the Pueblo tie, he told her that Murph was tailing Shipley, Pete on Alfie Doolittle, and that he had just left Goobie Crenshaw's. He also informed her of Thompson's reveal that the Connecticut investigators were tracking a Winnebago. With the hunting photo of the cabin, he let her know that he believed that's where the kids were taken. He also filled her in on Murph's research into three unsolved cases involving missing women.

"That's interesting," she said. "But you're talking significant time in-between. May be coincidental."

A pause. "They vanished," he said. "Not a trace. And if the same individuals are behind this…"

She felt for him. She wasn't about to harp on why he wasn't collaborating. The Chief is armed and ready for that.

"Why not speak to Russo?" she floated. "He'll listen to you, you know that. Maybe he'll bring the FBI resources to bear."

To Benny, Trish made a fair point, supporting why he called her.

In listening to her, while she felt the odds against the same operators taking his niece and boyfriend because of the decade-long timeframe, she didn't rule it out either. She recalled a Pennsylvania case six years ago in which three young women were captured and held as sex toys until they were killed over a 12-year timeframe.

"Puts a wrench into the quicker rhythm theory." She paused. "If you scope the prior cases, it will take time. I'd advise you to stay with the three you've locked onto. Glad you called. Where are you and Murph staying?"

"With my sister's neighbor. He's two houses away and has been a huge help."

"Have you spent time with Anne and John like I told you?"

With silence, Trish had her answer. "Put yourself in her shoes. Can't imagine the anguish."

Aware of his relationship with his sister, Trish believed Anne's angst stemmed from being underappreciated, the spotlight given to the star athlete and highly decorated Navy Seal.

Benny almost forgot to ask about the internal affairs investigation. "Thompson shared about Pete Williams. Anything else I should know about?"

"With Carney and now Williams, I don't think Thompson is going to let this string out for long."

"What gives you that impression?"

"To protect Sheila Morgan or simply worried about the full extent of the findings. Think about when this becomes public. Dozens of

Blacksburg police on the take? Doesn't bode well for the department and he'll take the brunt."

Benny was reluctant to raise Murph's connection to Williams which, he knew, she was familiar with. "Use your influence to draw this out. It's the only way. And be watchful," he cautioned. "If you start to get odd looks, it's probably because they sniffed it out."

Dropping off with her, even though Trish advised against wasting time on the missing women, he contacted Dom Scalia, the Rhode Island state police head. Though the missing person cases were largely under Connecticut jurisdiction, he asked Scalia for a favor, requesting that he obtain the files from Connecticut. It would be common to share files between states.

"You're putting me in a tough spot," Scalia said. "It's not the files. It's allowing you access."

"I wouldn't ask if I didn't feel it important."

Crossing his fingers, Benny felt relieved when Scalia said, "If Russo didn't vouch for you, I wouldn't be doing this." He told Benny that he would be notified when the files were available and that he could access them at their Rockford office.

Delighted, Benny drove to Fred's Smoke Shop to confront Shipley. Getting out of his car, he reached for the photo of the eight men standing outside the hunting cabin and spotted Murph's car across the street.

Walking over, Murph lowered the driver's side window, "You're ruining my cover."

"Come with me, while I stoke this asshole."

As they neared the counter, filled with containers of smokeless tobacco, as if taking inventory, Shipley's expression was priceless. Not only was surprised at seeing him again but he had this monster of a guy tagging along.

"My friend and I are in need of Pueblo," Benny said, sarcastically.

Shipley ignored them, continuing to stack smokeless tobacco bins.

"Murph, you know who smokes Pueblo. That fine fellow Alfie Doolittle whom I spoke to you about. In fact, he enjoyed a smoke right in front of me at the golf course. He's the guy in this photo."

Shipley chose not to look up, continuing to shuffle the tobacco tins.

"If you don't look at this photo," Benny threatened, "my friend here is going to come around that counter and ram his foot up your ass."

When Shipley pulled out his cell, Benny slapped it away.

"Hey, what the hell…"

"That's a laugh. You calling the police. I'd like nothing better. But take a gander first. There's you. And there's Alfie Doolittle."

"Where did you get this?"

"Never mind that. Tell me where those kids are or my friend's going to rearrange your face."

Murph menacingly stepped closer to where he could reach across the counter and yank Shipley over it.

Completely rattled, Shipley said haltingly, "I don't know them. That photo was taken in a Vermont hunting lodge. They were friends of Alfie's."

"Don't hand me that bullshit! That cabin is around here. I'm going to give you ten seconds."

"I want my lawyer."

Benny exhibited a phony laugh. "Murph, what a sorry ass. We don't give a rat's ass about laws, lawyers, and least of all, you. Murph, rearrange his face."

As Murph reached over the counter, a customer entered and Shipley screamed, "Robbery! Dial 911! Robbery!"

The man ran out of the store with Benny in pursuit, not before the guy managed to dial 911. As Benny rushed to tell him he was a detective, it was too late. A few minutes later a patrol car swung in.

Benny and Murph presented their shields. "Officer Smith," Benny said, reading his name above his breast pocket, "we are with the Blacksburg PD in New York. It was my niece who was kidnapped at Beach Pond. We had a few questions for Mr. Shipley, and he panicked."

"Panicked, bullshit! He threatened me! Arrest them!"

"Calm down," Smith said. With that, three other cops burst in. "I'm trying to get to the bottom of this," Officer Smith said to the others. "They claim to be New York detectives, that one the missing girl's uncle. The store clerk claims to have been threatened with physical harm. I'll call it in."

With Smith turning at an angle, to make it harder for them to listen, Benny hoped for some sort of reprieve. He didn't get it.

"Inspector Falcone seems particularly interested in what's going on," Smith said. "Why don't we all relax until he gets here."

CHAPTER 22

Waiting for Falcone seemed to take forever. It was bad enough being guarded as if you had intentions to rob the store, but Benny knew by Smith's stare that this was going to end poorly, that Falcone must have insinuated who was at fault. Even with Murph trying to raise his spirits, saying "what the hell can they do to us?" he couldn't imagine what was going to go down. The worst was making headway in finding Julie and Justin and likely being shut down for good.

Falcone arrived like General Patton, with all officers snapping to attention to pay homage.

"I've kept them apart, sir," Officer Smith said.

Falcone didn't acknowledge him and proceeded straight to Benny. "I thought I told you to stand down! Do you understand English?"

Benny absorbed the blows. Had to.

"And who are you?" he snapped at Murph.

"He's a colleague who came to help me find my niece."

Falcone reddened, the veins in his neck about to burst. "I asked him!"

"I'm Detective Dennis Murphy with the Blacksburg Police in New York and here to help a brother in need."

"Don't hand me that crap. You are thwarting an ongoing investigation."

"Thwarting?" Murph responded. "Mr. Thwarting is inside." He pointed to the store.

"Smith, watch them."

A few minutes later Falcone exited Fred's. "Tell me why you threatened him?"

"I'm certain he knows where my niece is."

"What evidence supports that?"

Benny took out his iPhone and showed him the hunting cabin photo. "See this?"

Falcone gave it a cursory look.

"Well, that's Alfie Doolittle right there and behind him is Goobie Crenshaw. And right there is the guy inside. He knows both of them and is stringing me along. That cabin is where I believe my niece and her boyfriend are being held."

Falcone pointed to the screen. "As I see it, no more than a bunch of guys hunting. I asked for evidence."

"Crenshaw and Doolittle were in a blind hunting when my niece went missing. It's no coincidence."

"For your information, I've spoken to Doolittle and he gave an account of where he was at the time of the abductions. It checked." A pause. "Smith, take him in your vehicle and…"

"You've got to be kidding me!" Benny protested, with Murph muttering from behind to remain calm.

"We're not going to settle this here," Falcone said. "We'll have a conversation at Divisional Headquarters and we'll see where we go from there."

Benny fumed. "And you're leaving him here? I told you he's involved or at the very least knows who is."

As Falcone turned his back, Officer Smith followed orders. Murph was told he was free to go.

At the headquarters, in Uncasville, Falcone followed Benny and Smith into a conference room. Not bothering to sit, he said, "I've gotten

Shipley to drop the charges...on one condition. That you leave New London County immediately."

"You've got to be kidding!" While Benny lost it, Falcone hardened. "You have a choice. Go to jail for harassing Shipley or leave."

Following the procession of state trooper vehicles to the divisional headquarters and listening in by the door, Murph was certain Benny was going to dig his grave. He knocked and stuck his head in.

Surprised, Falcone barked, "I thought I told you to go. Do you want what's coming to him?"

"I only want the right outcome."

Falcone grinned. "You two must think we're rank amateurs, that New York detectives are far superior."

Benny wished Murph had not interfered, for Falcone had Chief Thompson's ear. But by doing so, it did allow Benny to count to 25 and he calmingly said, "Shipley lied to me. One minute he's on his way to Denver to visit his ailing brother and the next minute he's back at Fred's. Tells me he thought twice of high-tailing it out of here and aims to lie his way through. He's rattled, for sure, and should be tailed as well as Doolittle and Crenshaw...one of them will lead us to the kids."

Falcone grinned again, this time shaking his head, "You talk as if you prefer jail."

"We're done," Murph said, recognizing it was useless to reason with someone unwilling to listen.

"That's more like it," Falcone said. "Besides, a nationwide search is on for a Winnebago that is tied to the abductions."

Murph coughed, staving off Benny. "Might I have a moment to speak with my colleague?"

"Take all the time you need."

After Falcone left, Murph closed the door and spoke with a voice barely above a whisper. "Let's face up to it…we're not going to get anywhere with him. Most important, we need to get the hell out of here."

"Attached to that damn Winnebago like lemmings," Benny murmured.

Murph wasn't so sure Falcone wouldn't pick up where they left off, in pursuing the parties in question. He just wasn't going to admit it, unwilling to give Benny credit for doing the legwork.

"Listen to me. Let's play nice. What good is it being confined?"

Murph, working long enough with Benny to know that he had come around to his way of thinking, went to the door and opened it.

He found Falcone in conversation with State Trooper Smith.

"We're going back to comfort Anne and John," Murph said, "and we'll be dropping any further pursuit of the teens.

Falcone stepped into the doorframe to take in Benny, who nodded. "Don't cross me. Next time you'll be in the cell down the hall. And to show what a good guy I am, I'm not going to bother my friend Chief Thompson with any of this."

"And we appreciate it," Murph said, stepping to the door.

As they were leaving, Benny overheard an excited trooper confronting Falcone and sharing that the Winnebago in question was found in Pennsylvania and, in interviewing its owners, it was determined they had nothing to do with the kidnappings. The reason they left the campground in a hurry: one in serious pain with kidney stones.

Crouching to pretend to tie a shoe, Benny caught it all. In the parking lot, he exploded. "Can you believe that?"

"He'll pick up where we left off," Murph said. "They have no other choice." Murph felt for sure that Falcone would dig deep into the cabin angle, with the Winnebago behind him.

Eyeing his cell for messages, Benny spotted a voicemail. It was from Pete, relaying that he had followed Alfie Doolittle toward Pachaug Forest until a car got between them and he lost him. He claimed that Doolittle had vanished into thin air. He told Benny he was headed to Dunkin' for coffee and would await his call.

"You can't be doing this," Murph said.

"She's my niece, Murph. Let them put me in jail."

Catching up with Pete, he led them to a stretch of Route 165 and pulled over, with Murph pulling alongside. Rolling down his window, Pete said this is the area he lost Doolittle. On given it thought, he figured Doolittle could have ditched into one of the houses, though he didn't locate his vehicle in any driveway and doubted whether he could have pulled into a garage that fast.

Benny got out. He looked up and down the road, before coming between the two vehicles. "Where does that leave us?"

As they considered their next move, Pete floated that maybe Doolittle went off road. "There are all sorts of entrances to the Forest, though I'm not aware of any established ones along here."

Suggesting that they proceed slowly to see if they might locate one, darkness worked against them. When Pete suggested going to his place to review maps of the area, Murph said he'd stop for sandwiches. Benny felt it was a good time to check in with his sister and found her in conversation with Joan Edwards. When she deliberately didn't look his way, John nodded to the deck.

"We just heard the news that the Winnebago didn't amount to anything," he related.

"Did they share anything else?"

"Only that they are following up a number of leads. Seems like more than a few people saw kids resembling Julie and Justin."

As Benny reflected on the possibilities, the sliding doors opened, slammed aside. "Stop talking to him!" Anne yelled. "You heard what Falcone said! He needs to leave! Couldn't even make the church service. Go!"

Attempting to apologize, she wouldn't let him, angrily storming inside.

"I'm sorry," John said. "I guess you'll be heading back?"

A long pause, as Benny stood with his hands on the railing and stared out at Beach Pond. "That would be right thing to do. But when have I ever done the right thing." He stared in the direction of Pete's house. "I'll check in with him."

On his way, he sat on a tree stump after noticing the moon's reflection on the pond. It presented a good time to connect with Charlotte and he gave her a pretty good account at what had transpired, though leaving out Falcone's directive to return to Blacksburg.

"With Anne being the way she is, why don't you come home? You tried."

"I can't babe. I feel so close."

"Leave it with the state police. You gave them enough to gnaw on."

A pause, after which Benny asked Charlotte about her day and was told of a horrendous crane collapse on a Bronx construction site, injuring more than a dozen workers, keeping the Jacobi ER busier than usual. Benny half-listened. His mind was fixed on finding that forest entrance, the one Doolittle likely ducked into. He spotted Murph pulling into Pete's driveway and getting out with a large paper bag that had to hold more than sandwiches.

"That was awful," he said, as Charlotte wrapped up. "You must be taxed."

"Not any more. Sitting here with a glass of Jacuzzi Cabernet and wishing you were with me."

Benny visualized her in comfortable sweats, with her legs camped underneath in reading a book and at peace. "Listen, I'll be home soon and will gladly open another bottle and rub your feet."

"I know that trick," she said, playfully. "Never stops at the feet."

He smiled. "I love you."

"And I love you too," she said. "When can I expect you?"

"Maybe tomorrow. Have one thread to follow."

CHAPTER 23

Masterson did all he could to calm Shipley who had rambled, incoherently at times, about two men threatening him, one being the guy who had previously been into Fred's asking about Pueblo. What Masterson did decipher was that the New York detective sought the names of the individuals, aside from Alfie Doolittle and Goobie Crenshaw, in the hunting photo. He was glad to hear that the investigators didn't bother to detain Shipley. The reason behind Shipley's panic: the investigators returning to more fully interrogate him.

"They don't have any evidence connecting you to the abductions," Masterson assured Shipley, "otherwise you'd be in the round-up." After he received Shipley's guarantee that he wouldn't divulge anything should the state police return, Masterson texted each hunting group member to call into his business conference call number tomorrow at 10 a.m. to discuss what Shipley had conveyed. Though alarmed over the persistence of this New York detective, Masterson was more concerned over Shipley's inability to keep his mouth shut.

Whitey, one of the first to call in, said the presence of state troopers around town had gone up tenfold.

"Maybe they found Old Man Crimmins," Jackson joked. A widower, Crimmins' car was found abandoned at Beach Pond in 1977 and his whereabouts had been the subject of idle chatter for years.

At Markey's Bait and Tackle to get a reel repaired, Alfie reported that he heard Clete saying that the girl's uncle had been in asking questions and that a ransom is expected shortly.

"This electrician is proving to be a pain in the ass," Jackson stated.

"Did you speak to Clete directly?" Masterson asked Alfie, over Jackson's remark.

"No. He was into his usual bullshit."

"Well, I got news for us," Masterson said. "Shipley said the girl's uncle is a detective from New York."

A long pause before Dupree said, "I'm going to whip her ass for lying."

"That's why I thought we should talk. Maybe we end this now."

Dupree didn't particularly like hearing that the detective had been in to see Shipley twice. "That squirrel has no backbone. He'll give us up for sure. If you ask me, he needs to go."

When the others agreed, Dupree said he would take care of it.

"Well," Masterson posed, "the key question is do we bail or move forward?"

"With the investigators not interested in Shipley, I say what's the rush?" Jackson said, weighing in. "That detective has no jurisdiction here."

When Masterson disclosed that the New York cop had a hunting photo, with all of them in it, it was met with silence, until Dupree voiced, "So, what of it? Showed us hunting. No cause for alarm."

More silence, until Jackson said, "I feel we can go another night. Her uncle may be snooping around, but he has no authority."

Masterson waited a few seconds for other comment. "It's agreed then. We meet tonight."

* * *

When Shipley arrived at the cabin, Masterson greeted him like a long-lost brother. "Don't you miss being here with us?"

Shipley lied. "Of course, the late-night card games and the hunting…a lot to miss."

"And our other adventures?"

Though Shipley nodded, getting immediately what Masterson alluded to, he wished he had gotten out sooner. He couldn't believe that they followed through on Dupree's and Whitey's idea of kidnapping women. Except for that one night, he had nothing the authorities could hold him on. But he was there.

"You haven't said anything to anyone, have you?" Masterson re-asked.

"No. And the state police didn't come back."

"Good. A sign they didn't buy into that New York cop's yarn."

Shipley told Masterson that he got the impression the two detectives were in hot water with Falcone.

"What can you tell me about those two?"

"Well, the girl's uncle is the one to reckon with, though the other was twice his size."

"What's so intimidating about the uncle?"

"I don't know. He ain't much to look at. But he gives off vibes."

'What vibes?"

"That he isn't to be messed with."

Masterson didn't probe. "Come inside and have a beer." Shipley seemed hesitant. "What's bothering you?"

"I guess nothing."

Though expecting the teens to be at the cabin, Shipley could hardly check his surprise at seeing them fastened to the wall, with no fight left in them. On the radio, it was reported that the Edwards Family put up a $100,000 reward for any information, and he gave fleeting thought to claiming the money. But being skinned alive, as Masterson put it, was reason to drop the notion. Dupree's knife skills were legendary.

"What do you think?" Masterson said.

Shipley didn't know what to say. He thought the young man near death, for he hadn't moved. Her eyes gave no sign of life, as if she accepted her fate.

Masterson asked, "You surprised? You must have known we had them. You'll have a ringside seat tonight."

Hearing a vehicle pull in, they watched Dupree cover it with a tarp. The alarm in Shipley's face was obvious. Masterson hadn't mentioned that Dupree would be joining them.

As Dupree entered the cabin, Masterson said, "Shipley's convinced the New York detective's on to us."

Dupree didn't acknowledge Shipley. "Whitey and I were drawing straws over who would kill him."

Masterson winked to Dupree. "Let's leave these kids alone to commiserate and go outside."

As soon as Masterson and Shipley descended the cabin's few steps, Dupree struck Shipley across his neck with an iron fireplace poker. He fell to the ground, his windpipe crushed.

"Are you clear to take him?"

"Yes." Dupree nodded toward the cabin. "Wouldn't mind feasting my eyes."

"Ok, but let's not ruin tonight's fun."

Back inside, Dupree poured a water bottle on top of Justin who screamed, gritting his teeth. "Wanted to make sure you were still alive."

Julie tried to comfort Justin but was even afraid to touch him. "Can you give me a towel or something?"

"I guess I can do." He returned with two bandanas. "He needs to be spruced up for tonight's performance."

After Dupree carried Shipley off and Masterson left, Justin and Julie heard the sound of a truck pull up outside. It wasn't long before Whitey entered the cabin.

"How are we doing this fine afternoon?" he announced. "Sonny, still feeling the whupping I gave you?"

With Justin attempting to say something, Whitey added, "I'll take that as a yes."

Julie's worst fears materialized, recognizing that he was here for one reason.

"I want you to stand up and turn around little lady, so that I can admire that fine ass of yours."

As Justin swung his arm over Julie's legs in a bid to protect her, Whitey rushed over and stepped on his ankle. About to do so again, Julie rose, lowered her bikini brief, and turned around.

"Woohooo! Isn't that a sight!"

As Justin attempted to stand, Whitey smacked him down. "Don't cry, little lady. Are those restraints bothering you? Let me undo them."

About to be raped, she heard the sound of another truck. Whitey peered outside and ordered her to pull up her bathing suit and sit down. Back outside, Whitey greeted Jarvis.

"A little early for the show, aren't you?" Jarvis stated, holding a McDonald's bag.

"Just checking to see that they're comfortable, that's all."

Whitey caught Jarvis noticing that Julie's restraints were undone. "Just felt she needed to stretch," he said.

"That's not your job. It's mine." Jarvis handed Julie the McDonald's. Ravished, they began wolfing down the fries before opening wrappers. Julie started drinking the large-sized Coke but, after a few sips, indicated she had to go to the bathroom.

"Just pee there in that fireplace," Whitey snapped. "We ain't going through that shit again."

Jarvis paid him no mind and walked Julie out, not before warning Whitey to leave Justin alone.

When they exited, Whitey knelt. "Don't be telling him any lies about me, do you hear? You know what I gave you. I won't be so kind next time."

"You bastard!" Justin summoned.

"Now, now. I guess I'm just going to have to tan your hide some more."

When Jarvis returned, Whitey had removed his belt.

"What are you doing!" Jarvis demanded.

"Keeping him in line."

"Put your belt on and take a hike!"

Whitey thought about taking him on. But nixed it. He had his sheathed knife but Jarvis was a force to be reckoned with. He looked over at the four-foot-long knotty branch hanging on two deer hooves. Jarvis had used it to ward off a pack of coyotes. Almost unable to make it back to the cabin, he told them how he used it to kill two coyotes and wound others, before the pack ran off. In disbelief, they visited the site, discovering the two dead coyotes with their heads bashed in. Masterson put the branch on permanent display.

Totally pissed off for losing out on raping Julie, Whitey looped his belt. He addressed Justin. "If you aren't up for it tonight, I'm going to stand in and take real good care of your girl. She deserves a man first time around."

Hearing the truck drive off, Justin thanked Jarvis. Understanding that this guy wasn't like the others, he pleaded with him to let them go, saying that his father would pay anything.

Jarvis didn't respond. He wished to have separated from the group long ago. He did speak to Masterson about ending the lease arrangement on the property, but Masterson pleaded with him to continue on, reminding him that we are all in this together. Jarvis caught his drift.

To him, Whitey and Dupree were demented. No telling what Whitey would have done to the girl, both of them for that matter, if he hadn't come. He had witnessed their brutality and killings. The latest, Shipley's, reinforced that they had no regard for human life. To date, he escaped killing or abducting any women, and didn't intend to. His contribution was in maintaining the cabin. But hearing what Masterson reported on this morning's call, it was clear their time was nearing an end.

"Your uncle isn't an electrician, is he?" The turn of her head and non-response confirmed it. "He's a cop, right?"

She nodded.

"And I bet from what I'm hearing, a damn good one."

As he was reapplying her restraints, Justin said angrily, "and you know what else he is…he's a war hero, a navy seal, and a detective. You can look it up."

"What's his name?"

"Justin, that's enough!" Julie pleaded.

"That's ok. I don't need to know." A pause. "Listen, whatever they ask you to do tonight, just do it. It's the only way to keep breathing."

CHAPTER 24

From Pete's large bay window, Benny admired the pond and the majestically shaped clouds rolling so low, almost touching the pine trees on the other side and casting mirror-image shadows on the stillness of the water. He asked why there were just a few houses directly across and Pete shared that the Rhode Island side was mostly state property, protected land. As to the few homes, he pointed out that they had been grandfathered in.

"Fewer homes mean purer water," he said. "It is a common belief that septic tanks destroy lake water but lawn pesticides inflict more harm."

"Aren't there regulations to prevent that?"

"They exist but not enforced."

"Then they should fine the lawn maintenance companies. That should do it."

"First someone has to complain. I guess homeowners prefer lush grass over pristine water."

Murph washed the last mouthful of his meatball hero with a second Budweiser from the six-pack he bought. "This lake isn't anything like the one I grew up on. Needs heaping doses of seaweed."

Pete called Benny over to the coffee table to review a few maps. "Here's the strip of road where I lost Alfie. I'm still befuddled that he was able to disappear. I wasn't far behind."

For the moment, Benny's eyes didn't settle on the road at Pete's finger but the extensive forest and the chances of finding Julie and Justin somewhere in it.

"How do we hook up with a forest ranger?" he asked, figuring consulting with one was the only way forward.

Pete suggested stopping by the bait and tackle store in the morning to confer with its popular owner, and Benny wished he was available now, eager to not let nightfall kill the day's momentum.

"Why don't you sit and eat?" Murph said. "I bought the low-fat turkey for you."

"And you had the low-fat meatballs? What happened to the diet you were on?"

"Pete, he's not up on the latest medical research. I'm sure you heard…everything in moderation. Thinking of it, I've been too strict lately."

Benny frowned. "If everything in moderation is key to a long life, then you need to be dieting for the rest of yours to offset eating like a horse up until now."

"Pete, isn't it wonderful how he looks after me. Just like the little brother I never had."

Pete enjoyed their spirited banter and, though only in their company a short time, he admired the deep connection between the two.

"I'd like to see my sister," Benny put forward. "But I believe I saw the welcome mat floating in the lake."

"Let me go over there and test the waters," Pete offered. "It will also allow me to do the neighborly thing and see if they need anything."

After Pete left, Benny sized up the turkey sandwich and bit into it. "Not bad. Generous with the turkey."

"That's because of my strategy. When I place my order, I display a menacing, angry look…like this. Always works."

As he did, Benny raised his eyebrows. "More like the deli worker matched the sandwich size to your frame."

In a moment of quiet, Benny winced when Murph bridged to a topic that he wished to avoid, asking about the assignment that he and Trish were handed by Chief Thompson.

With a mouthful of food, he had a moment to mull an appropriate response. He opted to be tongue and cheek. "I'd have to kill you first."

"Don't give me that bs," Murph said. "You can trust me."

Brought into the investigation in confidence, Benny had to hold the line. He did feel that Murph would make a great addition to the team with his decades on the force and his familiarity with the majority of Blacksburg's officers. But he didn't raise this with Thompson and he hated to be evasive to Murph.

"You're putting me in a bad spot," he finally said.

A long awkward pause, before Murph said, "Will you and Trish be angling for Thompson's job when he hangs it up?"

Offput by the left-field ask, Benny asked, "When is that?"

Murph enjoyed turning the tables. "Why should I tell you?" He rose, making his point, and walked over to Pete's bay window. "Has to get mighty lonely here. Don't know how Pete does it."

"Many people live alone. Seems happy enough."

Moving to the coffee table, Murph pointed at the map. "The hounds would die of exhaustion trying to cover an area the size of that."

Benny had given thought about their use, only they hadn't yet carved out an area to unleash them. Otherwise, it was taking a stab in the dark.

With Pete back from the cottage, he told Benny he was wise to stay put as his sister was angry at the world.

A knock startled them all. Pete moved to answer it, thinking it may be John. Instead, he came face-to-face with an attractive woman, professionally dressed in a navy skirt and white blouse.

"Am I at the right place?" she asked. "Can you tell me if there's a rather large individual here and a smaller one claiming to be detectives?"

She winked, extending her hand. "You must be Pete, the neighbor. We spoke. I'm the one who warned you about that guy over there."

"You're Trish."

"That's right."

Benny stood, surprised to see her. "Thompson's going to have a fit with all of us out of town."

"We won't all be out of town. I'm exchanging places with Murph."

"I'm not signing up for that," he shot back. "I'm good here."

"The only way. He wants you back. And he wants me in twenty-four hours, though I guess I can squeeze out another half day."

Though delighted to see her, Benny didn't want her in hot water and placing another colleague at risk. Only hours earlier he and Murph were threatened with jail time, and he knew State Police Senior Investigator Falcone wasn't going to take too kindly to having another New York detective interfering.

"You wasted your time coming here," Benny signaled. "I was just about to see Falcone and apologize. Tell him I'm standing down."

Murph laughed. "Funny, you had no such notion a minute ago."

"Listen, I can't put you two in Thompson's crosshairs. Pete and I will continue on."

"Pete, no offense," Trish said. "But two isn't a team."

"Neither is three," Benny responded.

"That's why I'm staying," Murph countered.

"No. You're going," Trish said, forcibly. "That's the bargain I made. Pack your bag."

Murph turned to Benny for sympathy but got none. "Do as she says," he said. "If you can clear the weekend, come back."

Murph caught himself. He wished to say that that would be too late. Heading to the bedroom and returning with his duffle bag, he shook hands with Pete.

"Why not stay the night?" Pete suggested. "It's late to be driving and we have room."

Murph appreciated Pete's offer but also knew his quarters were limited. He eyed both Benny and Trish. "It comes down to not being wanted."

"That's right," Benny said. "And Pete, look what you'll be saving on your food bill."

At the door, Murph turned, "Pete, not even hard-boiled eggs for him."

Believing that Trish and Benny might like to speak in private, Pete said he had some reading to catch up on and went into his bedroom.

Alone, Trish didn't know how to bridge to the conversation she needed to have. But did. She told Benny that she and Thompson met with Sheila Morgan this afternoon, sharing that Morgan got Johnny Egan on tape talking about his years of taking payments that contributed to the funding of a summer house for his wife and kids.

Benny caught the sensitivity. Egan was Murph's best friend. The two couldn't be closer. They played on rival high school football teams and were sworn in together as rookie patrolmen. As he thought through the implications, what bothered him was Murph's second attempt to extract information.

Trish saw Benny's troubled gaze, which matched hers earlier. She refused to believe that Murph would have anything to do with being on the take. But even if he didn't accept money, he must surely be familiar with those who did.

"This is deep…many are going down," she said, gloomily. "I had to get it off my chest."

"Glad you did. Don't hide anything from me." A pause. "Murph is clean. I'll stake my life on it."

CHAPTER 25

In checking in on Anne and John, Pete had walked into a firestorm. Anne continued to be down John's throat, holding him accountable for Julie's free spirit, claiming that she had her father wrapped around her fingers. She chastised him for giving in to Julie after she stood firm to her requests. John defended himself. He countered: "you're not being fair. Our daughter's disappearance isn't a result of me being a pushover."

Things really heated up when John blamed Anne for conceding to Julie's request for birth control pills.

"She wanted them. What am I supposed to say with her going off to college. I didn't deny Danielle and I'm not putting my head in the sand with Julie."

"Well, this is what you get!"

"What do you mean?"

"What do I mean? It's obvious Julie went over there to have sex with Justin."

With Anne sobbing, Pete felt terrible. He could no longer be a fly on the wall. "No one is to blame for their disappearance. "You're both great parents. Don't forget, I know. I've had a ringside seat all these years."

After Anne stormed upstairs and John moved to the deck, Pete asked Joan Edwards if she needed anything at the store. He found the Edwards' seemingly in shock and probably constrained in voicing much of anything being guests of the Stapletons. After receiving a short list, she tried handing him two $20 dollar bills but Pete refused to accept,

"I'll pick this up first thing tomorrow. Let's settle up then." He had no intention of doing so.

Back in his house, he hoisted the bottle of Woodford Reserve. "Where are my manners?"

"Only if you join us," Benny said.

"Can't. Woodford and I had a fond run but it's over. Doc told me we had to part ways or I'd be six feet under. But you guys, please do. A little refreshment never hurt anyone."

"Pete, I'll have to pass," Trish said. "Have to get to Foxwoods. Meeting up with a friend." Benny's smug reaction set her off. "What's your problem? My business is my business."

"So, who is this guy?"

Trish acted like she didn't hear the question. "Pete, how long will it take me to get there?"

"I'd say about twenty to twenty-five minutes."

With Trish coy, Benny was certain of a male acquaintance and was happy to hear it. He had encouraged Trish to date following her divorce from her abusive husband and was tired of her using her job and daughter as an excuse. He, though, was intrigued as to who it could be. For, other than a few college boyfriends, she hadn't spoken of anyone. He would have teased her more, if they had been alone. He updated Trish on the investigation and told her that the Connecticut investigators believed his niece and boyfriend's disappearance was tied to campers but it proved false.

"Where do we go from here?" she asked.

"Pete and I were reviewing the off-road accesses into Pachaug forest." He showed her the map with notations. "And we need to find a forest ranger who can hopefully guide us a bit."

He asked Trish if she would continue Murph's research on the disappearances of the three women. But after she protested mildly, feeling that it would take too much time, she signed on. He had asked Pete to continue to tail Alfie Doolittle. Already having been interviewed and released by Connecticut investigators, Benny felt Doolittle would be comfortable moving about and might lead them to the teens.

"Why don't you let me have a word with Falcone?" Trish asked.

"For what reason?"

"Hello, anyone at home…a collegial approach, of course."

Benny shook his head. "It will backfire. You're forgetting he's ordered us off. And he'd only be more upset with yet another out-of-state detective here."

Benny handed Trish the photo of the men in front of the cabin. "Would you call these guys upstanding citizens?"

She took a few moments to scan each of them. "I'd say not Lion's Club material." She felt her phone vibrate and wondered if it was her sitter. It was Chief Thompson.

As she moved towards Pete's front window, Benny didn't hear much.

"What gives?" he asked, when she got off.

"He wanted to know if Murph was on his way back."

"That's it? You were on longer than that?"

A pause. "With Murph and Egan friends, he's considering tailing Murph."

"That's a bad, stupid move," Benny erupted. "Murph will pick up on it. Why didn't you fight him?" After saying it and seeing Trish tongue-tied, he realized he shouldn't be angry at Trish. "Sorry. The right play is for Morgan to get deeper. This can't be rushed." A pause. "Even the DA admitted that if this takes years, it takes years. The Chief is an asshole and I'm going to call him."

"No, you're not! That's the bourbon talking. Do you really think he'd listen to you?"

Benny emptied his glass. And when Pete reached for the bottle to refill it, Trish waved her finger. Annoyed, she went to the bathroom. Emerging, she said smiling for Benny's benefit, "Don't wait up."

She stood facing him, waiting for a retort, and it came. "Pete, looks like someone is letting her hair down this evening. Listen, if you wind up at the Roulette table, play number twenty-four."

"What's lucky about twenty-four?"

"My jersey number in football."

She smiled. "I figured you for a bench warmer."

"That will be the day."

With Trish gone, Benny poured himself another bourbon. He debated whether to call Murph about the investigation but realized it would be a bad move. If Murph was stupid enough to get involved, he had to face the consequences.

"Good night," Pete said, while pointing to the bourbon. "Help yourself…going to waste anyway."

Benny raised his glass. "Thanks for everything. What time does the sun rise?"

"Six forty-two."

"And Clete?"

"Before the sun."

"You're a wealth of knowledge."

"Comes with time on my hands. Appreciate you deputizing me. It's a big deal to be engaged in something, though I wish it wasn't this."

"You and me both."

Keeping his voice down, Benny called Charlotte. "All ok on the home front?"

She could tell he had been drinking. "Tell me what's going on. I thought I would have heard from you earlier."

Benny shared much of what happened and what they had planned for tomorrow but, though interested, Charlotte zeroed in on Anne.

"She will not see you?" Charlotte hoped Julie's disappearance might bring them closer.

"She's in a world of hurt."

"I get it. But you're only trying to help."

"She'll come around."

"I hope so. How long do you think you'll be there?"

He thought of an appropriate response. "Let's make plans for Valentino's Saturday."

"That's in two days. Are you stringing me along?"

"I'm not."

"So, are you saying this will be over by then?"

"One way or the other."

"What does that mean?"

"Means that if they aren't found by Friday, they don't have a snowball's chance in hell of making it."

CHAPTER 26

When Whitey got to the cabin for Masterson's pre-show meeting, he had no intention of sharing the conversation he had with one of Falcone's deputies, who had asked where the photo was taken and who else was in it.

It was easy to sidestep the questions. He knew the officer. In fact, he had been called by him to tow a car following an accident only yesterday. He felt he responded rather convincingly that the photo was taken years ago in Vermont and that he was unfamiliar with the others, only able to identify Alfie Doolittle and Goobie Crenshaw who had invited him on the hunting trip. He knew the investigators already had their names.

To him, why raise this with Masterson who would panic and forego the evening's festivities over fear that the investigators were drawing close. Masterson didn't need to know that yet another of them was being questioned.

With Dupree pulling up, Masterson sought to get him alone. "Did you take care of Shipley?"

"He's resting very comfortably."

Ronald Jackson was the last to arrive. "What are we playing for?" he asked.

"Not there yet," Masterson replied. "Since the conference call, anyone hear anything?"

Jarvis Wingo said he stopped at Markey's Bait and Tackle to strike up a conversation and the talk of the day was on across the board fee increases for gaming licenses.

"That's it?"

"I'm getting to it…he said a news reporter had been in."

"Did he say what the reporter was interested in?"

"Didn't but it's obvious, isn't it. Anyway, I wasn't going to appear too interested."

Masterson shook his head. "Not good. Don't need those bastards snooping around. As bad for us as the cops."

"So, they snoop," Alfie said. "That's what they do. A few more days they'll be snooping onto something else."

Jarvis agreed with Masterson. "I didn't get the feeling this reporter was the quitting type."

"Stay away from Markey's," Masterson demanded, eyeing them all. "Let's not give gossiper Clete anything to gnaw on."

"He's a crook anyway…the bastard charges four dollars for night-crawlers," Goobie said. "I'll get my worms someplace else."

Masterson didn't feel he got his point across. "The moment you begin showing you're faces more than usual, the more risk for us."

"Enough with the bullshit," Whitey snapped. "You treat us like kindergartners. Nothing's happened and nothing will. Our cabin is in the middle of nowhere."

Whitey proposed that he would give them each $200 to have the girl for himself and carried on about it being a sweet deal. Masterson let him go on, fully knowing the others would reject it.

"Big ladies' man," Dupree said. "Thought you could get any woman you wanted?"

"That's right. But this is a special occasion and I aim to get twelve hundred worth."

"What do you think of his proposal?" Masterson asked.

"I think it's a fair price," Alfie said. "Need cash to go home with. My wife's getting a little ornery."

Goobie sided with Alfie, as always.

"I'm not signing on," Jarvis said, staring at Whitey. "Don't need his money."

Whitey already figured that Jarvis would vote against him as well as Masterson and Jackson. He stared at Dupree. "You owe me."

Knowing he did, Dupree almost caved. But the thought of seeing that girl lose her virginity wasn't worth giving in.

Whitey didn't let up. "You mean to tell me that we're going to let that piece of shit have had her when one of us can?"

"That's just it," Dupree said. "You answered your own question. Only one of us can undo the virgin, the rest getting sloppy seconds. I'd rather go for the show, this way we all get a rise."

With others agreeing, Whitey blasted, "You're all a bunch of pussies."

Seizing on Whitey's defeat, Masterson said, "That settles it. Ante up five hundred and write down your time."

"Wait a second," Dupree raised. "What are we anteing up for?"

Masterson thought that maybe for once they could move forward without bickering. He said that he would hold the timer and instruct the boy to screw her, the timer stopping when he climaxes.

"Remind him there's no pulling out," Whitey said.

"What if she sings Dixie first?" Dupree stated.

"Are you kidding?" Whitey voiced. "She ain't singing nothing, I can tell you that."

The others laughed.

"Hold on. What if he fails?" Jackson floated. "She had to take control last night. And with him being whipped and all, he might be incapable."

"If that's the case," Masterson said. "We'll reconvene outside and draw up a new plan. Agreed?" With no naysayers, Masterson provided them slips of paper.

After collecting, Jackson insisted on knowing what the plan was after tonight.

"Can we hold that until after the show?" Checking their faces, he had no choice. "I've come up with a few possibilities we can vote on. Scenario one: put the girl up to the highest bidder to do what he may. Scenario two: draw numbers for each of us to have a turn with her, with the higher numbers paying more than those on the bottom rung. That settle it?"

"Not quite," Jackson said. "How do they get disposed of?"

Masterson saw them eagerly waiting for his response. "The highest bidder in either scenario disposes of the girl. And then we draw straws on who kills the boy."

"If it comes to that, I'll do the honors," Dupree stated. "Be my privilege."

While thinking what else he might have in mind, and the others possibly as well, Masterson had to ask, "that ok…anyone else want him?"

With silence, Masterson continued. "There's also something else to consider…selling one or both overseas. We can use most of the money for paying taxes and leasing this property and probably have some left to split." He paused. "Sound reasonable? Think about all I said and we can talk later."

Remarkably, much to Masterson's surprise, Whitey stepped toward the cabin and the others followed.

Julie and Justin heard the trucks pulling up and voices, bracing themselves as the seven men filed in and took the same seats. Julie squinted into the darkness but dropped her eyes to the floor upon seeing Whitey's grin. As before, the lights illuminated them.

Masterson, the only one who didn't sit, stepped forward. "Last night was the preview. Now we're back for the main event." He addressed

Justin. "What we want from you is simple: make love to your girlfriend. I wouldn't think that too difficult. I'm sure you've been waiting for the day. Well, your ship has come in."

Holding for the laughter and taunting to abate, Masterson squared back up to Justin, who had lowered his head and closed his eyes. "Look at me," he demanded. Justin did so. "Here's what's going down. Slowly remove her bathing suit and get into it. I'll start this timer when your clothes are off and stop when you have…"

"I'm not doing it!" Justin roared. "I'd rather be dead!"

Whitey rose. "And that's fine by me. I'll torture you first, you little prick."

"Sit down, Whitey!" Masterson ordered. "The youngster needs a moment. For some reason, he believes we care about him. Surely, he must know that if he doesn't oblige, we'll kill him and have a go with the little lady there."

"Kill me then!"

After Masterson nodded, Dupree rose. He removed his Damascus gut hook, hunting knife from its sheath. Menacingly staring at Julie, he stepped quickly to her and yanked back her hair. "I'm going to lop off your ear. With this beauty, you'll hardly feel a thing."

"Justin! Justin!" she screamed. "Please do as they say! Please!"

"Stop, you bastard!" Justin shouted.

"Dupree, please sit," Masterson said. "Your services are no longer needed. Finally, curtains up!"

CHAPTER 27

Courant reporter Jefferson Cartright missed the turn onto Beach View extension and then, finding it, got questioned by a homeowner in a golf cart believing him to be an intruder. Shaking that off, he prepared himself to meet with the parents of the missing teens, dispatched to write a feature story that would connect *Courant* readers to the distraught families. He got them to agree after telling them it was a way for them to connect with the abductors, in effect to make an impassioned plea to let their children go. They signed on. And while he would ask questions, while consoling and sympathizing, he knew he was taking advantage of them and hated it. But the plight of these parents sold newspapers, and Cartright expected the piece to be one of the most read in the country, a follow-up to his sensationalized breaking news piece on the missing teens that had blown out nationally.

As he sat on a kitchen chair facing the Stapleton and Edwards, he avoided, as best he could, meeting their eyes. And it was easy to do so as he scribbled notes, a back-up to his iPhone capturing it all. As John largely filled him in on the cottage and Julie's love of waterskiing, wake-boarding, he bridged to the morning of their disappearance, to which Anne began speaking about, until she couldn't, with John and (name) Edwards filling in as best as possible. He ceased writing notes upon hearing the name Benny Fidalgo.

"You mean the same Benny Fidalgo who caught the New York serial killer?"

"Yes, that's him," John Stapleton said. "He's Anne's brother."

Cartright took a moment. "And he's up here investigating?"

With John glancing at Anne, Cartright either felt he didn't wish to answer or was seeking permission to do so.

"He's here, yes," John confirmed. "The state police would rather he not investigate and my wife agrees with them."

About to delve into why, Cartright danced around it.

"And is Benny Fidalgo onto the Pueblo?"

"Yes, he is."

"Is he staying with you?"

"No, he's not!" Anne Stapleton responded sharply.

For an awkward moment, Cartright didn't know which direction to bridge to but continued to sense that delving into a family matter would backfire.

"If I can ask, where is he staying?"

"With Pete Lewinski, our neighbor." John pointed in the direction of Pete's house.

"How did he find out about the Pueblo?"

"Went to the abduction site and discovered it himself."

"So, he brought it to the attention of the investigators?"

"Not quite." John explained that Inspector Falcone and his team found the Pueblo and that his brother-in-law did as well. "He was warned to stay away but received permission to go over there from a contact with Rhode Island state police."

"Oh, I see. Who is the lead Connecticut investigator?"

"That would be an Officer Falcone."

It became immediately clear as to why Falcone made an end run around Falcone. In his limited dealings with him, he found Falcone to be abrasive, a bully, one who disdains journalists and who belittles any who questions his authority.

"And Falcone, I imagine, didn't want him butting in?"

"That's right." John glanced at Anne, adding, "But my brother-in-law doesn't take no for an answer."

Cartright nodded. He got the picture. Two pit bulls squaring off. What he remembered about the New York serial killings was Fidalgo's determination in matching wits with a renowned child psychologist behind it all.

Cartright reached for his iPhone. "Can you give me a moment. My editor wants me to check in. I'll only be a moment."

There was no editor check in. As he stepped outside onto the deck, Cartright saw himself changing direction and needed clearance to do so. Instead of drafting a piece on the families, he instead saw Benny Fidalgo as his meal ticket. With Fidalgo inserting himself into the hunt, this opened new possibilities of gaining inside information. He was grateful that his editor also recalled Fidalgo's successful capture of the noted child psychologist behind the killing of several boys under his care.

"Why should we miss out on a chance to shadow Fidalgo?" he reasoned. "You know these cases…they're usually over quickly. Since we're not getting any information from the state police, why not lean into him?"

"What makes you believe he'll be so accommodating?"

"He's got to be a fish out of water up here. I'm going to play to his having someone he can tap for information. Right now, he needs someone in his corner. He's in hot water with the state police and he has a sister not particularly fond of him at the moment."

"What's that all about?"

"Don't know and was about to delve into it."

A pause. Cartright waited for the green light and got it. "We've got to lean into this. So, if you can't make headway with Fidalgo, get back to the parents."

Back inside, Cartright had to be tactful and finesse backing out of a feature story that he had himself propositioned with the Cartrights' and Edwards'. He also couldn't reveal his new designs.

"What you have given me is very useful," he began. "But unfortunately, my editor has me headed in a new direction. Often happens in this business. I'll be back to you at some point."

Meeting blank faces, Cartright gathered that the adults before him were rolling with the punches, in a zombie state that no one wishes on anyone. He put two business cards on the kitchen counter. "In case you need to reach me."

In his car, Cartright searched the Internet to refresh himself on Fidalgo. Dozens and dozens of stories surfaced. In particular he honed in on a profile that captured Fidalgo's military exploits in Afghanistan. Spotting the term "The assassin," to describe the former Navy Seal. It wasn't surprising that the ego-driven Falcone wanted to keep Fidalgo at arm's length.

Pulling out another business card, he wrote a brief note on the back for Fidalgo to call him, in case he wasn't at the neighbors. After knocking and no response, he was about to place his business card under the door when it opened.

"Can I help you?" said a professionally dressed woman in black slacks, white blouse, and hair in a ponytail.

"Sorry. I was told that Pete Lewinski lives here and that a Benny Fidalgo may be with him. Are you Mrs. Lewinski or Mrs. Fidalgo?"

"I'm neither. Who you are?"

In being handed the reporter's card, Trish regretted answering the door. "I'm covering this investigation and have a few questions for Mr. Fidalgo."

"Well, he isn't here."

"Can I ask who you are?"

"A friend."

"A friend of Mr. Lewinski or Mr. Fidalgo?"

"Both."

Peering inside, Cartright saw maps spread on a coffee table. He gathered from her curt replies that this woman was fully involved.

"Can you pass along to Mr. Fidalgo that it may be good if we teamed up. I know he may be new to this area and I may be able to acquaint him with goings-on…and can be discrete."

As this woman's eyes bore through him, he felt it best to be on his way, not before giving his best pitch.

"I know that Mr. Fidalgo and the Connecticut investigators aren't exactly seeing eye to eye. I know my way around…"

"I've got it," Trish said, interrupting. "Have a nice day."

After closing the door, Trish knew the reporter's real agenda lay in gaining information to file a story. But there was something trusting about him and, as she thought it through, she would encourage Benny to speak to him.

* * *

Off to look into the disappearances of women in the area, Trish headed to Rhode Island state police offices in Rockford, to review the files shared by Connecticut law enforcement.

"We were expecting a Benny Fidalgo or a Dennis Murphy," a receptionist said.

"I'm a colleague." She displayed her shield.

Getting clearance, Trish was led into a rather dull office with a monitor. She got it, the uncomfortable, stark law enforcement holding place. The woman logged in. "Here you go. These are the links. I think they're self-explanatory but let me know if you're having trouble navigating."

"You're so kind. I think I'll be good."

Hitting the first link, labeled "Mother Missing," she delved into the investigation of the missing woman who left behind a seven-year-old daughter, the one possibly having affairs and who may have been abused by her husband. The information, obtained by Murph, was verified in the files.

Reading on, the investigators first believed she might have run off. But she hadn't packed, hadn't driven off in her car. Many were aware of her jogging routine, after putting her daughter on the school bus. But no one recalled seeing her that morning. Trish could only believe, as the report alluded to, that the woman was snatched leaving her home. Investigators believed she knew her abductors. But after exploring all acquaintances, they struck out. A posted $50,000 reward for information went uncollected.

With the missing Dairy Queen worker, there was more to go on. After reading her file, Trish came away feeling that it made no sense for the young woman to be a runaway, as some assumed. The file stated that she called her mother at 10 p.m. saying she had a ride home from work. Why would someone thinking about running away do that? She had been an 'A' student, active in school, working to earn money, and wasn't dating. Her disappearance left everyone in the community, including her classmates, dumbfounded.

In addition, with a $100,000 reward established by her parents, the only one coming forward was a tarot card reader who insisted that the young woman had been drugged and taken out of the country. The last file entry was more than two years ago. Her case was profiled on the television show, 'Maybe You Know,' which highlighted missing persons. But after it aired, no one came forward.

Trish could see why the Connecticut investigators hadn't linked the current disappearances to the Dairy Queen worker for that occurred nine years earlier. But with three missing, she couldn't believe the FBI wasn't called in and also pondered how many others were unaccounted for.

While the Dairy Queen and missing jogger gave her pause, the case of the missing college dancer got her attention. With the police report describing the severity of the snow storm, Trish could appreciate that it kept everyone indoors so there could be no witnesses. Sure, the young woman, as speculated, could have decided to abandon her car. But that would have taken some daring and she couldn't get very far...not in a violent snowstorm and unfamiliar with the area being from another state. The notes indicated that her parents said she always took Interstate 95 back to URI. But with I-95 closed, she obviously tried an alternate route. And it cost her.

Police notes indicated the car still had fuel. Even if she left her car and wandered off, she wouldn't have traveled far and her body would have been found.

What kept flashing through Trish's mind was the possibility of someone stumbling onto her. She ruled out truck drivers, most likely to be on the road, for they would more likely offer help. No, more likely someone local who took advantage of a stranded, desperate young woman.

Giving brief consideration to plow operators being out and about but, with the amount of snow, some three feet, they likely would have waited for the storm to abate. She saw a note that the state's Department of Transportation had all they could do with keeping the main roads open.

The more she reflected, tow truck operators came to mind. Only the crazy ones would contest storms like that. But that's what they lived for, possessing the warrior mentality to confront the ugliest conditions and brag about it over coffee. The file noted that Mel's Towing Service had been called to take her abandoned car. She made note of it. The only thing that troubled her is that the young woman hadn't called Triple A or tow truck services. But maybe she did and the active ones had more than they could deal with.

A text from Pete to join he and Benny at Hannah's came at a good time. Having skipped breakfast at the casino, and hungry, she responded that she would meet them there.

On the drive, her thoughts weren't on the investigation but her old college boyfriend. Several months back, after accepting a job as entertainment director at Foxwoods, he called to invite her to an Andrea Bocelli concert. But she declined being so recent after her divorce. Her heart not into it, she told him she'd take a rain check.

Understanding that Foxwoods was close to Voluntown and now a year after the divorce, she debated whether to reach out to him and was glad she did. After checking in, the bell captain led up to one of the penthouse suites. Texted to meet her friend in a lounge, they enjoyed a few vanilla Cosmos and dinner at Cedars Steak and Oysters, after which she invited him up to her room. Not with a male companion for quite some time and her daughter safely with her aunt, the adventure gave her chills, more as he began undoing the buttons of her blouse.

As she made her way to Benny and Pete at Hannah's she expected Benny's teasing and got it.

"I thought maybe you wouldn't be up this early."

"What can I say," she said, taking a seat at the four-person table. She wasn't about to provide details, though she recognized he would be a curious, pain in the ass until she opened up. She decided to begin and end it with the filet mignon, wine, and dessert at Cedar's.

"Is that a rash on your neck?" Benny asked, not allowing Cedar's to conclude her evening.

Embarrassed, especially in front of Pete, Trish had tried to blot the redness but obviously was unsuccessful. "Never mind. How did you guys make out this morning?"

With Pete around, Benny let her off the hook and shared that they had covered the seven-mile stretch where the truck disappeared and narrowed it down to two potential off roads. He said they eliminated others close to homes, figuring that anyone up to no good would avoid being seen. The few roads they charted could be accessed from the main road.

The problem, he told Trish, is that the off roads narrow to such an extent that pick-ups could barely squeeze by. "Difficult to turn around in there. Went for miles. Didn't know what we were getting ourselves into. Except for Pete's nerves of steel, we'd still be in there."

Trish held up her mug of coffee to salute Pete. "How about getting a piper or helicopter to scope?" she suggested.

"We spoke about that. But they might even have trouble with the forest being so thick. And, of course, that's state police territory."

Trish stared at Benny's omelet. "What's in there?"

"A nice blend of goat cheese, spinach, and mushrooms." He waved the waitress over and Trish ordered one. "I guess you didn't have time for a casino breakfast?"

"Very funny. I've just spent a few hours in Rockford. Of the three disappearances, I think the dance team member points the way." She had their attention. "A tow truck operator could very well be behind this."

Benny nodded, as if in satisfaction. "Did the report state who towed her car?"

"Mel's towing Service. Called by the police."

Pete was thrilled to be a fly on the wall during their back and forth. He had all the respect for Benny and now had the same for Trish who was handed the omelet. She took a forkful. "You're not right on much but this omelet makes up for past miscalculations."

"Don't start on me," he said. "Lest I do a deeper dive into the casino."

Trish turned to Pete. "A gentleman wouldn't pry into a woman's business."

"Who said I'm a gentleman? Let's just say I'm…"

"Let's leave it there, thank you," she interrupted. "Back to more important matters, I'm thinking Mel's may not be behind the dancer's disappearance, but can't rule them out, just yet. I'm thinking it's more an evil-minded tow truck operator who made off with her. He leaves her car there, with such significant snowfall, no tracks. Off he goes and the young woman with him."

Considering the possibility, Benny was amazed at Trish's ability to construct something the police hadn't considered, and in such limited time.

"That's not all," she said. "In dropping my things at Pete's, who comes to the door but a reporter looking for you."

"Me? Why me?"

"He's a reporter…probably caught your name when he was next door with your sister."

"And it meant something to him?"

Trish's eyes shot upward. "Are you forgetting that you're the big shot detective who put the mastermind serial killer behind bars?" A pause. "Anyway. He didn't come on strong, offered to be a local source."

Nodding toward Pete, Benny said, "Got my local source right here."

"True," Trish acknowledged. "But you have Pete a hundred percent invested, and this guy has access to records, Falcone, and who knows who and what else."

Benny grabbed the check from the table. "Fair point. But reporters shift like the wind. Let me think about it."

CHAPTER 28

Invited, Courant investigative reporter Cartright knocked on Pete Lewinski's door and was surprised to find the same woman answering. As she led him to the sofa, Cartright swept past and took in the view from Pete's window. "How picturesque!" he said. "I've read that viewing bodies of water like this, or mountains, adds years to your life."

"Pete," Benny called out, "you're going to live to be a hundred."

"That will be the day."

With Cartright sitting alongside Trish on the sofa and with Benny and Pete sitting on high swivel chairs on the flip side of Pete's kitchen counter, Benny set the ground rules. "We need to get a few things straight."

Cartright was all ears. Having been stymied by Falcone and his staff, he was set to embrace anything Fidalgo could offer.

"We can't have you working both sides," Benny put forward, "meaning, you can't take what we're providing you and run to Falcone with it."

With Cartright non-committal, Benny felt that maybe bringing him in wasn't a good idea. "That ok with you?" he prompted.

"I can't be handcuffed in pursuing leads," Cartright said.

Seeing a bit of a stalemate and recognizing that Benny was apt to send Cartright packing, Trish jumped in. "You need to appreciate that things are very fluid and we're working on borrowed time. One disclosure of what we're up to may interfere with our ability to locate the teens. We're just asking you to be mindful of that."

"I get it and I wouldn't do anything to jeopardize their lives."

"Good. What Benny is trying to convey is that if we bring you into our confidence, you must have some allegiance to us."

Cartwright nodded. "I get it. I came in good conscience to work with you."

To back that up, he told them that it was his intention to write a profile of his sister's family – "you know, the piece that sheds light on your sister's family, their attachment to the community…to gain sympathy for their plight. It will also serve to allow your sister to speak to the abductors." By checking the faces around him, at a loss, Cartright got to point. "Anyway, I ditched that piece. I felt guilty using them to gain readership. So, I got my editors to back off. And they bought in especially after I floated your name and the opportunity to align."

Uncertain that he had gained their trust, Cartright thought it best to engage. "Public opinion is that your niece and boyfriend ran off."

"Really?" Benny said. "They could disappear any time. They have cars."

"Agree. I'm not buying it. I'm only stating what I've heard. Personally, I think Falcone put too much faith in the Winnebago." A pause. "I'm into helping you but what's in it for me?"

Unsure of Benny's thoughts, Trish said, "we'll bring you on where we are and where we're going. That should mean something?"

"It does. How about this? Before I file a story, I'll talk it through."

"Seems reasonable," Trish responded.

"I'm gathering you're close?" He searched their faces, even Pete's, and didn't get push back. "Which tells me the next day or two are key."

Before Cartright arrived, Benny and Trish scanned the internet and became acquainted with Cartright's writings. He was no flyweight, one of the *Courant's* go-to reporters.

"Let me share where we're at," he said, recognizing he had to take a chance with this reporter. "Stop me at any time to further explain a point or if you feel there's something you can help us with."

In removing a small notepad from his sports jacket, Cartright noticed Benny offput. "I'm not quoting you. Need to jot key observations and facts."

Nodding, Benny covered the finding of the Pueblo, the questioning of Shipley, the connection to Goobie Crenshaw and Alfie Doolittle, and his theory that the abductors were close by. Pete raised the map and used a pencil to note where he lost Doolittle.

Benny disclosed the hunting photo, identifying Shipley, Alfie Doolittle, and Goobie Crenshaw. "We don't know the others yet. We were told this cabin is in Vermont. My gut says it's in Pachaug."

As Cartwright told Benny to hold a second, they waited as he scanned his cell. "I thought so. My paper published this hours ago: "Authorities are interested in speaking to Warren Shipley in connection with the disappearance of two New York teens. Anyone with information on his whereabouts are to notify the Connecticut State Police."

Benny eyed Trish. "They're unravelling."

"What do you mean?" Cartright asked.

"I'm thinking Shipley conferred with his hunting buddies after I questioned him about the Pueblo and they silenced him." A pause. "The parties who abducted my niece killed Shipley."

Thinking it through, Benny wasn't terribly surprised by Shipley's disappearance, though the fact that the state police were seeking to speak with him might cause the kidnappers to quicken their plans.

"I need a forest ranger to help us locate that cabin," Benny said.

"That I can help with," Cartright responded. "A former high school classmate is one."

"How soon can we speak to him?"

"A she."

When Conservation Officer Tracey Waters arrived, Benny could tell from the warmth of their greeting that she and Cartwright were close. Cartwright shared the time he and Waters had gone trout fishing. He said he had caught a 20-inch brown trout and showed them an iPhone photo of him proudly holding it up. "I intended to surprise my girlfriend with a trout dinner, only the trout never made it home. In saying goodbye to Tracey, I laid the trout on my back bumper and, halfway home, it dawned on me where I left it. I imagine some hawk had it for dinner."

While the story and laughter helped to bring them closer, it proved fleeting. For when Waters heard of their plan to search Pachaug Forest, she was dead set against working around Connecticut authorities. "Not the way we do things."

"Tracey, we don't want to get you in trouble," Cartwright said. "But can't you direct them to this cabin. They're all in on getting to the bottom of this and, in that regard, are not at odds with the state police."

Taking a moment, Waters scrutinized the photo. "Can't say I've ever come across it."

Pointing to the map of Pachaug Forest on Pete's coffee table, Cartright asked, "How much of the forest are you familiar with?"

"About eighty percent."

"Good," Cartright said. "Point to the twenty percent you're not."

Waters picked up a pencil. "May I?" After Pete nodded, Waters drew two circles. "These areas are very difficult to reach because swamps border them."

"Are you saying it isn't possible by vehicle?" Benny asked.

"Pretty much. Depends upon rain levels. You'd need a heavy-duty tow truck standing by to pull you out."

Benny eyed Trish, who nodded almost imperceptibly. Her belief of a tow truck operator behind the abduction of the URI dance student may be key to unlocking it all.

CHAPTER 29

"I never thought he'd break her," Whitey said, gathering with the others outside the cabin.

"What did you expect with us gawking and drooling," Jackson said.

"I'd have finished in two minutes."

Masterson fanned the money. "I guess this is my lucky day."

"Who needs to hear your crowing?" Whitey said. "Let's move on."

Masterson put the thick wad of bills into his pocket and told them to come to a decision on the options he presented earlier.

"She should go to the highest bidder plain and simple?" Dupree voiced.

"Fine by me," Whitey seconded.

"And, if no one has problems," Dupree raised, "I'd be interested in carrying off that weak piece of shit."

"All agree?" Masterson said. There were no objections.

Masterson considered the matter closed. "Ok, lets bid."

"Five hundred," Whitey said, immediately.

"A paltry sum…I'll up it to a thousand," Alfie followed. He had already spoken to Goobie and added in his $500, figuring he would win the bid and they both could have her.

"Two thousand," Masterson declared, calculating enough to end the bidding, though he couldn't discount that the wealthy Jackson mightn't trump in. He didn't.

"That's bullshit!" Whitey protested. "You're using our money against us. You shouldn't be bidding at all."

"Too bad, my fine sore loser," Masterson said, beaming. "Just be glad some of your money is winding up back in your pocket."

After the seven had filed out, Julie and Justin rushed to put on their bathing suits. Hearing discussion outside, they listened intently. But they couldn't make out much. With Justin lowering his head between his knees, Julie inched closer. Earlier, she implored Justin to do whatever they said, reminding him of Jarvis's advice to comply. While Justin flat out didn't wish to give in, he told Julie that he didn't think he could sexually engage under the lights and scrutiny. She reassured him, "focus on nothing but me."

When Masterson hit the clock, Justin removed Julie's bathing suit. As she laid on her back, he knelt between her legs but glanced at the men in the aluminum folding chairs. "Never mind us, asshole," someone shouted, "look at the beaver in front of you." Masterson called for quiet.

Julie blocked out their comments, except she couldn't erase the earlier one from Dupree who said he would skin Justin alive if he couldn't go through with it. Embarrassed and anxious about what was to happen, she saw Justin kneeling between her legs, paralyzed, and sensed this was going to end poorly. Mouthing, "relax," she guided him down over her. Holding him tightly, with his face into her chest, she felt him responding. Three minutes later, it was over.

As they whooped it up, tears rolled down her cheeks. For Julie, the past two nights had been a nightmare. If not for Justin's soothing voice and confidence during their long hours together, she wouldn't have been able to find the strength to get through this.

"I'm so sorry," she said. "This is all my fault."

He brushed her tears with his thumbs. "Don't ever say that again." A pause. "Julie, they may have plans for you. But I'm a goner. If I don't make a run for it, they'll kill me."

"You mustn't. They're right outside."

Julie tried to grab hold of his leg but he bolted out the door.

Outside, he almost made his way around his tormentors, if Dupree hadn't tackled him. Whitey stood over him with a pistol as Dupree went to his truck and returned with hand and leg cuffs. "This will hold him until I dispose of him."

It wasn't lost on Julie that they had caught Justin. Going close to the door, she saw Dupree and Whitey kicking him on the ground. Running and screaming for them to stop, a Dupree smack sent her flying onto the ground.

"Leave her alone!" Masterson demanded. "She's my damn property!" Taking Julie by the arm, he brought her into the cabin, before joining them outside. "All of you take your chairs, empty beer cans, and other belongings and clean up. No one need come back here for a while. In fact, let's not be on the prowl for at least a year or more until things cool. We've had our fun."

"That's bullshit!" Whitey said. "I'm not bypassing this hunting season."

Others agreed.

Masterson chose not to get into it. He took Jarvis to the side. "I'm leaving her in your hands. Let's make sure none of these assholes loops back in. I'll retrieve her early tomorrow."

Jarvis had already decided to sleep in his truck. He hated to think that these kids would be killed. Responsible for their care, he could tell they were decent kids and fought through their pleas to be released. He had gotten in too deep with this crowd and cursed himself for doing so. If and when the group was exposed, they'd all fry and he with them.

Placing the restraints on Julie's wrists, Masterson asked her to remove her bathing suit and took a photo. It was his intention to text his contact and sell her. The next morning, the contact responded with instructions to bring Julie to Gloucester for shipping to Saudi Arabia, for $30,000. His contact worked as a consultant in Riyadh for a major energy company.

Masterson had met the guy in an after-hours club several years earlier. At first, he thought he was nothing more than a braggard. But the more he went on about the sheiks' appetite for American women and their penchant for paying handsomely, he came around. Masterson kept the guy's card as well as his declarations about easy money in the back of his head. And that paid off when he picked up a runaway a year ago. Instead of calling the others and bringing her to the cabin, he reached out to the energy consultant. As it turned out, the girl, wanting to get as far away from her father as possible, fell for his pitch about a new start overseas. A week later $30,000 in cash was in his hands.

Masterson left a message for his boss that he wouldn't be in tomorrow. He had to think through taking Julie alone to Gloucester. His plan was to convince her that he was going to release her far away from here and, in the scheme, caution that they would kill her entire family if she identified them.

About to take her from the cabin, a Whitey text indicated that he would pay a grand to have sex with her. About to reject the offer, the money beckoned. With $1,500 left from his winning time and buying Julie, this $1,000 and $30,000 more would be nice paydays.

"I'll meet you at the cabin on your say so," Whitey suggested.

Masterson told him to be there at 11:30 a.m. tomorrow.

CHAPTER 30

Pretending to have car troubles, Trish called AAA. Fifteen minutes later a young guy, seemingly a year or two out of high school and with tattoos covering both arms and neck, jumped down from his tow truck. She had deflated her front tire.

"Don't see any nails," he said, before swapping it out.

Asking if he had a minute, Trish claimed to be a reporter with Tow Truck magazine and assigned to write a feature story on the nation's most daring tow truck drivers. "Know any?" she asked.

Out came the name Whitey Marsh. Asked why, he provided an account of Marsh pulling an almost completely submerged Mustang out of a creek. He said a state trooper warned him not to attempt it, believing they needed a crane. But when the trooper left to divert traffic, he said Marsh "pulled that sucker out of there quicker than I changed your tire. If I hadn't been there, I'd never believe it. He's as reckless as they come."

Trish asked where she could find Marsh and was told that he hangs at Clem's garage. After pulling Clem's up on GPS, she called Benny who was with Pete checking out accesses to the Forest. He opted to leave Pete, feeling it would be wise to double up on confronting Marsh.

On the way, Benny stopped in at the Bait & Tackle store to see Markey and showed him the photo of the men at the hunting cabin, asking if he recognized anyone.

"There's Alfie Doolittle and Goobie Crenshaw, some of my best customers. And here's Whitey Marsh. Everyone knows Whitey. He runs a tow truck business." He didn't know the others. "Are they involved in the kidnapping?"

When an answer wasn't forthcoming, he got the message.

"You have everyone riled up," Markey said.

"How so?"

"Well, since you had me float the topic, Marsh told me that campers had taken off with them."

Benny wondered how Marsh had obtained inside information.

"Did you tell him that I going to kill the assholes when I got a hold of them."

"I did."

"And what was his response?"

Markey hesitated. "He said cops haven't the balls."

Benny smiled. "Thanks for helping me out."

"What about you're end of the bargain?"

"Tell you what, next time I pass I'll have the fishing spot marked with a gold star."

* * *

A downtrodden garage with the letters "C" and "E" missing, Clem's had vintage gas pumps out front and two old jalopies without wheels on cement blocks on either side.

Meeting up with Benny, Trish had gone around back and hadn't spotted any tow trucks. They found the front door open. Hearing noise, a man in overalls slowly emerged from under a car. In his seventies, he held onto to the car to steady himself. "What can I do you for?"

Benny said that he was an old friend of Whitey Marsh and was told he might find him here.

"Be right most days but haven't seen him in a few. Must be hunting."

"Does he hunt around here?"

"In Pachaug, I believe. Come to think of it, he's never spoken of exactly where, probably to keep other hunters away."

"Can you tell me where he lives?" Benny asked.

"Likely won't find him there. Almost always on the road. Told me he doesn't need much sleep and makes tons of moolah working nights when his competition catches ZZ's."

Trish said, "Maybe we'll get lucky."

"Well, come to think of it, I don't rightly know his address. But here's what you do."

The mechanic walked out of his garage, pointing. "Take this road until you come upon a large cornfield on your left. When you clear it, make a right. Take that down until your first left. His house is a hundred yards on the right. The one with the huge oak in front and old tires hanging from it. You can't miss it."

"By chance," Trish asked, "would you have his cell number?"

Wiping his hands on an old rag, the mechanic proceeded to a cramped office that featured a few vintage Playboy pinups and receipts stacked on nails attached to pieces of wood. "Sorry to offend you ma'me." Running his finger over a desk calendar, he stopped over a number, ripped off a bill of service, and wrote it down.

"If you catch up with him, tell him we've been missing his money. He's a great hunter, big rib eater, womanizer, and a terrible, sore losing card player."

"When we knew him, he wasn't married," Trish probed. "Is he still single?"

"Bachelor and thank God. No woman should have to be saddled with the likes of him."

Trish smiled. "It's been said there's a woman for every man."

He returned the smile. "God didn't make the woman who could stay knotted to him. He's one of those guys who… well I can't rightly say in front of you ma'am."

After they pulled away, Benny banged both fists on the steering wheel. "We got him! In the photo, he's the guy with his arms crossed, in the short sleeved, muscle shirt."

"Why didn't you show him the photo?"

"Afraid he might have withdrawn."

"That mechanic? As good as an open book."

Whitey's house, set deep off the road and well clear of other homes, was a perfect property to hold abducted teens.

Benny and Trish, not seeing a tow truck or any other vehicle, walked up a few stairs to the front door of an old farmhouse, boxy-like. It appeared as tall as it did wide. They put gloves on. No one answered the door bell, which they could clearly hear.

"I can't leave without getting in there," Benny said.

With no Trish protest, he walked around the side, removed a screen, and found the window unlocked. Climbing inside, it seemed to be a bedroom with only a bare mattress on the floor. Across the hall, clothes lay in a pile on a bed but, before going in any further, he opened the front door for Trish. They split and covered each room, including the attic and basement, until they were satisfied that Julie and Justin weren't there.

"At least he can put the dirty dishes in the dishwasher," Trish said. "This is one of the worst bachelors pads I've seen."

"I guess you're the expert."

"From the job, Fidalgo," she responded, adding, "The mechanic was right…no girl in her right mind would be married to him."

Benny double-backed to the main bedroom. Opening an end table, he held up handcuffs, nylons, and rope. "Well, I guess our man Whitey likes to have his way."

*   *   *

As Whitey Marsh neared the off-road into the forest, he saw a driver standing beside a Silverado. He stopped and asked if he could help.

With his antennas up as the tow truck slowed, Pete's heart skipped a beat when he recognized the driver from the hunting photo. "Don't actually know. I believe some kind of engine troubles."

As Pete held a map, Whitey asked, "Going hiking?"

"Oh, this. Taking my grandson into Pachaug Saturday. Just trying to find a good intermediate level trail."

"Best ones are about eight miles up along the basin. Why don't you start your engine."

Pete did and it turned over easily.

"Sounds better than mine."

"Sorry to have troubled you. She's ornery every now and then. Leaves my mechanic befuddled all the time."

When Whitey left, Pete nervously pulled out a cigarette. After a few draws, he called Benny. "You're not going to believe this, but the muscled guy in the photo just left. He's a tow truck operator."

"Is there time to follow him?"

"He's gone off and, anyway, I think he has me pegged."

"We'll be there in a few."

In greeting Pete, he described the tow truck as massive, showcasing fiery dragons on the door panel. They could see how shaken he was, as he reached for another Marlboro. "Didn't buy my story about going hiking. He could very well have been trying to enter the forest somewhere ahead and saw me."

"What entrances have we marked closest to here?"

"Less than a quarter mile up there's one."

Trish gathered that it was time to speak to Falcone and told Benny so, realizing that they had put Pete in a tough situation.

"But what do I tell Falcone?" Benny declared. "That we believe a tow truck operator is behind this."

"Yes. Something like that."

"We have no proof."

"We have him in the photo, which he's familiar with?"

Benny shook his head. "I bet Falcone or those close to him are familiar with this guy as they call tow trucks all the time. The fishing store owner said he's popular, which adds up to Falcone not believing a word we say."

Benny noticed, as did Trish, Pete's hand shaking in lighting another Marlboro. He caught the Trish look. Against his judgement, Benny called Falcone. Told to wait there, they did. Arriving in an unmarked car, Trish extended her hand but Falcone didn't shake it.

"Where's the other guy?"

"Back in New York."

"And you are?"

Trish shut him off. "Doesn't matter. Listen to what he has to say."

Benny showed Falcone the photo and pointed to Whitey Marsh, who was alongside Alfie Doolittle and Goobie Crenshaw. "We believe he is tied to the abduction of my niece and boyfriend and was attempting to get into the forest along here."

"Haven't we gone over this? And didn't I tell you that I can't arrest hunting buddies without proof? And I didn't I tell you to stand down?" A pause. "So, from what you said, he stopped to see if he was having car troubles. He's a damn tow truck operator. That's what they do."

"Where's Shipley?" Benny pivoted.

"He's missing."

"No, he's dead."

"You have proof? I suppose you think Marsh is the killer."

"I didn't say that. But sure as hell one of these bastards are. And they have everything to do with my niece's abduction."

"Listen," Falcone said, trying to reason, "We've spoken to Crenshaw and Doolittle. They had alibis. And maybe Shipley did go to visit his brother."

Trish stepped in. "Why not rule out the cabin?"

"And just who are you?"

"A detective in Blacksburg."

"That figures." A long pause. "Doolittle, Crenshaw, and Shipley all told us that photo was taken in Vermont. But to satisfy your wild hunches, I'll contact the Department of Conservation and maybe they can advise on how to find this cabin."

Stepping forward, Pete unfolded the map. "We think it could be in these remote areas marked by swamps… not easy to access."

"How did you come up with that?"

Benny jumped in. "If I was up to no good, that's where I'd be." He was not wishing for Pete to be under the radar of local law enforcement and wasn't about to surface contacting Conservation Officer Tracey Waters.

Falcone shook his head. "Listen, we'll scan that area from above. But when I'm through, I'm done with all of you."

"Thank you," Trish said. "That's all we can ask for."

Benny couldn't help himself. "Can I ask where you stand with the investigation?"

With that, Falcone turned to one of the three state troopers standing by and said, "will you listen to this guy. He hasn't cared a rat's ass with what we've been doing."

"I asked you a question," Benny demanded,

"Are you representing the Stapleton family? The answer is no. Ask your sister if you wish to know anything on our end."

As Falcone drove off, Trish said, "I wish you would have kept quiet."

"Sorry, but he needs stirring up. Did you see how he disregarded what we disclosed about Marsh?"

Trish put herself in Falcone's shoes, recognizing that he was not about to provide greater detail, especially to those outside the official investigation.

She tried to reason. "He out to find the cabin, has interviewed Crenshaw and Doolittle, and says they are tracking after those who claimed to have seen Julie and Justin. We've got to give them the benefit of the doubt."

Fuming, Benny stormed off.

CHAPTER 31

"Dad, he's going to kill me!"

Dupree yanked the cell away. "Kill him, yes, but I'll have a little fun first."

Shocked, Dave Edwards slowly lowered his cell, his son's frantic voice numbing, along with the remark, 'having fun'. The abductor's demands of $200,000 and explicit instructions not to contact the police stuck as well.

Joan screamed when Dave shared what he heard, causing John and Anne to rush in from the deck. They were equally stunned.

"Did he say anything about Julie?" John asked, after giving Dave and Joan a moment.

When Dave shook his head, John insisted they contact Inspector Falcone immediately.

"No, no, no!" Dave roared. "He said they'd torture and kill Justin."

"Let's connect with Benny," John encouraged. 'He'll guide us."

"Are you kidding me!" Anne shouted angrily. "He'll only make matters worse. We need the police."

Dave Edwards pushed back. "This is our call. And I'm arranging for the money."

"You can't divorce yourself from us," Anne pleaded. "Our Julie is out there too!"

Joan gazed at Anne sympathetically before heading inside to pack. John tried again, "Dave, at least let's consult with Benny."

"He's a cop, isn't he? I can't take that chance. I may lose our son."

Leaving the deck to not be heard, John reached Benny who asked that he delay the Edwards.

On their way to the cottage, Trish tried to make sense of the ransom call. "Seems late in the game, don't you think?"

Benny didn't know what to think, stuck on why Julie wasn't mentioned. "Sorry, my mind is whirling. It does seem rather late for them to be dickering around." A pause. "Seems like they should be on the back end of whatever they're up to."

Trish spotted a missed call from Chief Thompson, followed by a text: 'Call me about Murph.' She shared that. "This can't be good. Since we have a few minutes, let me return the call."

Deep in thought, Benny hardly heard anything, until Trish told him of DA Sam Barrett's intention to speak with Murph as he was a close friend to Johnny Egan, the latest to be identified accepting bribes. What they surmised is that once the DA questions Murph, it would be the beginning of the end for him. They were well aware of Department rules to report any knowledge of criminality in the ranks.

"What I don't understand is the need to confront Murph at this stage," Benny questioned. "The right path is to let Sheila Morgan continue to work it."

"Barrett knows Murph's history in the department," Trish said. "Maybe his aim is to entice Murph to corral the others."

"He'll never go for that."

Sharing that they expected to question Murph in a few days, Trish felt conflicted. While she felt it important to assist Benny in Voluntown, she had to assist the other detective she cared deeply about. "I'll call Barrett to ask him to delay."

"Leave immediately," Benny voiced.

"Let's see."

Arriving at the cottage, Dave was rearranging suitcases in the trunk of his vehicle.

"Listen, Dave," Benny said, in as calm a voice he could muster. "It is important for you to work through the police who have experience in these situations."

Disregarding Benny, Dave walked towards the cottage to help Joan carry other bags. Benny walked alongside him.

"Your chances of finding Justin alive decrease exponentially if you go it alone."

"Leave him alone," Joan said angrily. "What good have you done?"

"We believe we're close," Trish said, stepping in.

"Close?" Joan challenged. "I'll tell you what's close. I got a demented bastard threatening to molest my son."

With packages in hand, Dave began walking back up to his car. "You're holding me up. This is my son we're talking about. I heard his voice."

Trish said calmly. "I can only share that if Justin was my child, I'd work with the police." She paused. "Get to Falcone. His team and the FBI need to be involved. It's the only way."

In the middle of trying to make everything fit in the car, Dave began sobbing and Joan came to him. Trish and Benny left them be. After a few minutes, Dave offered, "We just had a major argument with John and Anne."

Recognizing that the Edwards had listened, Trish seized on it. "Give me a sec." Stepping on to the cottage deck, Trish heard raised voices and caught Anne's frustration on why the kidnappers didn't mention Julie.

Entering, she introduced herself. "Sit down, please. Both of you. Anne, I heard you. Difficult to tell why they didn't call about Julie. But hearing Justin's voice is a good thing. I believe if he's alive, she is too."

Anne teared. "We have the money."

"Listen," Trish said, reassuringly. "Things are fluid. Who can figure on why they had Justin call and not Julie. But it's best to play this out and Dave and Joan are prepared to work through the police. They are outside and not leaving. Might they come back here and stay with you?"

"Of course," Anne said. "Is my brother out there too?"

"He is."

"I'd prefer that he not come in here."

Trish tried to turn her. "Don't be harsh on him. He's all in and remains convinced Julie is nearby."

Trish winced in hearing, "I'd have more faith if it was you who felt they were nearby."

With the couples reuniting, Trish slipped out and saw Benny making his way toward the cottage.

"Leave them be," she advised. "Have you called Falcone?"

"I have."

"Good."

"I just told your sister a white lie and I don't feel very good about it."

"What did you say?"

"That Julie is alive based on hearing Justin's voice." She saw Benny deflated. "Sorry. I'm not losing hope."

Arriving and slamming his car door, Falcone marched past Benny and Trish without saying a word, with two troopers in tow. But when Benny called out, "Have you searched from the air?" Falcone stopped abruptly, "I'll make like I didn't hear that," before continuing along.

Benny regarded Falcone as a pompous ass and had seen many like him in the military chain of command, using their rank and power to make lives miserable for underlings. He pitied the troopers for having to listen to his bullshit.

After watching Falcone enter the cottage, he thanked his lucky stars that Trish was by his side. "McGlucas, you certainly have a way of restoring order."

"Am I getting a compliment?"

"You are. But I still don't know if you came here to help me or get to the casino."

"You aren't going to let it go, are you?"

Trish enjoyed the praise and, equally, his banter. She respected him immensely and was forever trying to demonstrate that she could handle herself though he continued to protect her. Her only comfort was in knowing that he saw himself as a protector of all.

As Trish stepped toward the cottage, Benny asked, "Where are you going?"

"Let me find out about the air search."

"Really? You're asking a lot."

"Ye of little faith."

As Trish disappeared inside the cottage, Benny thought of the many times she saved him from himself, either stepping in front of him to deal with Chief Thompson or advising him to calm when he was about to lose it. She benefitted from a wealth of knowledge from her NYPD captain dad who supplemented what she learned at the academy and on the street. He had none of it. His learnings came as a result of his tours in Afghanistan, for which he'd trade none of.

What he didn't have is McGlucas's ability to count to twenty-five. Polished, she rarely allowed emotion to interfere in getting to the right end in an investigation. Yet, as much she cautioned him to relax, he admired her for allowing him to free-lance, to take calculated risk. Point in case is that she didn't try to dissuade him from his sole focus on Pachaug, when it was easy to argue otherwise.

As he awaited her exit, he also respected Trish for not stating the obvious: the slim odds of Justin being freed post ransom and the even slimmer odds of finding his niece alive.

CHAPTER 32

"You did good," Dupree said to the tied up, blindfolded, and gagged Justin across the back seat of his truck. "Real good."

Only minutes before, Justin pleaded with him to call his father, saying his dad would pay anything for his freedom. And while Dupree had promised the others he wouldn't seek a ransom, he decided to pursue things his way.

"I'm a nice guy at heart," Dupree said aloud, to his audience. "Really don't need the cash? I lead a simple life."

In his truck, Dupree pulled up his favorite song, Psycho Killer, and yelled loudly in unison with the Talking Heads:
"Psycho Killer
Qu'est-ce que c'est
Fa-fa-fa-fa-fa-fa-fa-fa-fa-far better
Run run run run run run run away oh oh oh
Psycho Killer…"

Hearing him, Justin's only comfort was in knowing his father would meet the demands.

Calling ahead and getting the all-clear signal, Dupree arrived.

"Come along tiger." He led the blindfolded and gagged Justin next to a stately sycamore tree. He ordered him to kneel, put the handgun inside his belt, and picked up the shovel leaning against the tree.

Finished and exhausted, he said, "that should do it." Pulling Justin closer to the hole he had dug, he struck him on the back of his head, the impact sending Justin into the grave. After doing so, Dupree shoveled dirt onto him and spread it over evenly. Taking the hose near the well, used to fill the bison troughs, he liberally doused the entire area until it was muddy. Satisfied that no one would be able to distinguish the grave from any other piece of ground, he took the shovel and left.

* * *

When Whitey got to the cabin, he saw two tarps covering trucks, assuming one belonged to Masterson, the other to Jarvis. He thought by now Jarvis would have finished cleaning up but remembered how anal he was about everything.

At the doorway, Jarvis sprayed and wiped the door handle. "If you're going in, put gloves on. I'm not doing this again."

After doing so, Whitey entered the cabin and saw Julie sitting on the one remaining aluminum chair. Masterson, sweeping the floor, stopped as Whitey spoke of the individual he bumped into on the side of the road holding a map of Pachaug Forest.

"You sure he wasn't a surveyor?"

"No. Gave me some bullshit about his engine acting up, and she turned over like a charm."

Masterson called Jarvis over and told him what Whitey had related, urging them to speed up.

"Let's talk about her," Whitey said.

"Not now. Help Jarvis."

Julie took comfort in having Jarvis around. Unlike the others, all predators, she couldn't recall his face as she was force to have sex with Justin. Not only had he fed them, but he seemed genuinely apologetic. The fact that they were spending so much time cleaning up, led her to believe that the police were drawing near, or maybe her uncle.

Later, after checking and rechecking the cabin to ensure that they had thoroughly cleaned it, the three huddled.

"Where are you taking her?" Whitey asked Masterson, anxious to have a go at Julie.

"My brother's. He's got a house on Beach Pond."

"Of all places." Whitey couldn't believe the balls on Masterson. "Got to be a million cops over there."

Masterson didn't divulge that his brother's property was on the opposite side of the pond. He figured he could keep her safe there, with his brother and family in Europe, until he could arrange for her to be sold overseas.

"Let me have a go here," Whitey said.

"We just spent hours cleaning up."

"Then I'll do her outside."

"You'll do her when I tell you. You have the money?"

"Yeah. And I don't want you standing around either."

Before being taken off, Julie pulled a few strands of hair and left them on the cabin floor.

As Masterson wound his way, it dawned on Julie just how deep the cabin was in the forest. As he drove, she rubbed her head on the seat enough to dislodge the blindfold. Exiting the forest, she saw that they were proceeding through Voluntown on Route 165 and was shocked when they passed the turn-off to the cottage. About a mile farther, he turned left.

Taking her out, he reapplied the blindfold but she had caught enough to know exactly where she was…the chalet with the massive windows on the Rhode Island side of the pond, that she often passed while kayaking. As he took her by the arm, she squirmed to get free. That led him to pulling her more aggressively up the stairs. At a door, he fumbled for keys before pulling her inside.

"I'm going to undo the gag," he said, "so you can tell me what the fuss is about."

All Julie could think of was evading Masterson. "I'm cold and hungry."

"Anything else?"

"Yes, badly in need of a shower."

"Food will be here shortly." He led her upstairs to his niece's bedroom, where he handed her a robe, before taking her into the bathroom. "Go for it." He stood inside the door.

Having been naked several times before him already, she wasted no time taking off her bathing suit and climbed into the stall. Letting the hot water pour on her, she shampooed her hair. Finished, she reached for a towel and caught him watching her.

"What are you going to do with me?"

"Never mind that. You're alive, aren't you? You should be grateful."

The way he expressed it, she thought of Justin. "Where is my boyfriend?"

"You mean, lover boy?" he said, grinning. "Do you wish to be with him?"

Julie hated to think what that implied. "Did you call his dad?"

"Not interested in any ransom or him. It was you we wanted. You should know that by now."

If he hadn't been standing in the door, the thought crossed her mind to run down the stairs and outside where she could keep on running and/or call for help. She had heard Whitey expressing an interest in her and she feared the worst. She rinsed her bathing suit, wrung it out, and he said she could use the dryer downstairs. He held out a robe and she put it on.

As she descended the stairs and with Masterson behind, she loosened the bathrobe and flung it back at him. Naked, she bolted for the side door leading to the deck but struggled to unlock it, before he grabbed her. As he covered her mouth to muffle her screams, she bit down hard on his hand. Slapped, she fell and saw stars. Yanked by the hair, he smacked her again. As she watched him nervously gaze out the window facing the pond, she hoped someone had heard. But as he turned back to her, satisfied that no one had and plenty angry, she curled up, afraid of being struck again.

"That was the wrong thing to do," he said, sucking his hand, "and now you'll have to pay for it."

CHAPTER 33

When Benny and Trish caught up with Pete, they saw he had company. Alongside him was Sergeant Norma Peterson and Trooper Bobby Uhl. Also with him was Conservation Officer Tracey Waters who Benny had convinced to help find the cabin.

"Are you the one causing all the ruckus?" Peterson said, half-smiling, and reaching out to shake hands."

"I am he," Benny said, "meet Detective Trish McGlucas who is here to keep me out of further trouble."

"That's good. Well, Trooper Uhl and I have been given orders to keep you company. I understand we may be doing some hiking."

"Not exactly." Taking in the chunky Peterson, Benny pondered if she had ever hiked. Trooper Uhl, dead-serious, didn't bother to shake hands.

Benny didn't want chaperones but didn't have a choice. He took the Pachaug map from Pete and pointed to the two circled areas. "We're headed to find this cabin." He showed the photo of the hunters and she reviewed it while glancing at the map.

"What makes you so sure you're going to find what couldn't be found by helicopter? We're talking thousands of acres."

Every minute spent dealing with questions was another minute wasted. Seeing Benny tense up, Trish responded.

"Of course, we don't know for sure. But we think these guys may be set up deep in Pachaug and are crafty enough to cover their tracks." A pause. "That's why Tracey has graciously given us her time. She's very familiar with the forest."

Trish waited for Sergeant Peterson to respond but she didn't. She had probably told the troopers before they got there that she considered this an exercise in futility.

"I suggest," Benny said. "That you two go with Pete in his truck, while Trish and I go with Waters."

Trooper Uhl objected. "Not happy with that? Orders are that one of us needs to be with you."

Benny thought fast. "We won't lose connection. Pete, you stay on our bumper."

Seemingly annoyed with Uhl for speaking up, as she was the lead, Peterson felt that would be fine and Uhl got the message.

As Waters drove her Jeep Cherokee Trailhawk deeper into Pachaug, Benny appreciated her skills in traversing water-filled ditches and over and around rocks. As she did, she spoke of her experiences searching for missing people. That reminded Benny of the time he got lost on a middle school nature trip and embarrassingly had to scream his way out. Waters never seemed confused, knowing when to take right or left forks and didn't blink when the off roads morphed into more narrower lanes with bushes brushing the sides of her Jeep.

Stopping, Waters said aloud for their benefit. "Cannot rule out going left but, if I'm not mistaken, there's a greater chance the right leads to the swamps."

She turned to face Benny who said, "Don't look at me."

After another mile, Waters faced a similar decision. "Could be either way. Best if we let them scope one and we the other."

"I don't know how well that's going to go over," Benny said.

"Yes, and what happens if they get lost?" Trish added.

Waters smiled. "They'll always be found. I've come prepared." Getting out, Benny and Trish joined her. She opened the Jeep's hatch.

Waving up the others, Waters explained the predicament. "I believe we're close. But I'm not sure which way," she said, pointing. "Pete, take this," she said, handing him a red spray can. "Mark every turn. This way you can find your way out. Since we have no cell use in here, use this." She handed over an air horn. "If you get stuck, use it. It's quite powerful. I suggest you plug your ears before activating it. Continue to use it every five minutes or so and we'll find our way to you." She also handed over flares. "In case you need them."

"And who is going to find you?" Peterson said, half-serious.

"I'll be fine."

Benny and Trish could tell that Peterson wasn't too happy with this arrangement.

"Why don't we just proceed like we were doing," she suggested, "and if don't find anything on that route, we'll take the other."

Waters deployed the right tone. "Because that will take hours and, according to him, the kids don't have hours."

After they split up, Benny noticed that Waters proceeded more deliberately. She also got out at times to stick a tree limb into water-filled holes to gauge depth. Occasionally, he had to jump out to remove tree limbs. Approaching an open area marked by dead trees, she stopped the Jeep.

"Here's our swamps. This is the area I know the least about."

Following what appeared to be a lane winding around the swamp, Trish complimented Waters on her steadiness. She attributed it to years of locating hikers "who bit off more than they could chew."

On the far side of the swamps, she stopped the Jeep, got out, and walked up to an off-road coming in from another direction. Benny and Trish joined her.

"What do you make of it?" he questioned.

"Several threads from large vehicles. Used much more than the one we're on. Tells me that the cabin we're looking for is ahead."

Back in the Jeep, Waters continued very slowly, until Benny thrust his right index finger at a cabin, seemingly the one in the photo.

"Trish, let's use the trees as shields, until we get close. Tracey, stay put for now."

Drawing their weapons and ducking behind trees, Benny noticed several black tarps to his left, alongside ruts from heavy vehicles. Ignoring them, he stared ahead and could now tell the dwelling was the same one in the photo.

As he and Trish ran out of trees to hide behind, they sprinted to the cabin, charging up three stairs to the door. Knocking, he yelled, "Police! Police!"

Not hearing a sound, he opened it and he and Trish bolted into a large, unoccupied room.

"Not your typical hunting cabin," Trish said. "Seems like they had a maid."

"Don't touch anything," Benny cautioned. "We may need forensics."

Trish frowned. "There you go, Fidalgo, like I was a rookie."

"Sorry, for the fiftieth time. Can't help myself. It's from years in Afghanistan trying to keep the boots from blowing themselves up."

Trish bent lower. "Check this out."

She pointed to a few long, golden strands of hair. "You could eat off this floor. Wasn't left by accident."

Benny tried to remain calm. He had kept from thinking about Julie the Niece while he focused on Julie the Abducted. As Trish held the strands aloft, she placed her hand on his shoulder, to comfort him.

With Julie closer to Charlotte, especially as they had a myriad of subjects to talk about, Benny had little in common with Julie. On visits to his sister's, he either played soccer or video games with his nephew, or talked sports with his brother-in-law. Yet, he loved Julie for the independent, confident person she had become. Only a few weeks ago, in bidding her farewell to college, he had said, "if any of those college guys get fresh, you know who to call." With those words coming to mind and the hug that followed, he withdrew.

"You ok," Trish asked. A pause. "Of course not. The good news is that she's alive."

He nodded. "But we missed our chance."

Trish text Sergeant Peterson, and her message read 'undeliverable,' as expected. After conferring with Benny, he thought the best bet was to send Waters to catch up with Pete and the officers. He felt she could guide them out to cell coverage to connect with Falcone and forensics.

With Waters agreeable and off, Trish, embarrassed, said "Fidalgo, I have to pee, so stay here."

"What do you take me for…a peeping Tom?"

Heading around to the back side of the cabin, to a few bushes side by side and about to squat, Trish spotted a Victoria's Secret tag, secured by a rock.

Hearing Trish call out, Benny came running, holding his firearm. "Geez, I thought you were being…"

"Look, Julie must have left this as well."

Benny knelt. "To think she had the wherewithal."

"I know where she gets it from."

Her comment went over his head. "Leave. I still have to pee."

When Conservation Officer Tracey Waters returned leading Pete and the Connecticut troopers, Sergeant Peterson said she had contacted Falcone who was expected by helicopter. When they heard it above, they were to shoot off the flares.

With Troopers Peterson and Uhl going into the cabin, Trish saw Benny walking over to a tree, that had missing bark. He inspected it closely. "What do you make of it?"

Seeing indentations, Trish shook her head, before kneeling. "Toeprints pointing in."

Trish didn't want to say it but Benny did. "As if someone was getting whipped…"

With Benny visibly shaken, Trish left him and went to review the tarps, which she felt were used to hide vehicles. She pondered how a helicopter could have missed the cabin, until she saw how three huge maples hovered up on its sides. She also considered whether the helicopter crew didn't go deep enough, or maybe didn't spend enough time at it.

Approaching Benny, she told him about the tarps. "They were careful. Any thoughts?"

With Falcone soon to be focused here as well as on the ransom caller, Benny felt he had time to proceed independently. "We'll have Pete take us out via that other trail, the one they used in and out."

"Will Peterson permit us to depart?"

"She will if we give her the impression we're done after finding the cabin."

Trish knew from experience that he was holding onto more. "Where to when we get out this forest?"

"To hoist a tow truck operator up by his grab hooks."

CHAPTER 34

Sitting with the Stapletons and Edwards in a cramped cottage that couldn't house a pool table, Falcone felt claustrophobic waiting for the kidnapper's call. When Sergeant Peterson called to say they had located the cabin and had obtained evidence that the teens had been there, he didn't waste a moment heading out, assigning a trooper to remain behind in case the kidnappers followed up about the ransom.

Before boarding the helicopter, upset that Fidalgo had been right all along, he ordered Alfie Doolittle to be brought in again for questioning.

Accompanied by Sergeant Peterson, he couldn't believe how deep into the forest Peterson was directing the helicopter pilot.

"What do you think of Fidalgo?" he shouted to be heard above the helicopter's whirring.

"Terrific thinker with solid instincts," Peterson answered. "Did you know that he's a Navy Seal with several commendations?"

"Didn't you think I ran a check!"

'Then why did you ask,' Peterson said to herself. As the helicopter circled the cabin, the pilot scoped the area and settled down in the one spot he felt comfortable with. As they got off, a forensics team member approached and cautioned them not to touch anything.

"Do you know who you are speaking to?" Falcone barked.

Overhearing that brief exchange, a senior forensics investigator intervened and shared about the finding of strands of hair and the

Victoria's Secret label and explained that he didn't expect to get much else inside the cabin "was it was scrubbed to the bone." He showed Falcone the wooden club hanging on the wall.

"Any ideas about that?" Falcone asked.

"Haven't the slightest, except that some of the markings appear to be dried blood." He led Falcone to the cabin door and pointed. "There's canvass coverings over there, large enough to cover vehicles. You may have a wish to look at them."

It took Falcone only minutes to inspect the empty cabin and Peterson had joined him.

"Where's Fidalgo?"

Peterson braced. "He left with the neighbor on Beach Pond."

"And you let him!"

Expecting that nothing she could say would pacify him, she kept quiet.

"Didn't I give you instructions to not let him out of your sight."

"He said he wished to go see his sister."

Falcone steamed. "She doesn't care if he falls off a cliff." A pause. "You fell for his bullshit."

Storming outside, Falcone was drawn to the yellow tape around an oak tree. Peterson followed.

"I guess these guys were into torture," he said, inspecting the grooves.

"You have a keen eye sir." Not wishing to rile him up, she withheld admitting that it was Fidalgo who discovered the markings.

Expecting Alfie Doolittle in custody, Falcone boarded the helicopter. And upon landing outside regional headquarters in Uncasville, he proceeded directly to the interrogation room.

"Let's go over your hunting again, shall we? Admit you hunted the day those kids went missing."

"I told you it was days before. Didn't see any kids."

Falcone handed him the photo. "Isn't this your face second from the right?"

"Yes. That's me."

"Didn't you tell me that cabin was in Vermont?"

"Yes, that's where it is."

"Well, I was just standing in it a half hour ago. And I wasn't in Vermont."

"Must be a duplicate. Cabins tend to look the same."

"Don't give me that shit!"

Continuing to stand, Falcone leaned in. "You'd had better begin to tell the truth. We found hair belonging to Julie Stapleton in that cabin. Where is she?"

"How would I know. Just told you I hadn't been there."

Doolittle felt he had gone too far in mixing it up with Falcone, clearly against Masterson's instructions to wait for representation. "Release me or let me call my lawyer."

"And who would that be?"

Doolittle didn't know. "Ain't I entitled to a call?"

Falcone left the room momentarily and brought in Doolittle's cell. "Don't waste it on a wrong number."

Waiting for Falcone to leave, he dialed Masterson. "I'm in trouble. The troopers have me in Uncasville and have a photo of all of us at the cabin."

Masterson blanched at hearing Doolittle's rattled voice but had to focus. "Who have they identified in the photo?"

"Me, Whitey, and Shipley."

"Don't say another word."

Masterson believed Alfie Doolittle would hold the line but he needed to get a lawyer there quickly. He called Frankie Adamo, a fine trial lawyer who had an insurance policy with him, and Adamo accepted the case. He recognized also that it wouldn't be long before they corralled Whitey and likely the rest of them. His top concern, however, was in unloading Julie.

Calling Whitey, he shared what Dolittle had said, including that the investigators would be soon coming for all of them.

"So, we hunted," he said.

"Agree. They have no bodies to pin anything on us. When they catch up with you, you know the drill. What we need to do right now is get rid of the girl. Can you help."

Whitey smiled to himself, amused over Masterson exhibiting his true cowardly colors. "I'll take her off your hands."

Fifteen minutes later, Whitey arrived at Masterson's brother's place on Beach Pond.

"Where are you taking her?" Masterson asked.

Whitey raised his middle finger. "Isn't that breaking one of your rules? You know the one…the less you know the better. Anyway, she's my property now."

"Where's my thousand dollars?"

"You cocksucker. You should be paying me."

As Whitey faced Julie on the sofa, he thoroughly enjoyed seeing the sheer terror in her eyes. "Not glad to see me? Don't fret. He doesn't want you anymore…and I want you more than anything else."

He leaned over and smelled her hair. "You've cleaned up for me. How nice. We're going to go on a little ride and I don't want a bit of trouble. We'll walk out of here like boyfriend and girlfriend. Got that."

With his mother in a nursing home, Whitey took Julie to his old bedroom, adorned with football trophies and various photos of him and his teams. He plopped her in his desk chair and tied her to it. Receiving a call from a woman stuck on the side of the road on Route 138, a few miles away, he figured to respond, which would give him an alibi.

"Don't worry your pretty little head," he said, before closing his bedroom door. "I have to make a little cash, but I'll be back to snuggle."

Terrified, Julie beat herself up for not being able to evade Masterson. She knew he would never have caught her if she made it to the pond and swam until she could attract the attention of a boater or someone along the shore.

Trying to free her arms and legs, she heard a car door slam. Since Whitey had already left, she figured he forgot something. Yet, when she didn't hear anyone rush in, she felt it wasn't likely him. Finally hearing the front door open, she hoped it might be rescuers. But not hearing anyone call out, she nixed that too. As she listened intently, plodding footsteps ascended the stairs.

CHAPTER 35

When Whitey pulled up alongside the Honda CRV with car troubles, he nodded to the woman behind the wheel while pulling his tow truck in front. Exiting his cab, a man appeared out of nowhere. He recognized immediately that he had been duped.

"What do you want?" It was clear he was speaking to the girl's uncle.

"Don't give me that shit! Where is she?"

"Don't know what you're talking about. Have a nice day." Turning to leave, he felt a hand on his shoulder. Violently swinging his elbow back intending to connect, instead he found his left arm twisted up his back.

"Tell me where she is, you rat bastard!" Benny yanked his arm.

"What the fuck? Let go and I'll tell you."

Benny slightly relaxed his grip and pushed Whitey against his tow truck.

"Where is she?"

"I'll lead you to her."

"Asshole, you're going with us. Leave the tow truck where it is."

As Whitey spun around, swinging wildly, Benny warded off the blows and kicked Whitey in the groin, sending him to the ground.

"Easy," Trish said, "or he'll be no good to us."

As Whitey moaned, Benny added, "he ain't seen nothing yet. He'll wish he was tied to a tree and whipped."

Not knowing what he had in mind, Trish said, "Listen. You can't go half-cocked. Let's connect with Falcone."

Trish didn't know if Benny heard one word, being so charged up. But this reinforced why she came to Voluntown. With his niece's life at stake, Benny was apt to do anything.

He stood over Whitey, who writhed on the ground with his hands clasping his privates. "Let's head to Pete's. I'll take Whitey in the tow truck. You follow."

Trish shook her head. "We need to hand him over."

"For what? Another turn style release. No, he knows where Julie is and I need to get it out of him."

"This will backfire."

"Trish, if you want out, I understand. I'll take it from here."

A pause. "Let's go."

Hearing the sound of a truck outside, Pete flipped his outside light and was startled to see Benny pushing the tow truck driver down his steps.

At Pete's front door, Benny said, "Pete, sorry to get you in deeper."

"Do what you have to do."

Pulling his weapon out, Benny jumped on Whitey's chest, pointing the gun inches from Whitey's mouth.

Stunned, Trish felt he had completely lost it. Talking him down, he ignored her.

"I had nothing to do with it," Whitey pleaded. "Shipley took your niece."

"That's bullshit!"

"That's what I heard. Find Shipley and you'll find her."

"Asshole. That weak-kneed Shipley couldn't kill anyone We're way beyond Mr. Shipley. What about my niece's boyfriend?"

Benny grabbed Whitey's throat with his left hand, while training the gun on his forehead.

"I don't know where the hell he is," Whitey voiced quickly.

"Ok, the real dope," Benny said, more firmly digging his fingers into Whitey's neck. "Don't play the innocent bystander card. My friend here met you on the side of the road leading into Pachaug. You know exactly what went down. Take me to my niece."

Eyeing the crazed uncle, Whitey unloaded. "Alfie Doolittle abducted the two kids and arranged for us to see a show."

"Now we're getting somewhere. What show?"

"We paid $500 apiece to watch that kid make love to the virgin."

Trish and Pete stared incredulously. Benny relaxed his grip but kept the gun inches from Whitey's mouth. "Keep going."

"That's the full story. I paid and left."

"So, you watched and didn't do anything about it."

As Benny shoved the gun into Whitey's mouth, Whitey closed his eyes, believing he was going to get his head blown off.

"Benny, I'm coming behind you." Trish walked slowly. "Give me the gun."

Benny didn't flinch.

"Give me the gun," she said, more assertively, knowing not to touch him. "Let's take him to the police, where he can report what he's told us. It's the only way."

After pulling his weapon back a few inches, Benny rose, his eyes never leaving Whitey's.

"Pete, call Falcone and tell him to come here," Trish said, relieved.

Trish fully appreciated the trouble they were in.

When Falcone arrived with two troopers, Whitey yelled, "I want him arrested! He's a fucking lunatic! Just had a gun down my throat!"

"He's making this up," Trish said.

"Fuck no!" Whitey shouted. "You bitch!"

"We brought him here to question him and he tried to punch Benny."

"Why are you questioning him?" the steamed Falcone questioned. "Why didn't you call me?" A pause. "You were warned. I've had it up to here."

Leaving for Trooper offices in Uncasville, Trish saw Benny's brother-in-law watching them walk up to the vehicles. She pondered whether Whitey spoke the truth about the supposed show, numbing as it was.

At Troop headquarters, Falcone laid into Benny and Trish, who told him about Whitey's intent to go into Pachaug and his revealing about a show at the cabin. "See what he'll tell you. He admitted to being there."

Falcone stormed off. Imparting about the show to Doolittle, Falcone believed it to be true as Doolittle didn't contest it outright. For Doolittle, he couldn't believe Whitey had revealed what he did. He figured his best chance to extract himself out of this was to continue to deny everything and wait for his attorney. He told Falcone he hadn't seen Whitey Marsh in some time.

Falcone left Doolittle, confronting Marsh. He told him that their conversation was being recorded.

"Tell me about the show at the cabin?"

"There's no show," he said. "I made it all up to get that lunatic to stop threatening me. I'd be a goner if that bitch hadn't stepped in."

"Are you charging Fidalgo with assault?"

"Damn right I am."

Going to the door and telling a trooper to retrieve a complaint form, Falcone calmly pulled a chair in front of Whitey. "So, you had nothing to do with this cabin and the kidnappings?"

"Damn right. Don't need to be spending my hard-earned money on beaver. Can get all I want."

"Are you sure that's the route you wish to take?" A pause. "I have Alfie Doolittle down the hall. And he might just decide to help us. And when that happens, we don't need you. Get my point?"

"If he fingers me for anything, he's a liar."

Knocking, a trooper informed Falcone that Attorney Frankie Adamo had arrived to defend both Doolittle and Marsh. Proceeding to the main floor, where Fidalgo and McGlucas had been waiting, Falcone pointed at Benny. "Whitey Marsh has filed charges against you for assault and reckless endangerment."

"He doesn't know what reckless is."

"Be quiet," Trish angrily told Benny. "What did Marsh say about the show in the cabin?"

"That he made it up to avoid being killed."

"Well, he's lying."

"And you know that, how?"

When Trish didn't attempt to disprove it, Falcone pounced. "I'd suggest you go back to Blacksburg before I toss you in jail as well." He ordered a trooper to transport Fidalgo to a cell.

"Grow a pair!" Trish said, alone with Falcone. "At least he's been trying to get to the bottom of this. And you've been four steps behind."

"Retract that or face the consequences."

"Don't try and bully me."

Taking out his cell, Falcone put it to his ear. "Chief Thompson, sorry to bother you. But I must inform you that Benny Fidalgo is behind bars for threatening someone with a firearm. And I'm standing alongside Detective McGlucas. She'll likely be joining him unless you can talk some sense."

Handing over the cell, Trish had to listen to Thompson's rants before advising her to leave Fidalgo "before he takes you down the rabbit hole." Continuing, he said a black mark on her record could prevent her from ever becoming a Blacksburg chief. "The Town Board isn't likely to entertain a chief with an arrest record and lapses in judgement."

Listening, Trish tuned him out. She hurt for Benny, even more so in realizing how close they had been to finding his niece. As Thompson went on, what he didn't appreciate was her inability to abandon a colleague, in this case a friend, when he needed her most. She had to keep her head.

"Chief, everything you said makes sense. You'll not hear from Inspector Falcone anymore."

Ending the call, Trish handed the cell to the smug Falcone. "I hope after I leave that you'll do the right thing by Fidalgo."

"And what is that?"

"I shouldn't have to tell you."

Outside, she called Charlotte.

CHAPTER 36

"Keep away from me!"

Feeling the bottom of the bed shift, due to someone's weight, Julie began to panic, especially in hearing the sound of shoes hitting the floor followed by a belt buckle.

"Please leave me alone! Please!"

Hearing footsteps coming around the side of the bed, she felt a hand on her breast. Thrusting her legs violently accomplished little as two hands secured her upper arms and she found herself shaken like a rag doll. Frightened, she felt hands fondling her breasts.

"You're a frisky filly in need of a little taming."

The voice didn't belong to Whitey or any of the others.

Now feeling his full weight on the bed, she kicked out until hands grabbed tightly around each ankle and separated her legs. Trying to move, she couldn't and now felt fingers dig into her thighs, before his body on hers.

Powerless, she gave in.

When he got off, she wanted to crawl up into a ball but he reapplied the restraints. After he got dressed and descended the stairs, Julie let go.

* * *

When Whitey left state police headquarters, after several hours, he breathed fresh air. Masterson was right about securing the best lawyer. He was told that the DA wouldn't move forward without evidence, and he assumed they had obtained nothing from the cabin. That was good, and now he knew what to do.

On his way back to his mother's house, he called Dupree and Jackson and told them that Masterson dumped the girl on him and was panicking, no doubt ready to give them all up. Jackson was skeptical but Whitey insisted that Masterson was going to cut a deal to save himself. Jackson caved not knowing who to trust.

Whitey texted Masterson and asked him to come to Walmart's rear parking lot where he would divulge what he heard from Falcone at police headquarters.

"Have you lost your mind!" Masterson exclaimed, with the gun pointed at his chest.

"Shut up! We're tired of your bullshit! Let's go for a ride."

As Whitey pulled out of Walmart, Masterson knew where he was headed and tried to reason. "I've got tons of cash. Just take me home and it's all yours."

Whitey continued driving. "No dice. You are a complete wiseass. I expected that when Falcone gets a hold of you, you'll sell us out. I'm going to shut that mouth of yours for good."

"Why? Adamo will clear us. Killing me will only tag you as the mastermind."

Whitey laughed. "Me, really? No. Adamo will make certain that you're seen as the piece of shit behind all of this."

Masterson's mind whirled, with no cards left to play. He posited, "And you think you're going to get away with it?"

"You'll never know, will you?"

Marching Masterson to the sycamore tree, he killed him exactly in the manner as the others. After liberally soaking the entire ground around the sycamore with the hose, until it was mud, he let Dupree know he finished the job.

"Did he give you any trouble?"

"Shot off that mouth of his before he knew I couldn't be turned."

"Well, with he and Shipley gone, that's two big mouths dispatched of," Dupree declared.

"What about the others?" Whitey asked.

"Jackson is good. I'm not sure about Jarvis."

"Why is that?"

"He treated those kids too well if you ask me. As much as he's the big bad hunter, he's soft."

"I think he'll toe the line. They questioned Alfie but the lawyer came through. They'll bring in Goobie too but he's as dumb as a rock and will do whatever Alfie tells him. I think we're good for now."

"If they all need to go, I'm game," Dupree bragged.

Whitey didn't doubt it and feared that Dupree would turn on him too. He got Dupree to agree that they should lay low for now, comforted in knowing that Jarvis, Doolittle, and Goobie didn't know about the sycamore. And without bodies, reasonable doubt could always be spun.

Arriving back at his mother's house, he found Julie crying, lying handcuffed naked on the bed. "Can't be all that bad. Wasn't he kind to you? Calm yourself. I don't want no crying bitch."

Sitting on the edge of the bed, he patted her leg, as if attempting to comfort her but she pulled it away. "What, Whitey not good enough for you?"

"Hey, guess who I ran into?" he continued, getting aroused. "Your uncle. He isn't very nice. In fact, he's a royal piece of shit! But his ass is in jail. He won't be looking for you any longer."

Julie didn't know if he was speaking the truth. What she couldn't understand is why the despicable human being before her hadn't been arrested.

Finally, when he undid the tape covering her mouth, Julie sought to buy time before she was raped again. She saw that he couldn't keep his eyes off her privates.

"Can I shower?" she asked.

"You know what…that's a very good idea."

CHAPTER 37

After enjoying baked scrod at Hannah's, Trish returned to the state police post in Uncasville. Not permitted to speak with Benny, she remained in her car awaiting Charlotte's arrival. To kill time, she called daughter Emma who was excited about her role in a middle school play, before listening to a Bill Maher podcast. As Charlotte's white Mazda 5 entered the parking lot, she opened her driver's side door and waved her over. She didn't expect to see Charlotte in scrubs but, then again, she hadn't a chance to go home and change.

"Is he ever going to learn?" Charlotte said, hugging Trish. "Other brothers would have made amends with their sister and let local law enforcement do their thing. But not my husband."

"You know your guy."

Trish was surprised when Charlotte didn't rush in to be with him. "Have you spoken with my sister-in-law? I know he didn't."

"Anne's a wreck. Who wouldn't be. Your daughter goes out for a kayak ride and wham, this."

"Do you think she'll be found?"

Trish wasn't about to project doom and gloom. "Benny believes so."

"And you?"

"I honestly don't know. With each hour passing… Sorry, this must be tough on you."

Charlotte's eyes welled up. "She's such a good kid. You know, with us not having children, she's like one. I had made plans to go to Quinnipiac to spend a night with her and now…"

In the car ride, with her husband arrested, Charlotte once again regretted his accepting the detective's shield in Blacksburg. The aerospace firm that he worked for, after leaving the military, regarded him highly and kept boosting his salary. But money didn't drive her husband and never would. It was all about the adrenaline flow.

While she supported him in making the move, she now felt it was a mistake, in that he wasn't cut out for rules and boundaries and the politics. Also, he wasn't collegial, preferring to work alone, and frowned on those he deemed incompetent or lazy. While Chief Thompson hired him as a favor to a friend, she knew he and the chief were like oil and water. Also, she surmised, Chief Thompson didn't like his increasing popularity, with the Town supervisor and council members constantly talking him up after his closing of high-profile cases.

Charlotte sensed that his detective days might be over. While he served his first three years with distinction, he often expressed that he was bored. That she hated hearing, as she liked her job and home in Blacksburg. It was definitely a suburban town to raise a family. But the takeaway from this, she assumed, could be a nail in the coffin of his law enforcement career. And even if he chose to continue, she anticipated that he would beat himself up, second-guessing his decisions and effort over not finding his niece. She had come to accept his self-criticisms but it was wearing. Receiving the call from Trish that he was in jail, describing what had happened and sharing Thompson's ire, she felt the end near. She was, however, hard-pressed to think of a profession that suited him.

Why he remained a detective as long as he had, she could only attribute to the companionship and respect he had for Trish and Murph as well as his knowing that she was content in Blacksburg.

"Are you coming in with me?" Charlotte asked.

"I'd better stay here. Falcone believes I'm on ninety-five going south." Trish also knew that Charlotte and Benny needed to talk.

Asked to wait in a small sitting area, near an unmanned reception desk, Charlotte waited for Falcone. And it wasn't long before a square-shouldered, crew cut individual, in standard grey-blue trooper attire, appeared.

"Is your husband always this thick?" he said, smiling.

Warned by Trish of Falcone's brusqueness and confrontational style, Trish reminded herself to be respectful, mindful of the goal of getting her husband released.

"My husband lives and breathes his work."

"Well, up here, he wasn't on the clock, was he?"

Upset, Charlotte chose not to say anything as Falcone justified the arrest. "Sticking a weapon down someone's throat is something we can't ignore."

Trish let him go on.

"I can understand his angst over his missing niece but there are limits."

Charlotte kept her thoughts to herself. Specifically, if her husband was pursuing the disappearance of his niece on personal time, why the need to contact his boss?

In front of swinging doors, Falcone used his pass. "Jenkins," he called out. "Allow this woman in to see Fidalgo."

Although it pained her to do so, Charlotte thanked him, appreciating that he had the authority to make things difficult.

As Jenkins opened the cell door, Charlotte was overcome. Benny came to her.

"Charlotte, this isn't like you?"

As she tried to halt the tears, he pulled her close. "Honey, honey, I'm not being sent up the river."

"I know," she uttered. "I'm can keep a stiff upper lip but seeing you behind bars is…"

"Here, sit." Noticing that she didn't have time to change, it hurt him to think of the inconvenience on her making the three-hour trip. "Did you eat?"

"I'm not hungry. Listen, Trish is outside. She said she'd wait around until I felt comfortable."

About to say that Trish needs to get back to Blacksburg, as per Chief Thompson's edict, he checked doing so. Hoping to be in front of a judge soon, he'd tell her himself.

In jail, Benny had time to mull things over, beating himself up about the consequences of his actions on Trish, Murph, Pete, and Charlotte and feeling terrible about his poor relationship with his sister. But as much as he dwelled on it, he kept coming back to the players behind the kidnapping and abuse.

A few hours later, after he didn't contest the charges, he was brought to a courthouse in Norwich, with Trish and Charlotte following in their own cars. A judge released him on $25,000 bail. Asked by the judge if he had issues with PTSD, Benny frowned. The judge eyed Charlotte, "there's no harm in being checked out. PTSD can manifest years after serving."

As the trio walked down the courthouse stairs, Benny said to Trish, "I thought I told you to leave."

"Are you my boss?"

"That's right," Charlotte said. "Give it to him."

In the parking lot, standing by their cars, Trish unloaded. "Listen," she said. "I've been thinking through the disappearances of these women, specifically about where their bodies may be. Had me twisted up, until a light bulb went off."

Looking around for someplace to sit and not seeing any benches, Trish ditched that, seeing how anxious Benny was for her to speak her mind. "We know that these women were taken against their will and brought to the cabin. After these perverts had their fun, they knew they couldn't release them or be exposed. They had to be silenced. One would think they'd bury them near the cabin or at least somewhere else in the forest, but I now believe they were too smart for that."

Trish glanced at Charlotte and saw how she was also invested in what she had to say. "I'm thinking they'd be aware of an intense search focusing around the cabin and forest. Even though the forest is dense and vast, I don't think they would bury the bodies off the trail leading in and out, easier to find. And can you imagine lugging bodies deeper? In any event, I think they figured at some point the entire forest would be scrutinized. That's why I'm leaning on the burials being elsewhere."

Benny harbored doubts. "I think you may be giving them too much credit. You're forgetting that I've been in front of Shipley, Doolittle, and Marsh. They are low on the totem pole of geniuses."

"Right," Trish said. "I'm with you. But one, or possibly two, are up on that totem pole or they wouldn't be able to operate as long as they have."

Trish reached into her car to retrieve the photo of the hunting group outside the cabin. "These four are spoken for, right? Shipley, Doolittle, Marsh, and this other guy you saw working the golf course…I gather not genius material either. That leaves these others."

Benny studied the faces of those remaining. "Go on."

"See this one," she said, pointed to a clean-shaven individual at the far end, not in camouflage and not holding a weapon. "I predict he's calling the shots. And if I'm right, he wouldn't bury those bodies in the forest. He'd have law enforcement chasing their tails in twenty-eight thousand acres."

"So, we need to get hold of him," Benny said.

Trish glanced at Charlotte, who got the message. "Honey, that's for Falcone."

Benny smiled. "I've also done some thinking. Being behind bars does that to you. We need Russo."

Trish couldn't believe it. "Charlotte, he did have a come-to-Jesus moment behind bars."

"Will he get involved?" Charlotte asked, pleased at finding her husband willing to rely on others in law enforcement.

"My creds are good with him following the psych center killings. Right now, we need FBI firepower."

Benny told them of another idea. He intended to call *Courant* reporter Cartwright, figuring that a feature story would out them all.

"Are you sure of that?" Trish asked, knowing what that could also mean for the teens.

Benny couldn't look at either of them. "In that cell I shed more tears that I have in a very long time." He didn't convey that while incarcerated, he also thought of the deaths of his four closest buddies in Afghanistan, who lost their lives while he was on leave. And that, in the cell, he had prayed to God and to them to give him strength.

With glassy eyes, he continued. "I have to lean on every resource and Cartright needs to get the public stirred up. The hope is that someone will step forward and identify that guy right there." Benny pointed to the unknown, professionally dressed individual in the photo.

* * *

When Cartright arrived at Pete's, he accepted Pete's offer of some Entenmanns crumb cake and coffee. Charlotte had left to visit with Anne and John. Benny, up and energized, updated Cartright. He told him about the clean cabin, the strands of hair, and the Victoria's Secret bathing suit tag as well as Pete bumping into Whitey who was attempting to get access to the woods. Benny concluded with what Whitey Marsh had intimated, that Kelly's boyfriend had been murdered.

Pete chimed in. "Hate to think it true but the Edwards' haven't heard another word on the ransom."

Benny softened the blow. "Hopefully he's wrong. They have or have had Alfie Doolittle and Whitey Marsh in custody. Maybe they can get one of them to own up to something."

Cartwright, trying to digest all he had heard, challenged the legitimacy of what Whitey Marsh had shared about a show, "It wreaks fiction, with him willing to say anything to gain his release."

"These guys are tormented," Benny said. "And besides, Marsh couldn't have concocted such a yarn with the duress I had him under."

Benny showed Cartright the hunting photo and identified Alfie Doolittle, Warren Shipley and Whitey Marsh.

Pulling out his iPhone, Cartright shared an alert from the paper about a missing person by the name of Blake Masterson, a local insurance agent.

"Too much of a coincidence," Benny said. "I bet he's one of them."

Cartright called the newsroom and received a description of Masterson. It matched the person they deemed to be the mastermind.

"He's not only missing, he's dead," Trish said. "They silenced Shipley and now Masterson."

Feeding into Cartwright's thirst for details, Benny tossed him the largest bone. "Others have gone missing in this area over the years."

Cartright abruptly stopped jotting notes. "You believe were talking serial killer?"

"Killers," Trish said. "There have been at least three young women missing that we're aware of."

"But the police must have made the connection?"

"One might think so. But these guys are clever. By stretching the disappearances years apart, they're able to disguise what they have been up to."

"This is unbelievable," Cartright voiced, incredulously. He volunteered to help identify the others in the photo and also to check in with Falcone as to the results of the cabin forensics. "This needs to be blown open."

"Go for it," Benny said.

Before drafting the piece, Cartwright said he'd check in with Falcone for comment to confirm why they are holding Alfie Doolittle and Whitey Marsh. He also said he'd find out more about who owns the cabin and property surrounding it. He turned to Benny, "I'll be using your comments in my piece, but I won't identify you by name."

Benny nodded.

It didn't take long for Cartright to discover that Restaurateur Morton Anderson owns considerable property deep into Pachaug Forest. Calling him and finding him quite talkative, he confirmed that he leases property to the Sequoia Hunting Club and that a Jarvis Wingo is his contact.

"Did you get a number?"

"He wouldn't without speaking to Wingo. I told him never mind."

According to Cartright, Anderson labeled Jarvis "a hunter extraordinaire, a real Daniel Boone." He described him as having facial hair but tailored and always with a camouflaged, baseball cap pulled down covering much of his forehead. Reaching for the photo, Benny turned it around. In it, was the man as described.

Checking the Internet, the name Jarvis Wingo turned up, and they wasted no time going to his home. There, they found him on his deck collecting strewn toys. After Benny introduced himself, Trish, and Cartwright, he asked about the hunting property. Wingo ignored them, continuing to place toys in a bin, until Benny shoved the photo in front of face. "This is you. This is Whitey Marsh over here, Alfie Doolittle… and who could forget Shipley."

"Nothing wrong with hunting, is there?"

"Depends on the kind of hunting," Benny said, pointedly. "What do you know about the show at the cabin?"

"What show?"

"The naked boy and girl having sex show."

"Just who are you?"

As Benny took out his shield and Trish did the same, he said, "I'm the uncle."

Jarvis fought to keep his composure. He had to contact Masterson. But as the reporter laid out the story he was planning to write, Jarvis's knees buckled, especially so in hearing that Masterson was missing. There could be only one explanation.

"Are you here to arrest me?"

With that question, Benny had him. "No. But tomorrow your name and this photo will be on the *Courant*'s front page."

Thrown, Jarvis thought about his wife and invalid son.

"Tell us where the teens are?" Benny demanded.

With Jarvis's world turned upside down, he said haltingly. "The boy I believe is dead. Dupree took off with him. The last I saw of the girl she was with Masterson and Whitey at the cabin." He looked them straight in the eye. "If I knew where she was, I'd tell you."

CHAPTER 38

When Attorney Frankie Adamo finished speaking with Alfie Doolittle, he couldn't believe he had been contacted to defend an individual accused of kidnapping the missing teens, the extraordinary event that everyone was talking about. As he listened to Doolittle, in starts and stops, he had concluded that his client was guilty.

He didn't buy Doolittle's yarn about hunting near Beach Pond days leading up to the teens' disappearance. He had defended plenty of lying Doolittle types who slowly melted, or sometimes rapidly, when evidence piled up.

While Doolittle surprisingly kept calm as Adamo shared a number of details floated by the *Courant* reporter, who had contacted him for comment on a story he was filing, he unraveled when informed that Masterson had gone missing.

"Are you sure?" Doolittle asked, rattled. "Can't be."

"Let me assure you that the reporter is neutral in all of this...he wouldn't be making shit up. He told me that a hunting photo with you and several others will appear in tomorrow's paper."

Doolittle winced and rubbed his hands through his hair. He bent over, until he recovered, defiant. "Let them publish it. We were hunting."

Adamo but his lip, in a bid to prevent himself from erupting. "If I'm expected to successfully defend you, I need the truth. Start by you telling me where the teens are?"

"How the hell would I know!" he said, thrusting his chair back and waving his hands in the air.

"The evidence against you is mounting?"

"Do you believe me or them?"

Adamo pushed his briefcase to the side, as if to have no barrier between he and his client. "The Courant wouldn't publish what it has without certainty or face a libel suit." A pause. "You expect me to believe you were hunting within fifty yards of the teens a few days before their abduction. You expect me to believe that your friend's comment of a show in the cabin was false. That the New York detectives have it wrong. That the Connecticut state police have it wrong. Is that what you expect me to believe?"

Doolittle felt like a young buck meandering through the woods, unaware that a hunter had him in his sights. Based on what Adamo revealed and with Masterson dead, he had to trust the lawyer.

"We took them to the cabin."

"Who is we?"

"I can't tell you. He's my friend."

Adamo was all too familiar with brothers-in-crime solidarity, until the walls crumbled with everyone out for themselves. "I need bargaining chips."

Unable to consult with Masterson, Doolittle disclosed all he knew, naming Goobie Crenshaw, a co-worker at Brook Ridge Golf Course, as helping to abduct the teens. Through it all, Adamo took notes and couldn't believe what he was hearing, the extent to which they targeted the teens and ensnared them.

"I didn't harm her or him in any way," Doolittle said, wrapping up.

"But you abducted them. Where's the boy?"

"Dead. Dupree took off with him.

"That's make you complicit, facing murder charges."

Doolittle again ran his hands through his hair. "You've got to get me out of this!"

"Where's the girl?"

"Masterson took her."

"Where would he take her?"

With Doolittle's eyes glazed over, Adamo said, "Obviously something's troubling you. What aren't you telling me?"

Defeated, Doolittle posited weakly, "Masterson's dead."

With that, it was Adamo startled. "How can you be sure? I only told you he was missing. Maybe he saw the handwriting on the wall and left town."

"Listen to me," Doolittle implored. "He's dead!"

Adamo tried to remain calm, with the person who hired him out of the picture. "Ok, let me try and make sense of everything. You and this Goobie kidnapped the two teens. And you're saying you didn't have anything to do with the boy's death."

"That's right."

And that Masterson took the girl and you're saying he's dead."

"That's right."

"Then you're only chance of dodging life sentence is to help the police find her alive. If Masterson doesn't have her, who has?"

Exasperated, Alfie Doolittle posited, "I don't know. Maybe Dupree, maybe Whitey…yeah, likely Whitey. He wanted her most of all."

*   *   *

Glad to be released, assured that he sufficiently bamboozled the state police, Whitey picked up his vibrating cell and checked the number. With what was going on, he had to be careful. It was Jarvis Wingo.

"You think you're so smart!" Jarvis shouted. "A big shot! But you are nothing more than a double-crossing coward. Tell me where you are so that I can come there and kill you myself."

"That will be the day. Why are you calling me?"

"Because these New York detectives have me and everyone else in their crosshairs."

"They have nothing."

"They have nothing! You told them about the shows."

"So what? We had a show. Could be any whore? Do you believe everything the cops tell you?"

A pause. "Are you aware Masterson's missing?" Jarvis asked.

"I'm not his nurse maid."

With that response, it was clear that either he or Dupree killed Masterson. "I was so, so stupid to ever get involved. May we all rot in hell."

Ending the call, Jarvis headed straight to his basement and removed his Timber Classic Marlin from his large oaken gun cabinet. He walked out to his shed and closed the door. He put the barrel on the ground, fixed the end of the rifle under his chin, reached down, and pulled the trigger.

CHAPTER 39

Before proceeding to *Courant* headquarters, in Hartford, to meet with editors on what he was sitting on, Cartright relished every minute contacting those connected to the piece, including Alfie Doolittle's attorney who, not surprisingly, professed his client's innocence. Saving Falcone for last, he cherished confronting someone who always made him feel inferior. Instead of calling, he went to Uncasville taking a chance that Falcone may see him. Scribbling a note, he handed it to a trooper on his way in and asked for it to be delivered. While waiting, he viewed a number of bronze plaques honoring officers for meritorious service and settled on one in 2007 highlighting Falcone's successful raid of a cocaine ring.

Told to go to the second floor, he found Falcone alone in his office.

"I'm putting the finishing touches on a fairly explosive piece about the kidnapping of Julie Stapleton and Justin Edwards by a hunting party and am seeking official comment."

Falcone didn't even look up, reviewing a spreadsheet. "What's the precise question you're asking?"

"Is Alfie Doolittle a target of your investigation in kidnapping the teens at Beach Pond?"

He lowered the spreadsheet. "We are actively investigating and, as such, cannot disclose any information at this time."

Cartright wrote what he had often before. "I'm reporting the particulars in tomorrow's paper."

"Such as?"

Cartwright reviewed his notes for Falcone's benefit, concluding with the linkage to the other missing women.

Falcone leaned back in his chair. "That's a reach. You talking a spread of a dozen years."

"So, you're aware."

"It's my damn job to be aware! Let me add that you'll be whipping up this community unnecessarily for there's no connection."

"Can I quote you on that?"

"Absolutely not! People go missing for many reasons. Did you come up with that theory yourself?"

Cartwright wasn't going to reveal the extent of the research by Team Fidalgo. "I'll be on my way. I guess you don't have any further comment."

"Write that story and you're putting Justin Edwards at risk."

"What makes you so sure he isn't dead already?"

"We're working under the assumption that he's alive. But if you publish, the kidnappers will forego the ransom and kill him. Is the *Courant* prepared for that outcome"

"Don't hand me that bs. We've been told the boy is dead and the girl could be too for all we know."

"Are we off the record?"

Cartright nodded.

Falcone revealed that Julie had been at the cabin, as a result of hair sample analysis, and that Justin was there as well for the hounds tracked him in the woods. He speculated that either Justin had attempted to run off or was hunted down. He also shared that they were interrogating Doolittle. He concluded: "We know that Shipley and Masterson are missing, and Jarvis is dead."

"Jarvis?"

By the surprised reaction, Falcone knew he blundered in revealing that. It forced him to own up to it, knowing the news would circulate shortly.

"He committed suicide an hour ago."

Cartright thought to himself, 'and you're here pouring over a spreadsheet.' "That's three of the eight in the photo dead or missing."

"I see you're good at math."

"What about Whitey Marsh?"

"What about him?"

"Why isn't he in custody?

"We had him in and will be bringing him back in."

"I suggest you do."

"Don't tell me how to do my damn job!"

Not long after Cartwright left, Falcone received word that Whitey's tow truck had been located in the back of Clem's garage and that his troopers didn't find him at home.

CHAPTER 40

From what he gleaned from state police and local files, FBI District Head Hank Russo wasn't quite certain that the disappearances of the women over the years were tied to the Beach Pond abductions. But he wasn't betting against Fidalgo. He assigned Providence-based agent Christie Ambrose to provide an assessment and determine what resources, if any, were needed. In reaching Fidalgo, he cautioned to give ground to his agent.

Waiting for Agent Ambrose at Pete's, Benny received a call from Cartwright that Jarvis Wingo had committed suicide.

Difficult to absorb, he knew it was their visit and revelations that had obviously caused him to take his own life.

"We just spoke with him. Let me put you on speaker. Trish is here. He's a real loss to us. I don't know the extent of his involvement but he seemed to have a conscience and would have made a good witness against the others. How did you make out with Falcone?"

"Didn't provide much and I didn't expect much. But I get the sense he's more on top of things than we give him credit."

"In what way?"

"In that he was aware of the other disappearances. He may be looking into them and maybe wished to keep that under wraps. He tried to dissuade me from making that part of my feature."

Itching to finish his piece, Cartright told Benny he was heading to *Courant* offices.

Ending the call, Benny couldn't stop thinking about Wingo and what that meant. "If we felt Masterson was the ringleader and he's dead. And Wingo, at least presenting himself as reasonable, also gone. Who is directing this?"

Trish picked up the photo. "Leaves Whitey and these other two. This bearded one standing alongside the deer flashing the broad smile seems ornery to me. The other appears normal, a bit older. At a glance, his brown leather boots seem pricey, not the run-of-the-mill Sorells or Cabela's that these others have." She searched her iPhone. "Check these out. Similar cut designs. We're talking several hundred."

When Benny took hold of the photo, Trish could tell that he was anxious to head out the door. "Let's not get a head of ourselves," she warned. "Can we at least try to give a good first impression to the FBI agent?"

When FBI Agent Christie Ambrose did arrive, Benny was beside himself when she didn't delve right into the investigation, preferring instead to chat about the serial killer investigation he solved in Blacksburg. "Russo called it extraordinary work. He doesn't gush often."

With her continuing on, Trish saw Benny about to throw the good first impression message over the wall. "It had the usual twists and turns until Benny figured it out," she said. "It was numbing as to how many boys lost their lives…and right under our noses…like what we're dealing with now."

Benny saw how smoothly Trish bridged to the current investigation.

"With this case," Ambrose said. "I'm here to listen to where you are and where you're going."

Thankful, Benny brought her fully up to speed. And, when finished, Ambrose was thoroughly impressed at his ability to take abstract events and pull them into a meaningful manifesto. What got her attention was how he focused on the realm of possibility, believing that the kids were being held locally and charting a course to find them.

"I need to ask. Are you conferring with the state police?"

Benny didn't wish to give the FBI agent pause to think he wouldn't work with her either. "I don't see the harm in doubling up. I certainly wouldn't do anything to compromise them." He paused. "It's my niece we're talking about."

Ambrose nodded. She had already concluded that with Shipley and Masterson unaccounted for and Jarvis dead, all in a few days, this hunting group had everything to do with the teens' abductions. As with her boss, she wasn't yet sold on whether the other disappearances factored in.

"Give me a few seconds," she said, heading to the front door. "Have to check in with the boss."

When the door closed behind her, Benny felt like a caged rat. "Typical bs. She didn't let on anything as to how they're approaching this."

Trish frowned. "Will you relax. Give her a few. She needed to get the lay of the land. Just remember that she's an ally."

Feeling more comfortable returning to Blacksburg with Ambrose and the FBI on board, Trish told Benny she'd let him know what's happening on the home front as soon as she could. "You keep out of trouble here."

Benny had to stick the knife. "Pete, let's you and I sit down and tackle the jig saw puzzle."

Trish raised her eyes to the ceiling. "Yes do. And I'll take your photo. I'm sure Chief Thompson will appreciate the new and relaxed Fidalgo. Pete, if he flies solo, you're to call me."

To her surprise, Benny volunteered. "Can't thank you enough for coming here and..."

"We're not even," Trish interrupted, preventing him from getting emotional. For her, they'll never be even. She couldn't forget the night he came to her home to toss out her ex, her New York City detective husband, after he barged in drunk, ripped her clothes off, and had his way with her, while their daughter slept upstairs. All the police training in the world couldn't help fight him off. If she hadn't locked herself in her bathroom and fired off a text to Benny, she felt she would have been killed or maybe shot him. It wasn't Benny's swift actions in subduing her ex that she remembered most, but his compassion afterwards. He wouldn't leave until she ran out of tears. And he never uttered a word about it.

After watching Trish head off and catching Agent Ambrose still in conversation outside, Benny said energetically, "Pete, think hard. Who might know one of these two assholes?"

As Pete grabbed a light jacket, Benny said to himself, 'I love this guy.'

Benny left a note on Pete's kitchen counter for Charlotte saying he would be back soon and, outside, motioned to Ambrose that they were getting something to eat. She mouthed, 'I'm good.'

With Pete driving off purposely, Benny asked, "Where we off to?"

Pete revealed that his former high school shop teacher had an incredible memory and might recall either of the two in the photo. Not long on the road, he pulled his truck into a ranch house with a wheelchair access.

"Is Michael Broglio home?" Pete asked.

"Who should I say is calling?" said a woman who Pete thought could be his daughter.

"Pete Lewinski, a former student."

"Come in. I'm Mary Beth Armstrong, his daughter-in-law."

Leaving them in the living room, she wheeled in Mr. Broglio.

"Mr. Broglio. I'm..."

"Peter Lewinski!"

"That's right."

"MaryBeth, he was an outstanding student, destined for greatness. Am I right?"

"Fell short, I'm afraid. Spent much of my life in the navy."

"That's where you're wrong. There's greatness in protecting and defending our country."

Ushered into the living room, Pete endeared himself to Mr. Broglio by describing him 'the best teacher in high school.' He told Benny that Mr. Broglio had the students build racecars and sailing vessels that were timed for speed.

"Peter, I imagine you got top grades," Mr. Broglio said.

"Yes. But never understood why. My vessel sank and my racecar's wheels flew off."

While Benny and Mary Beth laughed, Mr. Broglio kept a straight face. "Never a factor in determining grades. Most important to me was the design, effort, and how the student presented their creations."

"Your projects were confidence builders, for sure. You taught us to tackle projects and not fear them. Saved me from paying plumbers and carpenters."

"You are so kind," Mary Beth said. "Can I get you some coffee?"

Pete eyed Benny and got the message. "I'm afraid we must be running. "This friend of mine," he said, nodding toward Benny, "is the uncle of the missing girl from Beach Pond."

"I'm sorry to hear that."

"And he's a detective."

"I see. I guess then you're not here to say hello. How can I help?"

"We've brought a photo and we're hoping you may be able to identify someone in it."

As Pete extended the photo, MaryBeth retrieved a magnifying glass.

They watched as Mr. Broglio hovered over each face. "Yes, that's Alfie Doolittle there," he pointed. "And that's Gerard Crenshaw," he said proudly, pointing to the tall, muscular man, alongside him. "Doesn't surprise me that they're together, inseparable as kids. Gerard was always chewing gum and sticking it under his desk. I kept him after school for two hours one day to scrape it all off."

He scanned the others. "I'm afraid I know only one other." He pointed. "I believe that's Marcus Dupree, though can't be certain. He's much scruffier looking but has those same mischievous eyes, the ones always trying to put one over on the teacher…though I must say that he built a dandy race car."

Benny saw that he was pointing to the one Trish felt was a suspicious character and one of the few remaining to focus on.

"Do you know if Marcus Dupree remained around town?" Pete asked.

"I don't." Mr. Broglio turned to Benny. "Are you after him?"

"It's still early," Benny said. Knowing his answer wasn't adequate, he added, "There's so many loose ends to tie up."

"Geez. I hope none of my students are involved? Are you sure you can't stay? My granddaughter just made what I'm sure is a delicious banana bread."

With Mr. Broglio clearly disappointed, Pete promised he would soon call again.

In his truck, Pete knew the answer but asked anyway, "You're going after him?"

"Pete, I'm up to my neck and throwing my head on the table."

CHAPTER 41

Recognizing that Agent Ambrose had to be wondering where the hell they were, Benny called Charlotte. Hearing his voice and already quite aware of how stressed Agent Ambrose was about his departure, obvious he didn't leave for food, she thought about going outside for privacy but had Ambrose staring her down.

"Pete and I are stuck. He's having his truck towed."

"I'll come get you."

"Charlotte, don't show surprise. He's not stuck. Tell Ambrose that we'll be back in an hour."

She spoke aloud, for Ambrose's benefit. "Are you sure? I can come can get you? Ok. I'll tell her."

Hanging up, he said to Pete. "Did I ever tell you what a wonderful wife I have?"

"As a matter of fact, you did."

Benny smiled, though it quickly faded. For not only was Charlotte faced with the awkwardness of being in Agent Ambrose's company, but she had to be worried about what he was up to.

Pulling to the side of the road, alongside the Brook Ridge Golf Course, Benny found Alfie Doolittle alone in the maintenance shed having lunch. He took a chance on him being there, as he easily could have been in Falcone's grasp for further questioning.

"Stay away from me!" Doolittle shouted, pulling out his cell.

"Put that away. I'm only here to ask a question." Benny showed him the hunting photo. "Who are these fine fellows?"

Though his lawyer had warned him not to speak a word, Doolittle felt the best strategy was to be obliging to this lunatic who wasn't going to leave without answers. He saw who he was pointing to.

"Ronald Jackson."

"Where can I find him?"

"At his bison farm."

"And who is this other fine fellow?"

"Mason Dupree."

"And where can I find him?"

"At Snake's Gravel and Limestone."

"See. That was easy."

Taking a step, Benny turned. "I see that Falcone has let you go your merry way."

"Had to. Nothing on me or the others. We were hunting."

"Sure you were. Shouldn't you be hiding somewhere?"

"Why should I?"

"Well, with Masterson and Shipley missing, I'm thinking you're next."

With that remark stoking fear, Benny enjoyed twisting him up. "You might consider deploying the Jarvis Wingo sayonara strategy?" It was obvious he hadn't heard. "Oh, you didn't hear? Mr. Wingo blew his brains out an hour or so ago."

With Doolittle stunned, Benny observed the big dude making his way toward him in a golf cart filled with rakes. He hadn't paid attention to him on his first pass at the golf course, but recognized him from the photo and Mr. Broglio's identification.

As he pulled in, Benny said, "Mr. Crenshaw, I presume."

With Crenshaw leaping from the golf cart, eyeing the sullen Doolittle and understanding who was before him, Benny calmly voiced,

"I wouldn't take another step if I were you, unless you want your face rearranged."

As Crenshaw stood not knowing what to do, Benny added, "Your buddy can catch you up, unless he drops dead of a heart attack."

In Pete's truck, Benny began searching GPS for the location of the bison farm, until he heard Pete say, "I know the way."

"Would you prefer I go alone?" Benny asked. "Totally understand if you do."

Pete reached for his package of cigarettes. With the FBI on board, he preferred to return to his place and provide what they had to the FBI. He still had Trish's parting words in his ear. But as he drew on the cigarette, it gave him the few seconds to think it through. "Point the way."

With the bison farm's stone entrance gated, Benny leaped from Pete's truck and tossed aside enough wooden fencing to allow Pete's truck through. Hopping back in and proceeding on, Benny rubbed his hands together, "Now for some bison hunting."

Pete braced for the worst, unnerved by Benny's callous disregard for private property. He hoped owner Ronald Jackson, a stalwart in the greater community, wasn't around. Following Benny's instructions, he pulled the truck between two oversized grey barns.

Far up into the field, they spotted a 4X4 streaming towards them. As the driver, wearing a cowboy hat and cowhide gloves, got out and stormed towards them, Pete knew this was going to turn ugly.

Halting 10 feet from his intruders, Jackson warned, "I'll give you three seconds to get off my ranch." Noticing his fencing removed, Jackson became more enraged. "In two seconds, I'm getting my shotgun and spraying you full of buckshot."

Standing beside Pete's truck, Benny held his right hand straight out, palm up. "See how rattled I am?" In his left hand, he held up the hunting photo and pointed to the individual wearing an identical cowboy hat. "I'd say that's you?"

Not bothering with the photo, Jackson reached into his jacket pocket. Not knowing if it was to retrieve a firearm, Benny rushed over and smacked the cell out of his hand.

"What the hell!" Jackson said, fully registering from Masterson's description who was before him. "I guess you're the asshole detective sticking his nose into business far from home."

"That's me. Pete, what we have here is all piss and vinegar. Where's my niece, tough guy?"

"How the hell would I know!" Jackson peered over his shoulder at his house, as if expecting aid.

"You watched the show, didn't you?" Benny said, angrily. "Asshole like you getting turned on..."

As Jackson charged forward, nearly connecting with Benny's chin, a kidney punch left him on one knee, gasping for air.

"Shouldn't be carrying all that lard," Benny quipped. "You're in a heap of shit, Jackson. It will not be long before the FBI is having bison steaks for dinner."

"Get out...now!" Jackson winced in rising.

Benny thought about pummeling him, only for Pete. "Where's my niece?"

"How the hell would I know!"

"Jackson, kiss this farm goodbye."

As Benny stepped backward and into the truck, Pete couldn't wait to hit the gas pedal, stopping at the entrance.

"Where are you going?" Benny asked.

"To put the fencing back up."

"Leave that right where it is."

Pete continued driving. "A little hairy back there," he managed to say, while fumbling for a cigarette. "Jackson is one of this area's most prominent land owners. I suspect he's on his cell now contacting the police."

Benny smiled. "Sure of that?" As Pete continued to stare in his rearview mirror, Benny added, "He's as guilty as sin. If he's contacting anyone, it's his lawyer."

Pete lit the Marlboro. "But we don't know if the teens are somewhere on his property?"

"I'm suspecting they're not. Too much activity here, too many hired hands about."

Clear of the ranch, Pete tossed the Marlboro butt out the window. "Where to?"

"To catch up with the other asshole Doolittle so kindly fingered." A pause. "I should really proceed solo."

After putting another cigarette to his lips, Pete said, "I'm good. The moment I get a little yellow, I think of your family and how fond I am of them." With that, Pete held out his hand, palm up, straight out over the dashboard, to signal, as Benny did to Jackson, that he wasn't rattled.

Benny grinned. "How far we got?"

"Not far at all."

Rushing into his house, Jackson went straight to his office and slammed the door. Plopping down in his easy chair while holding his side, he called Whitey.

"Don't dare bring that girl to my place!"

"Why, what's the matter?"

Learning of the New York detective's visit, Whitey assured him that he'd dispose of the girl somewhere else.

"Don't get your balls in an uproar," he told Jackson. "I'll get to Dupree and he'll have that bastard finished before the day is out. I'd do it myself only I have to get rid of the girl."

Not long after assessing what he needed to do, Jackson heard the sound of his front gate buzzer. With his staff attending a wedding, he went out to his porch and recognized the man standing there. He drove his 4X4 to him. Moments later, under the prominent wood carving, "Welcome To The Jackson Ranch," Ronald Jackson lay dead.

CHAPTER 42

When FBI Agent Ambrose entered the state police headquarters, she asked for Falcone. Expecting her, Falcone was eager to show off how aggressively and comprehensively they were approaching the case. On a sizeable, electronic white board were enlarged photos of eight individuals, with pertinent information in column form. Next to Shipley was his estimated height and weight, Fred's Smoke Shop, home address, and the date he went missing. Alongside was Alfie Doolittle's name, with known information, followed by Masterson, Crenshaw, and Jarvis, including the approximate time of his suicide.

"We're rounding them up," Falcone said proudly. "Shouldn't take long."

Ambrose nodded. Still upset over Fidalgo's whereabouts and suspecting he was free lancing, she had updated Russo, who was equally livid. He had told her to forget Fidalgo and partner with Falcone.

"Has Doolittle said anything?" she asked

"We'll have him momentarily. He's weak-kneed. I'm expecting he'll seek a deal before one of the others."

Ambrose asked to be a part of the discussion. She also asked to be taken to the cabin.

"We believe Whitey Marsh may be holding the girl," Falcone said.

Ambrose studied his photo and description. "Why do you think that?"

"Process of elimination."

Falcone brought Ambrose up to speed. Even though she received much of it from Fidalgo, she respectfully let Falcone go on. While Fidalgo had complained about Falcone's lack of interest in the investigation, from what she saw and heard, he appeared to be pulling all levers.

With one of his men waving from the door, Falcone excused himself. He got the news: Jackson had been shot and killed at his ranch. Sharing that with Ambrose, he said, "I think you'll want to come along. More interesting by the moment."

At the Jackson ranch, they entered the main house and saw a woman consoling two young boys at the base of a long, winding staircase. Falcone uttered, "his wife," and proceeded inside where several troopers stood. Jackson's body lay covered on a sofa. From what they were told, a worker found him at the front gate bleeding profusely from gunshot wounds to the chest.

Agent Ambrose allowed Mrs. Alice Jackson time, holding questions until the coroner removed the body and a housekeeper took the children upstairs.

"Did you see who shot him?" she asked.

"I didn't."

"But you must have heard gun shots?"

"I hear gun shots all the time. The guys are forever target practicing."

"So, you heard nothing?"

"I didn't say that. I did hear shouting an hour or so earlier and saw my husband arguing with two men."

Ambrose let her be as she wiped tears. "What did they look like?"

"One small in stature, black hair, in slacks, the other a bit taller and older, wearing a light jacket and jeans. He stood alongside a red pickup truck."

Falcone eyed Ambrose, as an acknowledgement of who they were. "After they left, what did your husband do?"

"He stormed into his office. I didn't think anything of it because he has these tirades." She began to cry.

Before leaving to get water for Mrs. Jackson, Falcone pulled Ambrose aside. "Sure as shit, it was Fidalgo and the neighbor Lewinski. The red truck's a dead giveaway."

With his cell vibrating, displaying Falcone's number, Benny debated whether or not to answer. He did.

"Agent Ambrose and I would like a word with you," Falcone said, angrily. "Where are you?"

Benny didn't respond.

"You paid a visit to the Jackson ranch, didn't you?"

"I can't hear. Who is this?"

Falcone raised his voice but Benny feigned difficulty hearing and cut him off. Pete, worried, caught it all.

At Snake's Gravel & Limestone, Benny was told Marcus Dupree was making deliveries and expected back shortly. Noticing two state troopers pull up, he ducked out and into Pete's truck.

"Seems like we're not the only ones looking for him."

About to go north on Route 138, Benny directed Pete south.

"I'm figuring Dupree more likely will be coming south to north, from three-ninety-five. Just pull over."

While Pete contemplated telling Benny to allow the state police to close this out, seeing that troopers were interested in Dupree, he didn't have time as a Snake's dump truck passed. Being told to step on it and after flicking his lights, as Benny requested, the dump truck pulled over. Benny rushed to the driver's side window.

"What seems to be the trouble?" Dupree asked, pulling the toothpick from his lips.

"I'm doing you a favor."

"Yeah. What is it?"

"Well, if you continue to Snake's, you'll find two state troopers eager to speak with you about what went on at the cabin."

It dawned on Dupree who was addressing him. "Well, I'll be damned...I'm speaking to the girl's uncle."

"Where is she?"

Dupree grinned. "Could be halfway around the world by now."

"What's that supposed to mean?"

"Well, the guy who took her is a real shylock, a money grabber if there ever was one. Hate to tell you this but your niece will soon be cozying up to some sheik."

"Get out of that cab!"

When Dupree did, Pete hurriedly exited his truck.

"I believe my niece is with some asshole named Whitey."

"Then you needn't worry. He'll take good care of her."

Reaching out to grab Dupree, Benny got spun around. As they fell to the ground, Pete attempted to separate them but couldn't. He backed off seeing Benny in control.

However, with Dupree taunting, "We got to see your niece get plucked," Benny started belting him until Dupree suddenly rolled under the truck. As Benny sprinted to the other side, Pete followed and saw Dupree waving a Jim Bowie knife.

"Keep coming, you bastard! I'm going to cut your gizzard out!"

Dialing 911 and describing where he was, Pete saw the two combatants come together. Moments later, he watched Dupree fall backward, the knife extending from his chest.

CHAPTER 43

Within minutes of the 911 call, trooper vehicles arrived from all directions. As they charged forward, Benny and Pete remained in place and raised their arms wide and high.

"Don't move, either of you!" one ordered.

After one trooper checked Dupree's carotid pulse, he said to the other, "he's dead," they cuffed Benny and Pete and had them sit well off the road.

Not long after, one trooper drove his vehicle about 50 yards down the road and began placing flares extending to where they were, in a pattern that effectively closed the lane. In the meantime, three other police vehicles arrived, and it wasn't long before Falcone and FBI Agent Ambrose did as well.

After checking Dupree's body, Falcone relished getting in Benny's face. "Couldn't help yourself, could you?"

"He pulled a knife," Pete protested. "It was self-defense."

"More like premeditated murder. Fidalgo, your actions are reckless, more than I've ever seen. First you gun down Jackson at his ranch and now this."

While cautioning himself to let this play out, Benny couldn't believe what he just heard and stared up at Falcone. "I had nothing to do with Jackson." It hit him that Jackson's death marked yet another of the hunters either missing or dead. But he could hardly reflect on it with Falcone breathing down his neck.

"Well, his wife claims otherwise. Heard you arguing right outside her damn house!"

Barking instructions, with Agent Ambrose seemingly lost in thought, Falcone barked to a trooper to call forensics. He ordered four others to take Benny and Pete separately back to the state police headquarters and sent another to Snake's Gravel to obtain personal information on Dupree so they could notify next of kin.

Off with Falcone to the command post, Ambrose was baffled by the rapid turn of events. Having been in Fidalgo's company, she respected him, knowing his stellar history and unflinching determination to find his niece. At the same time, she had to face facts over the individuals dead in his wake.

"Whoever hired him as a detective ought to go before a firing squad," Falcone chirped. "Even his sister thinks he has a screw loose."

Ambrose half-listened. She thought about contacting FBI command and Russo but, with things so fluid, felt it was better to wait until they had a full account of Fidalgo's whereabouts. But she also knew she couldn't wait long with the teens' lives in the balance.

"Can you run through the hunting party one more time," she asked Falcone who hadn't quit berating Fidalgo.

"Be happy to." He shared that Goobie Crenshaw and Alfie Doolittle were employed by a local golf course as maintenance workers and that they had previously questioned Doolittle but not Crenshaw and that both had been taken into custody. He reminded her that Blake Masterson, an insurance agent, Whitey Marsh, a tow truck operator, and Warren Shipley, a tobacco salesman, were all missing. He stated that Jarvis Wingo, a surveyor, had committed suicide.

"And you know about Ronald Jackson, the bison ranch owner. At least there's no mistaking who called Marcus Dupree."

To Ambrose, it was all numbing. "Can you drill down on Whitey Marsh?"

"He's the most familiar to us. As a tow truck operator, our troopers use his services as crash scenes." Falcone paused. "Fidalgo had to have killed Jackson. Who knows, he might be behind all of the disappearances and deaths."

Agent Ambrose studied Falcone to gauge whether he was serious. To her, someone would have to be psychotic to contact the FBI and invite them into the investigation, if the intent was vengeance. And he did have the company of Pete Lewinski, at least through much of what had transpired.

In the interrogation room, with Falcone and Ambrose peppering him with questions, Pete kept his cool. His intent was to tell the truth. But he was exasperated in not being able to change minds and of being interrupted repeatedly.

"How many times do I have to tell you?" he said, "we drove to Jackson's ranch and spoke to him about his being at the cabin. We wished to know where the kids were, and it got out of hand."

"I'll say it did," Falcone snapped. "Let's back up. You went to see Jackson. But his front gate was locked."

"That's right."

"And you moved wooden fencing adjoining the gate to get in."

"That's right."

"That's trespassing."

Pete slowly breathed in and out. "We've gone over this. Jackson came in his golf cart from deep on his property and Benny spoke to him for I'd say, less than five minutes."

"Go on."

"There is no going on. We left."

"How can you expect us to believe that?" Falcone challenged.

Frustrated, Pete angrily pushed back in his aluminum chair. "Give me a lie detector's test."

Agent Ambrose believed his account. "What did Jackson say about the cabin?"

Pete bowed his head, in resignation. "Said they were hunting."

An intimidating force, with his shoulders wide and squared, as if he was sticking his chest out to show off medals, Falcone paced, stepping menacingly toward Pete when asking a question.

"Tell us, don't you think Fidalgo capable?"

"Capable of what?"

"Of murdering those he believed kidnapped his niece?"

Pete quickly shook his head. "No way."

"Someone who even a judge intimated might be suffering from PTSD?"

Surprised in hearing that, Pete tried not to show it. "You're forgetting one key fact. I was with him at the Jackson ranch and nearly all other times. Like I said, give me the lie detector test."

Huddling outside the interrogation room, Agent Ambrose told Falcone that Benny and Pete, especially Benny, had more explaining to do but believed they had nothing to do with Jackson's death.

"At the ranch, Mrs. Jackson heard them argue and said her husband was downstairs in their house. I ask: How can Fidalgo and Lewinski leave in pursuit of Marcus Dupree and detour back and kill Jackson. From a time standpoint, doesn't add up."

"Well, Fidalgo could have returned to the ranch and left Lewinski to wait for Dupree to return."

"You're forgetting they had one car."

About to counter, Falcone caught himself. "But there's no getting around that Dupree is dead and that it was Fidalgo who stuck the knife in him."

"That he admitted…but in self-defense." Ambrose internalized, before continuing. "Fidalgo and Lewinski were completely in sync on what they told us. Remember, you had separated them, so they didn't spend time getting their stories straight. Furthermore, if Dupree pulls the knife, why didn't Fidalgo pull his gun? Tells me he wished to subdue him to obtain information on his niece rather than kill him." She paused. "Also, let's not forget both requested lie detector tests and didn't lawyer up. Can we get in front of the white board. Will help me to process before I call in."

In the main investigation room, Agent Ambrose plopped into a high-backed, swivel chair. "Feels good to sit." She saw Falcone not joining her, still heated.

"I can't believe you're giving Fidalgo a pass on Jackson. Isn't it obvious that he's out of his mind over what happened to his niece?"

"I'm not giving him a pass." Ambrose chose to end it there, for it's quite possible that Fidalgo had indeed lost it. She reached for a water bottle. "Let's put Fidalgo and Lewinski aside for a minute. We're losing sight of the teens. Let's presume these guys abducted them for this show. Plausible, isn't it."

"I guess."

"Then it's time to press Doolittle and Crenshaw for I'm sure they know a great deal about what went down."

"They've lawyered up, remember?"

"Then let's speak to their lawyer and make it plain what the clients can expect if they don't cooperate."

Falcone pointed to the white board. "Mightn't need them. My guys are closing in on Whitey Marsh. With the suspect list dwindling, he may be the one holding Julie Stapleton."

"How close are you?"

"Expect a call any moment."

CHAPTER 44

Cartright's sensational front-page news story, accompanied by the photo of the eight men reputedly attached to the missing teens in a Pachaug Forest cabin, had the entire region buzzing. Google and Yahoo picked it up on their news feeds and it became one of the most heavily viewed stories of the day. As a result of the coverage, so many local residents and others throughout Connecticut and nearby states were calling to report having seen either one of the men or the missing teens.

Inundated by the volume, Falcone assigned a special unit to triage the calls. In this way, he could hone in on those calling about the teens, which he had greater interest in.

With the *Courant* story nationally recognized, Cartwright's editors assigned four other reporters, especially in lieu of the Ronald Jackson and Marcus Dupree murders. Following appearances on morning TV news casts, Cartwright had enough. He didn't wish to seed what he believed was 'his story' to anyone. Anxious to get access to Benny Fidalgo, he was rebuffed and had to wait outside Trooper headquarters with dozens of other print and broadcast reporters.

Catching sight of a nurse leaving the Trooper building, and recalling that Fidalgo's wife was one, he watched as she waved off reporters who immediately impeded another individual who appeared to be in law enforcement.

Cartright drifted over to where she had parked. "You're Charlotte Fidalgo?"

Charlotte ignored him, proceeding to get into her car. But as she did and hearing his name and affiliation, she lowered the driver's side window, recalling that Trish had spoken of a reporter they had outreached to.

"Can you share your husband's status?" he asked.

Sizing up whether or not to speak to him, she threw out, "What my husband needs is a good lawyer."

"I can help. His name is Jacob Smiley. Doesn't come cheap. But he's the one I'd hire if my brother was in trouble."

"Thank you. I'll look him up."

"No need. Give me your cell and I'll text his contact information." When Charlotte did, he continued to probe.

"I assume they're not releasing your husband?"

She shook her head.

"Did he say anything about where he thinks his niece may be?"

"He thinks this Whitey Marsh character has her, if she isn't…"

"You mean the tow truck operator?"

"Yes."

If that's the case, thought Cartright, it won't be long before they bring him in. "Is Trish McGlucas headed here?"

Though surprised by the mention of Trish's name, it confirmed to Charlotte that this reporter had a connection. "She's expected shortly."

When a few reporters noticed Cartright in conversation, Charlotte apologized and hurriedly left the parking lot, determined to catch up with Pete who had been released. While she found Pete's front door unlocked and he not at home, she dropped off her bag and walked over to see John and Anne. That lasted all of a few minutes after hearing Anne say, "I guess that brother of mine is getting his comeuppance."

As she walked back to Pete's, she let the tears fall where they may, locked into thoughts of her husband's depressed state. "I don't care what happens to me" replayed over and over again. Even if this lawyer is able to free him, she feared he would be once again plunge into despair if Julie isn't found alive, like the years recovering from the deaths of his buddies in Afghanistan. The fact that they were dead and he wasn't, haunted him. What eventually snapped him out of it was the psychologist's insistence that his brothers in battle would want him to lead a fulfilling life helping others.

* * *

Trish proceeded straight to Uncasville. With Charlotte calling her about Benny's predicament, she couldn't leave them alone. And instead of tangling with Chief Thompson, she called in sick. Before leaving, she cornered Murph and told him what had happened and what she was up to. While he wished to go also, she convinced him to remain behind until she got the lay of the land.

Arriving, prepared to play hard ball, she was accompanied upstairs to meet with Falcone and Agent Ambrose.

"Are you not permitting me to see him?"

"In a minute, sit down," Ambrose voiced, calmly.

"This is clear self-defense," Trish replied, glowering. "What don't you understand!"

"Do I need to remind you that he was out on bail," Falcone said.

"Bail? Doesn't take a genius to understand what happened here."

"Detective," Ambrose said, appealing to the professional before her, "please appreciate that we can't let him go. He engaged with a party who lost his life."

"I beg to differ. As I understand it, said party pulled a knife. I know for a fact that Benny doesn't carry one." A pause. "To be honest, what also concerns me is your focus on him and not his niece."

"We haven't lost sight." Ambrose admired Trish McGlucas. It wasn't only over defending her partner. It was more in seeing an assertive, experienced, female detective go toe-to-toe in taking them on.

"Has the DA charged him?" Trish asked.

Agent Ambrose glanced at Falcone. "Don't think the DA is prepared to do that."

"We've received no official word," Falcone corrected. "Let's see where this nets out."

Agent Ambrose sought to reassure McGlucas, without contradicting Falcone. "We're holding him for his own sake. There's a slew of individuals dead in his path." Ambrose described Jackson's murder, which Trish hadn't heard about from Charlotte. "As you can appreciate, we don't need him meddling as we attempt to locate his niece."

Trish had no comeback. That seemed plausible for she also couldn't trust Benny's actions upon his release. Taken downstairs and peering into the cell, she saw him defeated, a shell of himself, sitting dejected and taking no notice of her.

"You've certainly gotten yourself into a mess," she said upon being permitted into the cell. A long pause. It was obvious he wasn't into talking, as Charlotte had indicated in their conversation on the ride up. "I don't think they can hold you."

Bent over, with his arms resting on top of his legs, he raised up. "Trish, I plunged that knife so far into his chest that I wanted it to come out his back."

Trish winced, and whispered, "Keep that to yourself, for crying out loud. Paints you as a crazy man." It wasn't lost on her that while his killing of Marcus Dupree was a clear case of self-defense, he had lost it. She knew he trained police units in New Jersey on close quarter fighting techniques and could deescalate situations better than anyone. She saw it firsthand with her ex.

He looked up at her. "I'm an officer of the law. There's no excuse for killing him. I didn't do right by the police, by Pete, by you, by Charlotte, by my sister, and certainly not by Julie and Justin...my stupidity has most certainly delayed efforts to find them."

With Benny again bending over and leaning his arms on his thighs, Trish had the antidote. On the way up, she had done quite a lot of thinking on the investigation. What she was about to put forward would surely snap him out of it.

CHAPTER 45

In the bedroom of his mother's house, Whitey Marsh checked that Julie's restraints remained secured. He liked seeing her naked and the sheer terror she exhibited every time he entered the room. On his last visit, he sat at his old desk and raised his feet up on it, and proceeded to pontificate about what a great high school football player he was, how he was scouted by top tier colleges. He told her he was set to accept an athletic scholarship to Michigan State as a tight end when he broke his shoulder falling into a fence trying to make a catch in a local softball game. "And, can you believe it, the bastards reneged on my scholarship. Probably a good thing for I would have screwed every sweet piece of ass on campus." Continuing his life story, he bragged about the money he was making as a tow truck driver, often exceeding a $1,000 a day, towing 'the suckers' and 'fleecing them' for an additional $100 dollars a night for the safekeeping of their vehicles.

Listening, Julie grew anxious when he spouted that he always dreamed of doing a girl on the 50-yard line and crossing that off his wish list. "Think you'd like that?"

Saying it to get a reaction, as he knew it was impossible to get to the football field unseen, Whitey knew his time was limited. Earlier, at Dunkin' for a breakfast sandwich and coffee, he couldn't miss the *Courant's* blaring front-page headline, "Teens Believed Targeted By Pachaug Hunting Club."

Flipping open the first page, the large photo of him and the others caused him to scan the store, worried that someone might identify him. He took some comfort in seeing the Pakistani owner busy with a customer purchasing lotteries, a mother buying milk and dealing with a rambunctious kid, and an old-timer facing away from him drinking coffee.

Whitey ditched getting Dunkin', tossed two dollars for the paper on the counter, and quickly exited. He worried that it wouldn't be long before the police tracked him down and hoped they hadn't yet established road check points. He now understood why the weak-kneed, coward Masterson dumped the girl on him. Figuring to have sex with her one more time, he'd bury her and head backroads to Canada.

* * *

In the main investigatory room and waiting to speak with Dolittle's lawyer, Ambrose saw Falcone charging through the door, saying they received a tip that Whitey Marsh was spotted going into a home on Shawnee Road.

In a parade of trooper vehicles, they reached the house and saw the tow truck outside. Huddling with his team, Falcone barked instructions. When one trooper asked if they should shoot to kill, Falcone told them to protect themselves, which was essentially his way of giving clearance.

After waiting for the officers to get in place, he clicked the bullhorn. "Whitey Marsh, this is Lieutenant Troop Commander Desmond Falcone, with the Connecticut State Police. Come out with your hands up."

Hearing the commotion outside, Marsh kicked himself for not leaving sooner as he observed state troopers crouching and sprinting along both sides of the house. Untying his meal ticket, he took her to the window facing the patrol cars. Casting aside his mother's sewing machine, he opened the window and, holding Julie by the back of her hair, pressed her face and naked upper body out.

"I'll kill her first!" he yelled. "Stay the hell away!"

"You are surrounded," Falcone replied. "Let her go and walk out with your hands up."

"Do you think I'm that stupid!"

When the two disappeared inside, Falcone turned to Ambrose. "I'm going in."

"No. Let's get a negotiator here. He's not going to kill her. He needs her. We need to wear him down."

"Listen, I told you we're familiar with Marsh. He'll listen to me."

"He's too crazed. You saw him. We need to play the long game."

Falcone handed the bull horn to a trooper. "He's deranged. He'll kill her for sure. I'll go in and talk him down. I'll not put her at risk."

Ambrose wanted none of it. "I'm running this!"

Ignoring her, Falcone put his bullet proof vest on and took hold of the bullhorn. "Whitey, this is Lieutenant Falcone. I'm coming in unarmed."

With Ambrose irate and vociferously demanding that he wait for negotiators, Falcone brushed her aside. Walking steadily toward the front door with his hands raised, he entered and disappeared from view. A few minutes later a shot rang out, sending Ambrose and half the troopers, weapons drawn, sprinting toward the house. About to enter, the door swung open and the naked Julie ran past. Ambrose and the troopers moved in.

"I'm in here," Falcone shouted.

On the floor lay Whitey Marsh, a bullet hole in his forehead.

Checking for a pulse, Ambrose holstered her gun. Two officers behind her whooped it up.

"Let's not lose our heads," Falcone said. "A lot of work to do here."

One of the troopers outside wrapped Julie in a blanket and put her into the back seat of a patrol car. Agent Ambrose came to check on her. "Are you in pain?"

Julie, in shock, shook uncontrollably.

When Ambrose asked again, Julie shook her head. "We're going to take you to the hospital to have you checked out. Are you cold?"

When she nodded, Falcone asked a trooper to retrieve more blankets.

"Have you found Justin?" Julie asked.

"We haven't. But we have a lot of people on it. Do you know where he is?"

In raising her eyes to Ambrose, Julie harkened back to her last image of him, sitting on the ground outside the cabin.

"Were you sexually molested?"

Pulling the blanket up to her face, Ambrose knew this wasn't the time and place to probe. She couldn't imagine what had happened to her in the days under their control.

Telling Julie that they would bring her mom and dad to the hospital, Ambrose couldn't tell if she was listening, appearing to be in a catatonic state, but had to advise her not to speak to anyone about her ordeal. She then asked Falcone to have a female officer present when they got to the hospital. Reaching John Stapleton, she delivered the news, telling him to meet them at Bacchus Hospital.

With John and Anne rushing from the elevator and attempting to go in, Ambrose prevented them as the medical team was still attending to their daughter.

"I'm her mother!"

"You'll have access in minutes. I assure you."

"Is she alright?" Anne asked.

"She's fine." She couldn't leave it there. "She faced severe trauma."

"Was she…"

Ambrose's face said it all.

"Oh my God!" With Anne burying her head into her husband's shoulders, Ambrose let them be. Minutes later she told the Stapletons what they could expect going forward, including Julie being seen by a hospital psychologist and their needing to interview her. She advised them to remain on the floor to be protected from the hordes of media gathering outside.

At the state police headquarters, Trish and Benny heard the roar and overheard one exuberant trooper tell his colleagues that Falcone had freed the girl, killing Whitey Marsh.

"Well, thank God for that," Trish said, yet noticing that Benny hadn't reacted, hadn't even lifted his head. "Did you hear that? Your niece has been found."

Nothing registered.

"The DA isn't going to hold you, especially with what Julie is likely to say." Still, getting nothing, she added, "You had it right all along."

Benny appeared to rebound following Charlotte's arrival, but it was only for show. After convincing she and Trish to get something to eat, above their protests, his mood turned sour. He couldn't take his mind off what those bastards did to his niece and that he failed to rescue her. He couldn't imagine the state she was in. What he did take comfort in was that Whitely Marsh was dead.

As he mulled over the sicko players involved and all that had gone down, what stuck in is mind is who killed Ronald Jackson? What he knew is that he and Pete had left the irate bison ranch owner and not long after, he's found dead. It could have been Whitey Marsh who shot him, but he figured Marsh to be preoccupied with his niece. It wasn't Alfie Doolittle and Goobie Crenshaw, as he remained convinced that they were minor players in all of this and had to be under the radar of law enforcement.

Noticing a trooper entering the cell area and hearing his name, Benny was surprised as a guard unlocked his cell. "I'm to drive you to the hospital."

Led out, Benny wasn't about to ask questions.

CHAPTER 46

Waiting to see her daughter was excruciating for Anne Stapleton, especially knowing the hold-up had to do with administering the rape kit exam. And then the hospital psychologist took longer than expected. She hardly listened to his words of Julie suffering severe emotional and psychological damage and that she needed time to heal. She wanted in.

Rushing past a nurse, assigned to standby for any signs of distress, Anne hugged Julie, not letting her go. In releasing her, she stared lovingly at her daughter while scanning for any physical scars from her ordeal. In holding her hands, she noticed the redness and bruising around her wrists and what that signified. She kept smiling, though the tears cascaded to such a degree that Julie had to reach for the box of Kleenex and blotted them.

Being warned by the psychologist not to probe about anything or approach any subjects that might trigger anxiety, Anne latched on to what she deemed a safe topic, the welcoming packages from Quinnipiac University.

It backfired, as Julie now used the tissues as it stirred memories of conversations with Justin as to how they could meet up after going their separate ways. She recalled Justin's determination to make it work, how he was trying to find a high school classmate who he could stay with at Quinnipiac when he visited, even considering reaching seniors at nearby schools.

Trying to comfort her daughter, Anne was at a loss as to what to say. Looking on, with his wife struggling, John stepped over and kissed Julie's forehead. "We love you."

"I know dad."

It was now John crying, and his tears flowed so heavily that he could no longer remain bedside. For some time, Anne held Julie's hand until she saw Agent Ambrose enter the room.

"Honey, the police need to speak with you. I'll be right outside."

When her parents left, Julie sobbed and raised the bedsheet up to her eyes. The nurse, witnessing everything, came over. "It's really going to be tough on you and them. Do you need time? Do you want me to have the police wait?" When Julie shook her head, the nurse added, "Ok, I'll remain by the door. Wave at any time and I'll ask them to leave."

The nurse allowed Ambrose and Falcone in.

"Thank you, sir, for rescuing me," Julie said. While Falcone nodded, he really cherished receiving the praise in front of FBI Agent Ambrose who had protested his actions.

"I have many questions," Ambrose said, stepping close to the bed rail. She considered sitting for a moment but felt that she would be at a disadvantage staring up.

As if a light bulb went off, Julie voiced, "Where's my uncle?"

Stupefied, Falcone asked, "You mean Benny Fidalgo?"

She nodded.

"He's occupied. He may see you later."

"I want him here now," Julie insisted. "While I waited for someone to rescue me, these men belittled him, called him "the runt" and cursed him. But it gave me hope. I told Justin that my uncle will find us."

With Julie distressed, the nurse took a step but Falcone raised his hand to stop her. "I'm afraid that's not possible," he said. "He's in jail."

Julie's eyes darted from Falcone to Ambrose and back again. "What did he do?"

"He killed a man," Falcone said.

"What man?"

Though upset at the direction this was going, Ambrose felt that at least Julie was conversing. "Someone by the name of Marcus Dupree," she said.

Julie's eyes widened. "You jailed my uncle for killing him! Tell me you're kidding! He's evil! He took my Justin!"

Rushing to the bed, the nurse declared, "she needs a break," to which Julie said forcefully, "A break? I'm not saying another word without my uncle."

In the hall, Falcone exploded. "That bastard's not coming here!"

Ambrose peered over her shoulder. "Keep your voice down. We don't have a choice now, do we?"

When Benny entered onto the hospital ward, in handcuffs, Anne pretended not to see him. Told by Falcone that Julie wanted her brother in the room, she was livid and insisted on speaking with Julie herself. "I'll get her to reconsider."

"That's not necessary," Ambrose said. "If she desires for him to be there, she must have her reasons and we must respect that."

"Well, I need to be there as well."

Feeling that Julie wouldn't be forthright in front of her mother, Agent Ambrose assured Anne that Benny's presence mightn't last long, as Julie may be embarrassed responding to questions in front of him. "I know this is tough on you but allow us to do our thing. I promise I'll come for you the moment I sense that Julie needs her mother."

Before entering Julie's room, Falcone warned Benny not to say anything at all. After he agreed, Falcone instructed the trooper to remove the handcuffs.

Entering, Julie raised her arms out to him. "Oh, uncle!"

Choked up, Benny didn't want to let her go. He thought to the time her pet rabbit, Roscoe, died and she blamed her parents for not giving Roscoe a companion. Hearing that she was taking it hard, he recalled telling her that Roscoe didn't die of a lonely heart because he had a beautiful seven-year-old girl to take care of him. He further told her that Roscoe is in a very special place with thousands of friends and telling them all about the lovely girl who fed him and let him run around in a backyard pen. Benny cherished that moment for, when he finished cheering her up, she had wrapped her arms around his neck, much as she did now.

"Uncle Benny, if it wasn't for you, I'd have given up all hope."

"Sorry I couldn't get to you, sweetheart."

Falcone coughed, a cue for Benny to step back next to the nurse.

Calm, Julie began by speaking of the kayak ride, even disclosing to them the intention of losing her virginity. But her account came to a screeching halt after she said two men "appeared out of nowhere." With Julie eyes transfixed to a place all her own, Ambrose patted her knee, which snapped Julie out of it.

"Julie, what did these two men look like?"

She described one as tall and muscular with long arms, who didn't say much; the other much smaller with a beard and salt and pepper hair. In handing Julie a dozen photos, Ambrose asked, "Are they among any of these?" She pointed to Alfie Doolittle and Goobie Crenshaw.

She indicated that the muscular one carried the kayak from the water and got Justin to help take it to a blue truck. She said she didn't know much more after that, being blindfolded until they were inside a cabin. "I knew we had gone off the main road for it got bumpy for a long time. I could hear the brush hitting the sides of the truck."

It was clear to Agent Ambrose that Julie was going to have a hard time from here. "Tell us in your own words what happened."

Julie nodded. "Seven men came inside and sat on folding chairs in a semi-circle. One man, the leader, held a clock. He gave us instructions on how to remove our clothes. He wanted me to perform oral sex on Justin."

After admitting that, Julie's face reddened, until Ambrose said, "there's nothing you're going to tell us that we haven't heard before. Unfortunately, there are evil doers in this world, and we're very sorry you ran into a few."

As tears rolled down her cheeks, Julie summoned the courage. "Justin took off my bathing suit and stood up. I tried but it wasn't working. The leader stopped the clock and said if we failed, he would kill Justin." A pause, the tears more significant. "Justin began yelling at all of them but they said he wasn't a man. I comforted him, told him to lie down and close his eyes. I…"

As Julie held the bed sheet up to soak her tears, Agent Ambrose didn't need to know the details. "What did this leader look like?"

Julie described him as more neatly dressed than the others, in a collared-shirt and slacks, and wearing a Red Sox baseball hat. Ambrose handed Julie another dozen photos. "Is he among them?"

"This one."

"What happened from there?"

"They left but said they were coming back tomorrow for the grand finale."

"So, you were left alone?"

"We were shackled to the wall. But then I needed to pee. And Justin did as well, or so he said. He ran off until a few with rifles went after him."

While she paused, they waited for her to regroup. "They caught him and tied him to a tree where they whipped him…making me watch."

As she raised the bed sheet, Benny went to her and squeezed her hand. "You are doing beautifully. Close your eyes if you need to. You'll get through this." After squeezing her hand, reassuringly, Benny went back by the door. He had all he could do to hold himself together.

"What was the grand finale?" Ambrose asked.

"They forced us to have sex. I heard someone say 'the virgin's about to get lit up.' Justin began screaming at them and they belittled him." Julie stared at the blank TV screen mounted overhead. "I convinced him to do it. I overheard what they said…they were going to kill him if he…" She paused. "He had difficulty, was shaking so much, until I relaxed him and put him inside me."

Shocked by her account, Ambrose nevertheless held steady to maintain the flow. "Tell us about the other men?"

"One was kind. Brought us food. Justin felt we might be able to convince him to let us go but it wasn't to be."

"What did he look like?"

She spoke of him having a full beard and responsible for the cabin because "he cleaned it up the day we were leaving." Benny knew right away that she was referring to Jarvis Wingo. Ambrose provided more photos and asked if he was among them. "That's him. He told us that if we wished to continue to breathe, we should do what they say."

"The other two?"

"One taunted Justin unmercifully."

"Can you describe him?"

"He looked like a leprechaun, only taller. He had large ears and heavy eyebrows. His hair was long in the back and the sides and his ears popped through. He's the one who taunted Justin, the one you said my uncle killed."

Julie glanced over at her uncle, seated next to the nurse, as Ambrose again put several photos in her hand. Julie identified Dupree.

Ambrose recalled what she had said earlier. "You mentioned he may have been responsible for Justin's death? Why do you think that?"

Julie related that after Justin unsuccessfully ran off, "Dupree stood over him like he was his slave, his property."

"And that was the last time you saw Justin?"

After Julie nodded, she seemed to withdraw. Realizing she was on borrowed time, Ambrose handed over another packet of photos.

"Anyone else you recognize in here?"

She identified bison ranch owner Ronald Jackson.

"Julie. Aside from these men, were there any others?"

Appearing at first to be thinking it through, Julie burst out, "No! Stay away! No! No!" The nurse rushed over, removed the pillow supporting her, got her to lie down, and pulled up the bed sheets. "You relax, darling. I'll get you something."

As the nurse turned from the bed to chase the law enforcement officers, she didn't have to. They had already left.

CHAPTER 47

Leaving Julie's room, Falcone waved over a trooper to handcuff Benny and ordered that he be taken back to their Uncasville command post.

"Do you think the cuffs necessary?" Ambrose raised, watching them head off. "He's not a flight risk."

"We are obligated to hold him until the DA says otherwise."

Agent Ambrose couldn't believe all that Julie revealed and was just grateful she had the composure to identify her captors. At a loss as to what may have happened to Justin Edwards, she remained confident that with additional FBI resources, she and her colleagues would get to bottom of it. With the nurse sharing that Julie needed at least a few hours of rest, she figured to use the time to grill Goobie Crenshaw and Alfie Doolittle. With Julie Stapleton identifying them, maybe they'd be more inclined to bargain with respect to the whereabouts of Justin Edwards. She also intended to probe about the disappearances of at least three women in the surrounding region.

In Uncasville, as the trooper walked him in, Benny spotted Charlotte and Trish in the lobby huddled with someone he presumed to be his lawyer, the one Cartwright recommended.

Introduced to Attorney Jacob Smiley, he was told the DA should drop the charges. Smiley beamed when Benny shared what his niece revealed about Marcus Dupree, being among her predators.

"That seals it," Smiley said. "The DA won't hold you. You'll save the state money."

Before leaving, Smiley apologized for what had gone down in his community. "We have some ornery folks, for sure, but to think we had deviants like this lurking about, it's hard to fathom. Ronald Jackson's a huge surprise. No one could have seen that coming."

"It can happen anywhere," Benny said. "Evil is an equal opportunity employer."

In his cell, Benny was thankful Trish and Charlotte were granted permission to see him. "Thanks for hiring Smiley. I owe Cartwright."

"Speaking of Cartwright, he's anxious to speak with you."

"The feeling's mutual."

Trish saw the fire in Benny's eyes. Julie's disclosures charged him up.

"Honey, can you do me a favor?" he asked. "I'm starving. Earlier, they served me up something that tasted like roadkill. Can you get me a sandwich? You know what I like."

Charlotte was only too happy to oblige. She was thrilled that her husband had rebounded and would soon be released, when only hours before she thought the worst. When Trish reached into her sling bag for her wallet, after requesting a chicken salad sandwich, Charlotte voiced, "don't be silly."

"You aren't hungry, are you?" Trish asked, once Charlotte left.

Benny shook his head.

"I thought so."

"We can't be hanging together. You're beginning to know me better than my wife."

"Men. Don't you think she knew you wanted to speak with me alone."

Benny didn't want Charlotte around while he shared details of Julie's capture and sexual abuse. Even though Charlotte faced the daily horrors of ER life, in Jacobi Hospital, one of the City's busiest emergency rooms, he knew she would hurt deeply in discovering what happened to their niece. It was bad enough for Trish to hear.

"Do you want me to stop?" Benny asked.

"Of course not, just don't look at me."

Benny took a moment. In hearing Julie speak of what happened, he managed to hold it together. He had to. At various times, he saw his niece look at him, almost to take his temperature as he nodded to her, as if to say, "we got this." But inside, he was a wreck.

"You ok?" Trish asked, seeing him lost in the moment. "It must have been tough on you in there."

Getting choked up, Benny turned his head away, saying "Trish, I died in there, listening." When he finished, he told her that Ambrose and Falcone were focused on shaking up Goobie Crenshaw and Alfie Doolittle.

"I guess you'd like too as well."

He shook his head. "Not really. Those idiots aren't going to offer much on Justin…and sure as hell won't compound jail time in revealing much of anything."

"What about the ransom call?"

Distracted, the question hung until Benny said, "We have to come to grips with the fact that Justin is dead. They likely abandoned the ransom feeling the heat."

"What were you just thinking about?" Trish asked.

"The one thing that will ensure these guys fry, at least the live ones…finding the bodies."

Trish flung her index finger into the air, smiling broadly.

"What's that for?" he asked.

"Because to that, I've been doing a great deal of thinking."

Trish eagerly let him know that she didn't believe the bodies were buried in Pachaug Forest. "Anyplace but," she said, "in an effort to keep the bodies a distance from the cabin. In this way, when and if law enforcement got tipped off to their activities, they would exhaust themselves in Pachaug. Without bodies, they knew it would be much harder for the DA to hang murder charges. But where?"

As both wrestled with the question, Benny suddenly snapped his fingers. "I got it! Of course! The bodies are buried on Jackson's ranch!" He paused. "Hear me out."

Describing his trip to the bison ranch, he spoke of beautiful, picturesque hillside and pastures, "a place where no one would imagine a graveyard and certainly not on the property of a leading entrepreneur." A pause. "None of these other assholes owned property. But Jackson did. That bison farm is huge. Think about the possibilities."

Trish couldn't disagree. But as was her nature, she played devil's advocate. "But he must employ quite a few people. How can they pull that off? Wouldn't the ranch hands, his wife, others notice suspicious activity or, at the very least, disturbed land?"

Benny considered for a second. "Great points. But we know these guys have been fooling people for a long time. It's not like they're burying people every month, for that matter, every year."

Trish suggested conferring with Agent Ambrose. "I think she's reasonable. Made a good impression on me." Benny agreed.

When Ambrose and Falcone finished round two with Doolittle and Crenshaw, it was Alfie Doolittle who cracked. He disclosed that Justin wound up in the hands of Marcus Dupree, who was "out to kill him and dispose of the body." Asked where that may be, Doolittle shrugged. "Might not find a body at all. Dupree's more likely carved him up and sprinkled his body parts here and there."

With Dupree dead, they planned on scouring his house and property as well as the commercial enterprise of Snake's Gravel & Limestone, where he worked.

Neither Doolittle nor Crenshaw admitted anything about the disappearances of other women, though Doolittle admitted that the hunting group brought in a whore or two at times for a strip show and "a little post-event entertainment."

When they tried to delve into that, the lawyer intervened. "You haven't provided one piece of evidence tied to these so-called missing persons. You're on a fishing expedition."

Catching Agent Ambrose eyeing Doritos in a vending machine, Trish approached and lowered her voice. "Benny thinks he may know where the bodies are buried."

"And where might that be?"

"Ronald Jackson's bison farm."

Trish acquainted her with Benny's thinking. And Ambrose didn't dismiss the possibility, sharing that at least three FBI agents were on their way to help in searching for Justin Edwards.

"What's with holding my colleague any longer?" Trish asked. "It's a bit ridiculous, don't you think?"

"I do. But, unfortunately, it's not my call. Falcone's one stubborn guy and unforgiving about out-of-state detectives operating on his turf."

Trish caught Ambrose's subtle way of telling her not to cross paths with Falcone. "Tell me. What do you hope to gain from Julie this time around?"

Ambrose almost let on about how they had left off with Julie. "We're most interested in confirming who sexually assaulted her. She left us hanging a bit."

Apologizing, Ambrose received a text that Julie was cleared to talk. "I'll catch up with you about the Jackson ranch."

CHAPTER 48

Before entering Julie's room, Falcone received the initial report from forensics. They were able to lift fingerprints of three individuals from inside the cabin, two of which were taken from a wooden club hanging on the wall. None matched anyone in law enforcement data bases. Other fingerprints obtained from several black tarps were tabbed "insufficient." Unable to obtain prints at the cabin from either Julie or Justin, they were able to determine that the hair strands matched Julie's as did her fingerprint lifted from the Victoria's Secret tag. From DNA, it was established that two individuals had intercourse with Julie Stapleton.

In sharing the findings with FBI Agent Ambrose, Falcone said that "I guess we can assume one was Justin's, the other Whitey Marsh."

As Ambrose mulled it over, she admitted that one had to be Justin's. "I'm not going to make any other leap." A pause. "Let's see what Julie is able to give us."

Entering Bacchus Hospital, to Julie's room, Benny blessed his good fortune in Julie insisting he be there and squeezed her hand before taking his place by the nurse by the door, not before receiving a slight nod from Ambrose, as a way to let him know that she and Trish had spoken.

"Julie, thank you for being so helpful yesterday," Ambrose began. "Whatever you can add today will be very helpful in putting your abductors away. Please let us know if…"

"Anything new on Justin?" she interrupted.

With Ambrose shaking her head, Julie squeezed her eyes shut.

Probing about the final hours at the cabin, Ambrose was relieved to see Julie more alert and talkative. She described their efforts in cleaning the cabin, even to the extent of wiping the pot belly stove two or three times and cleaning the door several times. She spoke of coming up with the idea of leaving behind a few strands of hair. "I had to wait until I knew for certain they were finished cleaning. Did you find my Victoria's Secret tag?"

Ambrose nodded. "You were so brave to do so."

"I can't tell you how difficult that was to do while being watched. I had to yank it a few times and was afraid of ripping the suit and them becoming aware of what I was up to." She paused. "At all times I imagined them taking me to that tree and whipping me."

As Julie teared, Ambrose waited. "And I believe you indicated that it was Masterson who took you from the cabin?"

She nodded. "Yes, and can you believe it, to a house on Beach Pond, opposite ours."

"Are you certain?"

Julie described the white house with the blue shutters, with a boat house near the shore.

"Give us a moment," Ambrose said. In huddling with Falcone who engaged with his iPhone, Benny thought it was probably to send troopers to that house.

"Sorry for that," Ambrose said. "Julie, please go on."

"When we got there, he had me take a shower, which I was grateful for. He didn't seem athletic. So, when I was coming down from the upstairs bathroom, I tossed off the robe he gave me and tried to get out of the house. I figured if I could jump into the lake and swim, I'd scream for attention."

Taking a tissue from the box at her fingertips, she blotted the tears. "The door was locked and I couldn't open it before he got to me and slapped me around." A pause. "It wasn't long before the other guy came and took me to another house away from Beach Pond."

Ambrose showed her the photo. "To be sure, this guy?"

"Yes."

"Whitey Marsh."

"He blindfolded me so I can't tell you where that is…only it wasn't too far. Maybe a ten-minute drive?"

"What happened there?"

Ambrose thought she lost Julie but, after blotting tears, she continued.

"He told me he'd kill me if I didn't tend to his needs. When I told him I didn't know what that meant, he took out his cell and shared a video of a woman having sex in every position imaginable."

"Was he in the video?"

"No. the image wasn't clear, like it was lifted from a TV or device."

With Julie pausing, Ambrose didn't push, hoping Julie would continue on her own, and she did. "At that point, I had decided to do whatever he asked. I recalled what Jarvis had said, "just go along with what they say to continue breathing."

Julie wiped the tears. "I gave in, accepted it. I was sodomized and raped. After that, I had given up all hope."

Listening, Benny closed his eyes. He thought back to being so close to finding her at the cabin and his overall failure to rescue her. He also thought about having had Whitey Marsh in his hands at Pete's house. He thought to himself, 'I should have pulled the trigger.'

"Of course, you did what you had to do," Ambrose said. "You desired to live."

As Julie teared, Ambrose let her be. When she continued, she went back in time, to her strategy of having Justin make love to her. "I was waiting for the right moment. I wanted it to be special. That's why I nixed doing so in the car. I recalled the kayak ride we had taken the year before, to the other side of the road, when I took him into the woods, under the pines, and took off my bathing suit. It was the first time he saw me totally naked."

"Why that location?"

Julie half-smiled. "My mother had sent me to find my sister Danielle and that's where she and Robbie were and…" In peering in Benny's direction, he nodded back as if to say 'it's ok.'

"So, I took Justin back there. It was supposed to be…"

As Julie paused, Benny tensed up, his rage brewing in that he couldn't rescue his niece.

"The men who took us had videotaped us naked on the pine needles and showed the video at the cabin to the others. I felt so vulnerable and ashamed. Little did I know what was to come, that I would be forced to have sex in front of them…I'll never be…"

As the nurse rose, Benny got her attention. He mouthed, "it's ok." Torn, she sat.

Ambrose knew exactly what to say. "We women are very strong. Each of us hold secrets, hurtful pasts, that we lock up. But the good news is that we don't allow troubled times to consume us. We have families to raise, people to take care of. We have love to give."

Ambrose took Julie's hand. "For with every passing year, there are new events, new blessings that push that hurtful past further away." A pause. "Indeed, you have some near-term burying to do. But let me assure you, you will rebound. You are a very strong young woman. The fact that you persevered is a speaker. Good things are in store for you. You'll see."

Benny admired Ambrose's bedside manner, similar to Trish's, and how women relate to women, in their own fraternity.

When Julie asked for water, the nurse refilled her glass from the pitcher on the tray table. Viewing it as a natural break, Benny saw

Ambrose and Falcone engage with their iPhones. It gave him time to think. In doing so, he had the answer to something that had been puzzling: how Goobie Crenshaw and Alfie Doolittle knew where Julie and Justin would be. It wasn't by chance. They had seen them the year before on a trail camera and counted on them returning to the isolated place for lovers. He figured they identified the teens, the yellow kayak, and the cottage, and bided their time. It speaks to how the hunting group operated for so long without being discovered. Their targeting was laser focused, waiting years for the right situation to present itself.

After the nurse backed off, seeming ok with her patient's ability to continue, Ambrose resumed. "Julie, yesterday you got very emotional over someone approaching in the home that Whitey Marsh took you to."

Ambrose thought she lost her, until Julie began speaking robotically.

"I anticipated something bad was going to happen when he tied my wrists to the headboard and blindfolded me."

"Who did this?"

"Whitey."

"To be sure, while Whitey abused you, you weren't blindfolded?"

"No. He forbid me to close my eyes. He blindfolded me before driving off. Right after, I heard another car." Julie stared ahead, in an attempt not to lose it. "This individual comes in and rapes me. He pushed my legs high in the air...I felt like I was being torn in two, his fingers indented in my thighs."

"Did he say anything?"

Julie nodded, cleared her throat. "You're a frisky filly in need of a little taming."

"Was it a voice you were familiar with?"

"I can't be sure but I don't think so."

"Would you recognize the voice?"

"I don't know, but he did wear an aftershave like my dad's."

"What happened after that?"

"I heard him putting his clothes on, and he left. Nothing else occurred until I was rescued."

"Let's talk about that. We saw you being thrust out the second story window."

Julie harkened back to the moment. "Yes. He pushed my face and breasts out. I could see all of the patrol cars, everyone looking up at me. I feared being tossed out. I thought he'd kill me. He was so out of control." A pause. "But after he took me back inside, I saw Officer Falcone." She gazed at him, admiringly. "That's when I was let go, and I ran. I heard the gunshots behind me."

"Did Whitey have a weapon?"

"Yes. He held it to my temple at the window. But inside, he had tucked it into his belt while using his cell."

While Julie had rather calmly related what had happened, they watched as the events of the past three days consumed her. She became hysterical, cupping both hands over her face and her knees to her chest. The interview was over.

In the hall, being handcuffed, Benny saw his brother-in-law John nearing, to see what he could learn. As he neared, Benny could plainly see the look of a zombie, battle-weary soldier who needed rest and relaxation, not another mission. For John, there could be no rest for the foreseeable future.

With his trooper handler receiving instructions from Falcone, Benny had but a moment. "John, Julie is hurting. Give her space. Don't probe," adding, "Consider this rock bottom. It will get better for you guys."

Feeling a tug and somewhat grateful for it, Benny felt helpless in being whisked to the elevator bank, especially after glancing back and seeing his sister pleading with the nurses to allow her into Julie's room.

CHAPTER 49

As Ambrose and Falcone departed Bacchus Hospital for the short ride to the state trooper headquarters in Uncasville, Ambrose thanked Falcone for allowing her to fly solo with the interview; in essence, for not interfering. While she felt it would be better for her to speak to a young woman recovering from such trauma, she had run into many ego-centric peers who had to be heard.

"Interesting what she revealed about the rape," Ambrose floated. "Any ideas on who it might be?"

"Whitey Marsh."

Ambrose cocked her head. "But she admitted to being raped by him. Why would he have her blindfolded and return?"

"Who knows how he got his rocks off. Forensics has evidence of her being raped by two. That's the boyfriend and Marsh." He added, "victims often get confused."

While that was true, Ambrose leaned toward the rapist being someone other than Whitey Marsh, as a result of Julie's chilling account of what had occurred. And she didn't feel inclined right now to get into a debate. Being driven to trooper headquarters, she needed alone time to think things through, unable to do so with Falcone harping on Fidalgo's recklessness. She was relieved when he changed subjects and spoke of locating Masterson and Shipley, or their bodies, which reminded her of the conversation she had with Trish McGlucas.

"How quickly can we get a court order to search the Jackson ranch?"

Ambrose felt Falcone's eyes upon her. "Probably in a few hours."

"That's good. Let's do so."

Arriving at the bison ranch with the search warrant, they were buzzed through the front gate and saw a number of vehicles outside the ranch house. Inside, Jackson's wife was being comforted by several people, including her brother who was extremely upset about the intrusion.

"What are you searching for?" he demanded to know. "Why aren't you after my brother-in-law's killer? Damn media is making him out to be a perverted monster."

As far as Ambrose was concerned, Jackson was a perverted monster. Fighting to keep her composure, she apologized again for needing to search.

Feeling constrained, Ambrose ditched going through Jackson's files and paperwork and led Falcone outside. Standing on a beautiful, wrap-around porch, the view was stunning. She noticed the hammocks perfectly positioned to admire the stately sycamore tree, a hundred yards away, and the rolling hills beyond it.

"You've been here before," Ambrose asked.

"Not on official duty. Jackson invites the community in to greet the new calves. Brought my children here a few times."

After scouring the hills, Ambrose had to ask, "Where are the bison?"

He pointed. "There are fields upon fields among those hills. But, as you can see, the bison are brought under that sycamore where, sitting here, he had the grandest of views."

In strolling toward a barn that had to be a least 100 yards long, it hit Ambrose on the difficulty in searching a property this size and sent a text to FBI headquarters requesting earth stealth scanning equipment.

"If you don't mind," Falcone said, "I'd like to take a look around."

"Be my guest."

As Falcone commandeered a golf cart and drove off, it gave Ambrose an opportunity to connect with Trish McGlucas. "I'm at the ranch and, let me tell you, this place is immense."

Trish caught resignation. "You're not backing off?"

"No. Not at all."

With Trish offering to get a piece of Justin's clothing and suggesting the use of hounds, Ambrose was all in. Realizing it would be better for Trish to maintain a low profile, as Falcone wasn't going to take kindly to her involvement, Ambrose said she would secure a service. And, in searching the Internet, she identified Number One Bloodhounds as being close and spoke to owner Rufus Randle, who was thrilled with the opportunity to work with the FBI.

Trish and Randle arrived at the Jackson ranch minutes apart. Trish brought the t-shirt that Justin wore to bed as Randle, in boots, tried to quiet three yapping bloodhounds.

Arriving back in the golf cart, Falcone wasn't happy in seeing McGlucas. "It's best you be on your way," he said.

"No, she stays," Ambrose declared, checking him. "This is an FBI matter. She's a help not a hindrance."

The standoff ended as they watched eager hounds pull Randle in three separate directions. Exasperated, he asked, "What do you want with my girls?"

"Girls?" Ambrose said.

"Yes. Easier to train and don't get distracted like the boys."

After Ambrose addressed the task at hand, Randle knelt and allowed his girls to sniff Justin's t-shirt. As soon as he unleashed them, they wasted no time scurrying around the main house and barns, before they picked up a scent.

Their journey ended quickly, under the sycamore. "Can't be that easy," Randle said, disappointed. Walking quickly to yapping hounds, he gave them a treat. Just before re-leashing them, he took a piece of red cloth from his pocket, that had a nail through it, and pushed it into the ground.

As he did, Falcone, Ambrose, and Trish McGlucas watched from a distance as the entire area surrounding the sycamore was muddy. With three huge water troughs nearby and a hose attached to a tap for filling them, this was a bison watering station. The ground stomped to such a degree that no grass grew anywhere around the sycamore.

Randle called out, "Glad I brought the boots." He came to where they stood.

Extending a business card, Ambrose didn't wish to get too close to the hounds. "Bill me at that address. But I warn you, it will take time."

"That's ok. Hope you can use me down the road."

"I promise to tout your service. Your girls get results."

With Randle off, Ambrose faced Falcone and Trish, "Well, who is up for digging?"

Trish couldn't believe their good fortune. A half hour ago she figured a search might take days, not minutes. Spotting Jackson's workers standing idle nearby, she waved them over. Explaining what she wished done, they returned with shovels and several long wooden boards that they laid down to the spot with the red handkerchief, which allowed the three law enforcement officers to get close.

After digging three feet down, one jumped out shouting, "Aqui! Aqui!" Peering into the hole, they clearly saw the back of a leg. A half hour later, the state police forensics team disembarked from a helicopter on the other side of the sycamore.

As they carefully removed dirt around the body, while photographing and videotaping, Ambrose said, "it is Justin alright," pointing at the whip marks across his back and torso.

When Trish offered to notify the Edwards, Ambrose gratefully accepted and received Falcone's approval to dispatch a state trooper to pick them up.

When the forensics team leader informed them that Justin had died from a blow to the back of the head, Falcone went to Jackson's home and requested that Mrs. Jackson join them at the sycamore. Getting an earful, her brother said he would represent her. As he neared Justin's body, the blood drained from him.

"You can decide what to tell Mrs. Jackson," Falcone said. "But we need her here."

Shaken, he went back to the house. The Jackson workers remained huddled as if waiting for further instruction.

Trish said aloud, "Let's not forget, there's Shipley and Masterson and everyone else unaccounted for."

Ambrose nodded.

Watching a vehicle make its way through the open, front gate, Trish dreaded speaking to Joan and Dave Edwards. She watched as they slowly walked towards the unearthed grave. On her cell earlier, she only expressed, 'I'm sorry to tell you this but we found Justin and the news isn't good.'

Both parents lost it. When the forensic lead folded back the sheet, Joan placed her hands around Justin's neck and pulled him to her. Falling to his knees, Dave raised his hands skyward, "why, why Lord!"

It pained Trish to see their anguish, as she knew the Edwards' to be good people. It was some time before they were able to remove Joan's hands from her son.

"He died a hero," Trish said, leading them away. "From Julie's lips, he was the calming voice who tried to find help. I'm so, so sorry." Reaching out with Justin's t-shirt, Joan buried her face in it, as Dave Edwards wrapped his hand around his wife and pulled her close.

After followed them to the trooper's vehicle, Trish reached Rufus Randle. "We need your girls again." He was only too happy to double back.

With articles of clothing from Shipley and Masterson, the hounds again went at it. As before, they halted under the sycamore. Not long after, the bodies of Masterson and Shipley were uncovered.

Trish realized how perfect a burial site this was, with the mud and hoof prints being perfect cover. When Mrs. Jackson neared, aided by her brother, Ambrose asked if she could identity either person. Justin's body had already been removed.

"Can't you see the state she's in," her brother pushed back.

"It will only take a moment."

When Mrs. Jackson moved closer, the forensic lead peeled back the white sheet on one and then the other. Both times she shook her head.

"There, you satisfied?"

No doubt filled with anxiety meds, in dark sunglasses, as she appeared to be in a world of her own, Mrs. Jackson emitted, "My husband loved sitting on the hammock and watching his beloved bison. He would spend hours at it."

Ambrose couldn't help herself. "Did you ever see him digging under the tree?"

"You despicable human being!" her brother snapped. "Are you insinuating that my brother-in-law was a murderer?"

Agent Ambrose, a bit embarrassed, refrained from following up, though she had to get to the bottom of Jackson's role. Even though it was still to be determined whether Jackson murdered anyone, he was complicit at what went on at the cabin and in permitting burials on his property.

In reading a text from Trish to come to Pete's, Ambrose left her FBI colleagues, who had arrived in another helicopter with the earth stealth equipment to scan the bison farm for other burials, most notably Warren Shipley's. She told them to use the state police headquarters as the home base, and that she would catch up shortly.

"I've had enough today," she said to Falcone. "In terms of investigations, this is surging up the Ambrose leaderboard. Right now, I need a shower and a Manhattan, and I don't care what order. Text if anything comes up."

"What about the press?" he asked.

"What about them?"

"They'll be here before you know it."

Ambrose reflected on the question before declaring that she would check with FBI brass. As she began walking to her vehicle, she heard, "Will the FBI leave us to complete the investigation?"

A bit surprised by the ask, Ambrose turned fully around to face Falcone. "I'll check on that too, a bit above my pay grade." A pause, as she gave it some thought. "I'll recommend we stay attached as there's still much to clear up, like who killed Ronald Jackson and who raped Julie Stapleton. And, of course, there remains the outstanding question as to whether this hunting club was behind the disappearances of the other women."

CHAPTER 50

Hearing doors slam, Trish assumed it was Pete, who had left to retrieve Benny from custody. According to what she had learned from Charlotte, their lawyer had threatened the DA with legal action if his client remained another minute behind bars. Aside for it being a clear case of self-defense, Julie had described Dupree "as the cruelest of them all." She had disclosed that he was last seen with Warren Shipley, wielded a hunting knife and threatened to lop off her ear, and that she saw him kicking Justin on the ground before leaving with him.

"You good," Trish said, as Benny and Pete entered.

"Fresh as a daisy."

Feeling her cell vibrate and seeing who was calling, she declared, "this can't be good." It was Chief Thompson. Watching her face grow alarmed by the second, Benny guessed it had to do with internal investigation into police corruption.

When Trish, clearly upset, voiced, "Why didn't you wait for me?" Benny knew for sure that Murph was involved and asked that she put the call on speaker.

As a seeming apologetic Thompson reasoned why he placed Murph on leave, while taking a major step to the right and attributing the decision to the DA, a shocked Benny and Trish, a step apart, couldn't look at each other. Not giving them time to protest, Thompson thrust Sheila Morgan into the conversation to share that, as she was told, Murph had accepted illegal payoffs from commercial property owners. Thompson quickly added that they had confronted Murph, and he didn't deny taking the payment.

Finally able to get a word in, with Trish shaken and unable at the moment to converse, Benny took the cell from her. "Why act so fast?"

"DA's request."

"But you signed on. Are we talking one or multiple payments?"

Met with silence, Benny fired out, "Dammit, you know the man!"

"Don't you think this was difficult on me? Let's not forget that I worked with him far longer than you have."

With Trish turning her back to him, Benny knew she was likely stifling tears. As close as he had become to Murph in his three years in Blacksburg, Trish had much deeper ties. He didn't mind stoking Thompson.

"When was this supposed to have happened?"

"Nineteen ninety-eight."

"Nineteen ninety-eight! That's twenty-five years ago. Was that the extent of his involvement?"

Met again by silence, Benny lashed out. "You ruined a man's career…a man's life over a one-time event! Tell me you're kidding! Why didn't you wait for Trish?"

"You're responsible for that!" Thompson snapped. "She's been investing her time with you when she should have been here."

Trish wheeled and angrily grabbed the cell. "That was my decision! You told me you'd wait for me!"

"Things are fluid here, McGlucas."

"Fluid, really? You gain one piece of information and it becomes the lightning rod to action against Murph. Why?"

"You're not to question a decision reached after serious consideration."

"Serious consideration? Really? Have you spoken with Carney, Williams, or Egan?"

"Not yet, but will do so shortly."

"But you felt you had to move on Murph...I don't get it."

Thompson let them know that DA Barrett didn't feel comfortable putting Morgan at risk, feeling that with several identified as taking bribes, one or two might implicate others in exchange for reduced sentencing. "Frankly, Barrett figured if Murph would help, and with his limited involvement, he could be especially lenient on him."

Benny, fuming, stepped over to Trish. "Did you actually believe he'd rattle off names? Proves to me you don't know the man."

"Fidalgo, that's enough out of you! Don't question my decision!"

After a few awkward seconds, Sheila Morgan volunteered that she heard one patrolman comment: 'if a church usher like Murph could take the cash, I'll get in line.' "Believe me, I was sorry to hear his name in this. Murph's been very kind to me. I know how you must feel."

"No, you don't!" Trish said, incensed. "You don't know anything about how I feel, so don't give me your shit!"

"Don't get angry at her!" Thompson bellowed. "She's doing a job! That's more than I can say for you. Get back here! There's a lot of work in wrapping this up."

After first placing his hand over hers on the cell, sensing that Trish was just getting wound up and apt to say things she'll later regret, Benny placed his index finger across his lips, whispering "easy, easy."

"I'll be back tomorrow," Trish said. "Don't proceed without me."

As Thompson ranted about being told what to do, Benny ended the call. "That poor bastard," he said of Murph. "Call me a Doubting Thomas, but I want to hear from the asshole who put money in his hand."

Trish could only shake her head. She also had a difficult time believing Murph accepted payoffs, but her law enforcement genes also knew that one had to pay for crimes committed and lapses in judgement. She dreaded returning to Blacksburg.

Trying to reach Murph, Benny was unsuccessful. "He knows why I'm calling."

Pained in seeing them hurting, and having just met Murph as well, Pete didn't know what to say to the two distraught individuals before him. As Trish went into the bedroom to collect her things, he reached for the bourbon. "Have a go. Sometimes this stuff actually works."

Numb, Benny tossed down a double shot. A few minutes later, Trish took a seat on the sofa. To Benny, the few minutes alone seemed to have done her a world of good, as she appeared composed. He always appreciated her recuperative powers, able to think clearly following stressful times, much quicker than he was able to do so.

Expecting FBI Agent Ambrose momentarily, Trish wasted no time updating Benny about the hounds obtaining quick results, the discovery of Justin's body, and his parents' anguish as well as finding the bodies of Masterson and Shipley.

Throughout, he didn't interrupt, which wasn't like him, prompting her to say, "Don't go down that rabbit hole of yours." Saying her goodbyes, not inclined to wait for Agent Ambrose any longer, with a long drive ahead, she asked Benny if he felt the missing women might also be buried at the bison farm. And he nodded, saying "that pattern was set long ago."

He added, "They'll get what's coming to them. Check that…not Whitey and Dupree. I'd have them begging for mercy. They met their ends too quickly."

About to depart, she saw Benny gazing at his empty shot glass. Not knowing if he was going to refill it, she cautioned, "Maintain a clear head."

Obeying, he placed the shot glass down on the end table. "According to what Julie shared to us, Whitey gave access to his mother's house to someone who raped her."

"You didn't tell me that."

"Well, I'm telling you now."

Trish mulled it over. "Maybe Dupree before he was killed?"

"Not likely. With Julie familiar with him, no need for the blindfold. Also, DNA links to Justin and Whitey, not Dupree. Which means whoever raped her wore a condom." He stared up at her from the sofa. "Had to be someone outside their merry ring…or, then again, someone who knew what they were up to."

With Trish fiddling with her car keys, intrigued, he invited her to sit. "Wait for Ambrose. Need for you two to challenge my theorem." A pause. "You too Pete."

CHAPTER 51

On the way to Pete's, Agent Ambrose briefed FBI Supervisor Russo, wrapping up by honing in on the missing women and the possibility that they too could also be buried on the Jackson ranch. He agreed that the FBI should stay engaged and signed off on additional resources, while also addressing the press conference. "This will be as explosive as they come," he said. "Kidnappings, sex shows, murder… let's refrain from tying in the missing women." He paused. "Do they still have Fidalgo detained."

"No. Couldn't hold him. The individual he killed was a central figure in this hunting group." A pause. "Fidalgo's everything you said he was. One step ahead of everyone else."

"Yeah, no quit in him. But, as you saw, his independent, bulldog side will be his undoing."

With only an hour or so in her schedule to play around with, Ambrose rushed to Pete's. She had to thank Benny personally for, if it wasn't for him, the teens' disappearance was destined to become yet another unsolved missing person's case.

"Hail, hail, the gang's all here," she announced, swinging Pete's door open. "Did you begin the party without me?" Entering, she noticed they hardly moved. "I guess the party's over."

With Pete holding up his bottle of Woodford Reserve, she said, "Pour me two fingers. I'd go for three only I'm needed elsewhere."

Benny rose to shake hands.

"What's that for?" Ambrose asked.

"For coming here and doing your thing."

In their relatively brief time together, Benny liked Ambrose who, he felt, listened, didn't take herself too seriously, and could handle the Falcone's of the world.

While waiting for Ambrose to arrive, he had watched his sister and brother-in-law trudge back and forth to their car for their journey home. All the while, Julie had remained in the car. As Pete bid them farewell, Benny thought the better of joining him. In reaching his mother, she cautioned to leave Anne be and that she would arrange a get together soon to mend fences. She tried to lighten his guilt in not finding Julie sooner by describing her granddaughter as a 'strong young woman,' using the word 'resiliente' a few times. But no matter what she said, he continued to be preoccupied.

"Sit beside Trish," he said to Ambrose, pointing to the sofa.

She raised her eyebrows and did so. "Are you making some sort of announcement?"

"Something like that." He took a moment. "I know who raped Julie at Whitey's mother's house. It was Falcone."

"Woe, woe, woe, woe…" Ambrose replied, almost spilling the bourbon and now cradling it. "You're way off base. Although he's a pain in the ass to work with, from the moment I first caught up with him in his war room, he never wavered from getting to the bottom of this."

"Just hear me out."

Ambrose eyed Trish for her reaction but Trish continued to train her eyes on Benny.

"Two things gnawed at me," he said. "First, who shot and killed Ronald Jackson? And second, who raped Julie besides Whitey Marsh. I now know it was the same person…Falcone."

Pete, he could tell, was the most startled, having never heard the full extent of Julie's ordeal. "Forgive me, Pete. This isn't going to be easy for you. What happened to Julie is numbing."

"It was Falcone," he repeated, assertively. "Thank God my niece wanted me in that hospital room or I'd never be able to put this together."

"But I was there," Ambrose said.

"True. But you were engaged with Julie. In the background, by the door, I could observe and digest."

Benny gathered his thoughts. "When she said she was blindfolded before being raped, I thought to myself, 'that's unusual, typically a rapist feeds off the person he's controlling.' But Falcone was allowed in by Whitey…fully knowing what he signed up for. It couldn't be one of the guys in the cabin for Julie was familiar with them. A blindfold wouldn't be necessary. For Falcone, though, it was and he wore a condom to avoid DNA evidence."

"Sorry, can't buy it," Ambrose said, shaking her head. "Falcone's a career ladder climber. Ambition drives the likes of him. He wouldn't risk the climb."

"Stay with me - I'm going to give you a lot to gnaw on."

Benny asked Ambrose to think about their time in Julie's hospital room. "Why did the ambitious and ego-driven Falcone let you take the lead?"

"Why not? I was running it."

"But he didn't ask one damn question."

"But he wasn't absolutely silent either. Wouldn't she have been able to identify his voice?"

"Julie said he uttered but one sentence while being raped. Not much to go by. Another observation: No one could hear what Julie said in that hospital room and not be shaken or at least show some emotion. I tell you Falcone was stone cold."

Ambrose continued to be a disbeliever. "He's programmed to project steadiness, calm, in the face of chilling accounts."

Undeterred, he continued. "We heard from Julie that her assailant wore after shave. You are aware that Falcone does?" Ambrose nodded. "Well, not once did he come near the bed."

Benny bridged to Jackson's killing at his ranch. "I think that when Pete and I left the ranch, Jackson called Falcone. He was rattled and contacted someone he knew well. Didn't dial the main number at state police headquarters. Had Falcone's cell."

"Not surprising that a leading businessman might have a connection," Ambrose contested.

"Granted. But I'm betting he wasn't in the headquarters building when Jackson was killed. More like he went to the bison ranch to kill him, conveniently leaving Pete and me as scapegoats."

Benny studied Trish to see if she was a buyer as she hadn't interrupted him. He could see she was mulling everything over.

"Put Jackson aside for a moment. Let's look at the circumstances surrounding Whitey's death. For starters, Whitey and Falcone knew each other really well."

"True," Ambrose said. "Falcone admitted to knowing Whitey as a tow truck operator."

"Right. So, while Julie is held captive and you surround the house, he tells you he's going in, largely based on his familiarity with him. Let me step back, how did you know Whitey was holding Julie at his mother's house?"

"Falcone said they had received an anonymous tip."

"Did you confirm how that came in?" By her expression, Benny could tell that Ambrose hadn't given it any thought. "Ok, he gets the tip. I'm sure you didn't want him to go into the house."

"I tried to stop him, but he wouldn't listen."

"Of course. What better way to free my niece, be the hero, and kill Whitey." Benny relished laying it out. "Think about what Julie told us. When Falcone entered the house, Whitey let her go. He let his meal ticket go? In his shoes, who would do that...only moments before he held her up at the window threatening to kill her. Falcone went in there with one intention. And we know that Julie heard the shot before she even made it to the door, which means there was no discussion between he and Marsh, the good friends. That tells me he didn't wish to apprehend him...he wanted him dead, out of the way."

"Are you insinuating that Falcone was tied to this hunting group," Trish put forward.

"Precisely. With them gathering for ten to fifteen years, well before Falcone's star began to shine, he probably hunted with them and withdrew at some point. But after he dropped out, Whitey Marsh continued to serve up women for him to rape. Think about it from their end... why not satisfy their former hunting buddy who is rising up in the state police ranks? They'd certainly desire a protector if things go south. And they continued to have a cozy relationship. From Julie's own account, we learned that her attacker came in, didn't rush up the stairs, slowly takes off his shoes and belt, rapes her, and exits without rushing...as if he had done this before, knew the routine."

"But why the need for a condom?" Ambrose raised.

"He wasn't taking any chances in trusting her handler, Whitey, to kill her and dispose of her body. No, he used the condom alright."

With the thought of Falcone raping Julie, also as a way to get back at him, Benny stared at the ground, losing his train of thought for a moment, before telling them that Falcone sought to eliminate all those who could finger him. "He convinces either Dupree or Whitey that

Masterson had to go. That was key, in that Masterson was the brains of the outfit. And with him gone, Falcone had to know that the others were apt to make mistakes without him."

"He benefits from Wingo's suicide. I do him a favor in bumping off Dupree, and he dispatches of Jackson and Marsh."

Locked in, Ambrose questioned why he hadn't killed Goobie Crenshaw and Alfie Doolittle?

He shrugged. "Good question. But I'm not sure how much those two know?"

"What do you mean? They were involved."

"I mean the disposing of the bodies, etcetera. They were on the front end, as we know with the kidnapping of my niece, but on the back end, of the killings and burials, I'm not so sure. It's certainly time to bang their heads together."

As Benny excused himself to go to the bathroom, Ambrose reached for the bourbon. "Whew…I need more than this." Turning to face Trish, she asked what she thought. "This from a man who hates Falcone."

"The feeling's mutual." A pause. "I don't care for him either."

"For jailing Benny?"

"Yeah, that too. But more for wanting to get into my pants." A pause. "Sorry, shouldn't have said it. Has no place here."

"Don't apologize. Speaks to his character." Ambrose knew that Trish didn't elicit that to brag, for she didn't have to.

"In answering your question as to what I think," Trish said, rising to depart, "Isn't the first time Benny has me a believer."

Sipping the bourbon, Ambrose smiled, "I bet he's a good chess player."

"He actually sucks."

"Are you talking about me?" Benny said, reentering.

Ambrose put her glass of bourbon back on the end table. "Let's say I'm a partial buyer. But with no DNA evidence connecting him to Julie's rape, the DA's going to want more than Falcone unaccounted for when Jackson was killed, and his acquaintance with the hunting club."

Benny grinned. "That's where you come in."

CHAPTER 52

Benny's strategy for incriminating Falcone called for major cooperation from Alfie Doolittle. But in order to get it, lawyer Frankie Adamo had to sign on. With Falcone attending at a state-wide law enforcement breakfast gathering in Hartford, where he could bask in the limelight for rescuing Julie Stapleton, Ambrose cornered Adamo. And she convinced him that, following Julie's account of being kidnapped by Doolittle and Crenshaw, it was in his clients' best interest to cooperate.

After allowing Adamo time to meet with Doolittle, she was invited into the interrogation room.

The experienced Ambrose knew exactly how to play it. "I'm here to tie up some loose ends," she began. "And you may be able to help me. If you are cooperative to what I'm about to ask, I will do my best to make it easier for you."

With Doolittle sitting back in the chair, with his arms folded and seeming non-interested, Ambrose watched as Adamo nodded to her and proceeded to lean over and whisper into Doolittle's ear. "We'll hear you out," he said.

"Tell me," Ambrose asked, "how far back have you entertained women at the cabin?"

"I've told Falcone all I know…that girl was the only one."

Ambrose grinned. "Is this cooperating? You've already admitted to having prostitutes at the cabin?"

"Oh yes, them. Several years, maybe."

"What about women other than prostitutes?"

Doolittle chirped, "What am I supposed to do, hang myself?"

Ambrose remained cool. "You are facing murder charges."

"Bullshit! I didn't kill anyone!"

"But your hunting buddies did and that makes you complicit."

"I'll take my chances with a jury."

"Ok, the jury hears that you triggered this entire nightmare by kidnapping the teens. How do you think that will go over?"

With Dolittle rattled, Adamo asked to speak to him alone.

When Ambrose re-entered, Adamo nodded, as if to say let's begin again.

"Answer me this," Ambrose began. "How long have you been a member of this hunting club? And what do you know about its history?"

Doolittle dreaded providing information that could deepen the case against him, but Adamo had convinced him that cooperation was the only way forward to avoid a life sentence. He reluctantly acknowledged that he and Doobie Crenshaw met Marcus Dupree at an after-hours strip club, where Dupree bragged about having real entertainment..."the kind that perform at a higher level with their lives at stake."

"When was that?"

"I don't know…several years back."

"What did he mean higher level?"

"Torturing and killing if she didn't do what he said."

"Tell me about women, other than prostitutes."

A long pause. "They brought in a hitchhiker one night and forced her to strip and perform. When she refused to provide sex, they threatened to kill her. She did so alright and Masterson concocted a bidding game to see who would wind up with her. I put in a measly bid just to go along, and Whitey took off with her."

"To do what?"

When Doolittle glanced at Adamo for guidance, Adamo simply nodded. "To kill her. They were afraid she'd report us."

"And where was she buried?"

"How the hell should I know? I wasn't a part of it."

"How long has the hunting club been operating?"

"Way earlier than when we joined."

"How do you know?"

"Because they compared that hitchhiker to others we didn't know about."

"Who was in the original hunting group?"

He reflected. "Masterson, Shipley, Whitey, Dupree, Jarvis and Jackson."

"Anyone else?"

"That's it. Though Shipley dropped out years before."

"Sure there was no one else?"

Noticing his client's anxiousness, and then abrupt comment, "I'm through with this shit," Adamo again asked to speak with Doolittle alone. When Ambrose closed the door, he asked, "Who is she trying to implicate?"

"Falcone."

"Falcone!"

"Keep your voice down," Doolittle said, alarmed. "While we were having beers one night, Whitey let on about being protected by a badge."

"That could be anyone."

Doolittle lowered his voice to just above a whisper. "When it was my turn to kill one of the girls, Whitey told me that he would take her off my hands. That was music to my ears. Curious, I followed him to a house and who do you think shows up?"

"Falcone?"

Doolittle nodded. "He went in and I didn't wait for him to exit."

Adamo contemplated the disclosure of Falcone's name to Ambrose. "So that's what she wants."

"Yeah, only if I give him up, they'll find me hanging from the ceiling."

"Look at the upside," Adamo said. "You're not dealing with the locals but the FBI."

After Doolittle reluctantly agreed to share about Falcone's connection, Adamo left to speak with Ambrose.

"I think I know why you're here, but you tell me."

"Is your client knowledgeable about Inspector Falcone?"

"Be specific."

"Is your client aware that Falcone was involved with the hunting club?"

Adamo smirked. "Let's say he is. What can you do for us?"

"I already shared what I can attempt to do."

"You were too vague. Not good enough."

Knowing the boundaries, Ambrose mulled it over. "I could lie to you and tell you that I can reduce his sentencing, but I think you know that's outside my purview. Let's say your client serves his time with inmates connected to white collar crime. With that, I have influence."

"I think he may be up for that."

Ambrose told Adamo of Benny's scheme. It called for Doolittle to speak to Falcone and tell him that the FBI is going to the Bison ranch to exhume the body of the girl he killed.

Incredulous, Adamo shook his head. "I don't think he'll have the nerve."

"Fortify his nerves, otherwise he'll be alongside inmates who know a thing about shows and torture."

A pause. "How's my client supposed to have knowledge of the dead girl at the bison ranch?"

"Just say he overheard the New York detective mention it. Listen, he needs to play his part really well. To make this work, he needs to ask Falcone for a favor in exchange for information."

An hour later Ambrose received a text from Adamo that Doolittle would confront Falcone. The following morning Ambrose received another text: message delivered to Falcone.

*   *   *

At the bison ranch, after the assigned FBI agents escorted Mrs. Jackson, her family, and workers to another location, Ambrose discussed details of the operation. It called for three agents to hide with their vehicles in a side barn, farthest from the house, and three others to remain hidden up into the fields and hills. Benny had figured Falcone, after hearing from Doolittle, would attempt to rebury the body of the woman he had killed.

Two hours later a sedan drove through the open gate. As Ambrose hid in a tractor, she saw Falcone emerge and proceed to the house. After ringing the doorbell, he went around to the side entrance and back to his car, driving off on a dirt road through the field.

Minutes later, an agent positioned in the hills text Ambrose and his colleagues that Falcone's car came to a stop under some apple trees. As advised, he waited until Falcone began to dig. When his feet disappeared, the agent notified the others and all raced toward the apple trees.

Seeing four vehicles streaming towards him, Falcone jumped into his and attempted to exit the bison farm. But with the gate now closed and two agents holding shotguns beside it, his attempt to escape failed as his vehicle flipped after skyrocketing in and out of a ditch.

They found Falcone unconscious. But by the time the ambulance arrived, he was coherent. The medics attended to him and placed his neck in a brace. Refusing to be carried off, though limping severely, the medics walked him to the ambulance were accompanied by two agents to the hospital.

As they headed off, Ambrose text Benny, 'I'll be there in fifteen. Your plan worked to perfection.'

Arriving at Pete's, she described to Benny and Pete what had gone down, including Falcone's choice curse words for her and him as he placed in the ambulance.

"You were right," Ambrose said. "He even brought a shovel. This connects him to the hunting group, likely way before they began using the sycamore." A pause. "When he and I had gone earlier to the Jackson ranch, he had taken off in a golf cart in the direction of the apple trees. At the time, I didn't think anything of it. Now I know why."

"I have to hand it to you," Ambrose added. "Russo said you had one of the sharpest minds he'd ever come across."

"He didn't add that I'm crazy."

"That too."

While they laughed, all three quickly morphed into recognizing that evil had had its way.

"Thank God, it's over," Ambrose said. "At least the first part, though we have a great deal of work ahead in trying to locate the other bodies."

Reaching for the Woodford Reserve, Ambrose poured shots. Pete waved her off. "Can I offer you a piece of advice?" she said to Benny.

"Shoot

"You strike me as someone who doesn't care whether he lives or dies."

It wasn't the first time Benny had heard that. In fact, the psychologist who treated him after the death of his buddies killed in Afghanistan said the same thing.

"If I go out for a good cause, so be it."

Ambrose winced.

"Sorry. But I regret not ringing Shipley's neck the first time I had the chance or Alfie Doolittle at the golf course. If I had, then…"

"A word to the wise," Ambrose interrupted, "no one can go at it like you and not pay the price."

She extended her hand. "I guess you'll be wanting to get far from here."

"I have to say yes, though that means leaving this man behind." He raised his shot glass to Pete and Ambrose did the same. She soon left.

Relaxed and with the bourbon doing its thing, Benny's eyes moistened, in thinking of Julie, his sister and brother-in-law, whose world had been rocked. He would have downed a few more shots but had a few errands. He first went to Hannah's to pick up a $200 gift certificate and then to the liquor store to buy a bottle of Woodford Reserve, before stopping at St. Thomas and St. Anne's, where he asked Father Arias to hear his confession.

Exiting, he said his penance and put $100 into Father Arias' hands to offer a few masses for Justin Edwards. But Fr. Arias told him that he couldn't accept it, as he had been doing so every morning.

"Then give it to someone who could use it."

"That I'll do. Before you go, can I tell you something?"

Amused, Benny said, "I thought what I said in there is sacred?"

Fr. Arias smiled. "Of course. That's between God and us. Have you ever heard of El Camino?"

"The pilgrimage from Madrid to the coast of Spain?"

"Yes. To Santiago de Compostela. The journey Saint James took. You should consider walking it."

"Did you arrive at that based on what I said in there?" Benny said, nodding toward the confessional.

"Well, yes and no. I have been following the news and you've got to be exhausted and haunted by what's gone on here."

"Comes with the turf."

"Granted. The pilgrimage will give you a chance to find peace, to explore your inner soul. Think about it."

Benny thought about telling Father Arias of his planned trip to Portugal but there was no way to squeeze in El Camino, but then again…

In saying goodbye to Pete, Benny felt indebted to him. "I'm going to miss hanging with you."

"I'll miss your company a great deal more. Gets lonely here when the summer folk hit the road. I'm very jealous of you."

"How so?"

"You're blessed. I watched Murph and you interact…there's brotherly love there. He really respects you. And while Trish is cerebral, she often defers to your judgement and has your back. Those are true colleagues. Don't come any better."

"Don't make me cry now."

Pete wasn't done. "And Charlotte is there to catch you when you need catching. You are made for each other. And before I shut up, Anne will come around. She and Julie really need you now."

Benny handed Pete the Hannah's gift certificate and the liquor. "To express my thanks for your hospitality and for putting you at risk. Completely stupid on my part."

"You didn't have to do this, though I will say my heart skipped a beat more than once these past four days."

As Benny took hold of his overnight bag, he said, "Pete, almost forgot, please give Clete the secret fishing spot we promised."

"Will have to make something up. There really isn't one spot. That landlocked salmon we caught was as much by luck than design. Someone upstairs was looking down on that Vietnan vet before he was taken from us."

Before heading off, Benny walked over to his sister's cottage and onto the deck. He draped his arms over the railing and gazed at the water. He breathed in deeply and paused in viewing in the direction of the Rhode Island side. Two young adults, one murdered and the other severely traumatized, conflict with the beauty and serenity his eyes beheld.

Instead of driving south and back to Blacksburg, Benny made a pit stop at the state police headquarters, where he met up with a surprised Ambrose who thought she had seen the last of him.

"Why are you here?"

"Need a favor. Can you give me a few minutes with Falcone?"

Ambrose shook her head. "That would be a major error in judgement on my part. Why are you asking?"

"It will help bring closure. I'll be good."

Ambrose smirked. "You don't have a track record of being good."

Entering the cell area, with Ambrose at his side, Falcone leaped up. "March that bastard out of here!"

Benny stood four feet away from the cell, as Ambrose instructed.

"You owe your life to me!" Falcone shot out. "Whitey wanted to kill you but I told him that he shouldn't waste his time…that you are nothing but a cocky little prick…."

Benny waited until Falcone's diatribe to end. "There's something troubling me. You knew Whitey was going to kill my niece, yet you had him blindfold her. I'll bet you didn't for the other girls."

Falcone moved menacingly toward the bars, as if he was going to reach through.

"That tells me you feared me closing in," Benny said.

"I said get him out of here!"

Benny grinned. "You were part of the twisted hunting group and continued to partake at a distance. How convenient. You protected them and they let you in on the action. You're nothing but a royal piece of shit and will pay for it."

"Take him away!" Falcone roared.

Feeling a hand on his shoulder, Benny turned to leave. They could hear Falcone's tirade, until the steel doors closed behind them.

"Now what did that accomplish?" Ambrose asked.

"Just cements his involvement. Didn't call me a liar, did he?"

About to say something else, Benny instead shook his head. What he wished to say is that he had prayed to be left with Falcone alone, so that he could beat the living hell out of him.

"You have your work cut out for you," Benny said. "I'd go back at least 15 years into all missing persons. I'll think you'll find bodies all over that bison farm."

"Just curious to how you suspected that Falcone killed and buried a woman at the ranch?"

"Just took a shot; well, half a shot. Doolittle spoke of the hunting group going back more than a decade. The odds are that Falcone had taken a girl in those early days, either before becoming a state trooper or right after."

"Think about this," Benny smiled. "Who took the hunting photo?"

A pause. "Falcone?"

"Who else?"

"But Doolittle's in the photo and he claimed he didn't go back that far?"

Benny smiled. "Doolittle's protecting his own ass. As you investigate, you'll find that some women never made it to the cabin. These guys operated independently, in and out of the group, and made arrangements with Jackson to bury them at his ranch. So, while Whitey served up women to Falcone, Whitey, Dupree and others allowed Jackson to rape women before they were killed at his place. They had tipped Jackson off so that he could find a time when his wife and children were off and his men engaged elsewhere. It explains something else that has been bothering me all along."

"What's that?"

"How these guys could be satisfied with only a few women abducted over more than a dozen years. There had to be others. While the sycamore holds a nucleus, bodies could be anywhere." A pause. "Can you tell Hank Russo that I was asking for him and apologize for my behavior."

"I will. But you don't have to apologize for anything. It's terrible what happened to your niece."

About to pull out of the parking lot, Benny saw Cartwright running toward him and yelling, "Don't' go anywhere. I have a profile of you to write."

Turning off his engine, Benny couldn't give Cartright the quick brushoff but what he wanted most of all right now is to get back to Blacksburg. He hadn't forgotten about Murph and craved squeezing Charlotte.

CHAPTER 53

Five months later

Benny and Murph stood in the hall waiting for the graphic artist to finish debossing the lettering onto the door of their new offices. When the artist stepped back, "Gotcha Inc." stylishly grabbed attention.

"What do you think?" Murph said, quite proud of the name they agreed upon for their new private eye business venture.

"I guess this makes it official," Benny said. "Do you know how many people will show tonight?"

"Lost track at thirty-five."

"What do you mean you lost track?"

"Thirty-five accepted. But this building is filled with lawyers and doctors, a bunch of free loaders."

"Did you order a spread of vegetables for the doctors?"

"You kidding? They'll be first going back for seconds of the chicken marsala and veal cutlet parmigiana." Murph extended his hands from his body but turned his fingers inward. "Don't fret. The Murph's got this."

When Murph was relieved of his duties as a Blacksburg detective, Benny suggested that they go into business together as private investigators. Murph had lost his pension of 26 years and his self-worth with it. He couldn't deny taking the envelope he found in the front seat of his patrol car, his second year on the job, which sealed his fate. Trish tried to defend him with Chief Thompson arguing for a suspension and making restitution, along with testifying against the others. But Murph, though thankful, didn't want her support or her sympathy. Being a devout Catholic, he had to confess, take his punishment, and live with it.

With private high school tuitions mounting and his mother failing, he had succumbed in a moment of weakness. Didn't matter that he had returned the envelope to the other officers on the take. He had to live with the guilt and the possibility that one day he might be questioned on it. And when that day came, when asked to identify others, he refused. Embarrassed, he left for Virginia Beach when the firing of 12 Blacksburg officers became public. Months later, ashamed every time he was out and about and all eyeballs on him, he listened to Benny's proposition. And with his wife and Trish's urging, he accepted.

When Benny had returned from Voluntown, he expected to catch hell from Chief Thompson but surprisingly found him sympathetic, messaging that it was understandable to get involved in a family matter. It took months to recognize the Chief's longer term, Machiavelli strategy at play. His aim: drown his subordinate in routine investigatory matters. And it didn't take long for his underling to come crawling, begging for stimulating cases. But as his colleagues got assigned suspicious deaths - like that of Deidre Esposito jumping from her dorm window, which he eventually got to the bottom of - he drew car thieves and graffiti artists.

After months tackling run-of-the-mill assignments, he had a sit-down with Charlotte about moving on. And it hurt him to do so because he knew she loved her ER nurse position and living in Blacksburg. But upon giving it further thought, the idea of beginning anew as a private eye checked the right boxes, as it would allow him to answer to no one and choose cases to his liking. The other box it checked was in lifting Murph out of his doldrums. Winning him over wasn't easy, as Murph wasn't going to be a charity case. But Benny wore him down, played the 'at wit's end card' with Chief Thompson and the need to relocate elsewhere. It worked. It did because Murph ran into a former colleague who bragged about getting choice assignments and who labeled Fidalgo as a "pariah." That Murph couldn't accept, for Fidalgo could run rings around the other detectives in the department, excluding Trish.

Securing their new office space, Benny was thrilled, more so when they received their first case. A woman in Montvale, New Jersey, with leukemia, was devastated when her husband left Mount Sinai Hospital in New York City to retrieve their car and didn't return to pick her up. To save on parking garage fees, her husband's brother, a retired fireman, arranged for him to park the car at the firehouse on 112th Street and Fifth Avenue, a half mile walk, which typically took 12 minutes. At 20 minutes, his alarmed wife texted and received no response. A camera outside a co-op building on 108th street had him walking briskly past, but he never arrived at the firehouse.

While she waited anxiously for news from New York City detectives, a friend advised her to hire a private eye, which led her to Gotcha Inc.

When Trish arrived for the Grand Opening, she couldn't believe the turnout. Spotting Murph, dressed in a gray plaid three-piece suit, with a pocket watch, she couldn't wait to catch him alone.

"What's with the get up?"

"Don't I look grand?" Murph turned three sixty.

"You look like you belong on an old movie lot."

"This was Benny's idea."

Trish greatly missed their antics and the opportunity to confer with them on cases. She had no real bond with any of the other Blacksburg detectives but refrained from making Gotcha Inc. a threesome. She had her father's genes in law enforcement and could hear him whispering to stick with increasing responsibility, steady hours, and a pension.

Catching Benny ending a conversation, she approached. "Nice duds."

"It was Murph's idea. Just went along with it."

"You guys had better get on the same page."

As he appeared puzzled, she said, "Never mind. Saw that Alfie Doolittle got twenty-five to life and Crenshaw should get the same." The FBI had discovered the yellow kayak buried behind Crenshaw's house. They also unearthed the bodies of nine women at the bison farm, five under the sycamore tree and four others scattered along the far reaches of the property.

The body under the apple tree belonged to 19-year-old Aleksandra Bosko, who had left Poland in 2008 to join an Appalachian Trail hike. What the FBI pieced together was that she left the trail in Eastern Connecticut to surprise friends in Rhode Island. While she had been warned not to hitchhike, she maintained that it would allow her to absorb more of the United States. It was the last anyone heard from her. The FBI was unable to connect her to Falcone, a rookie trooper at the time. With his actions in attempting to transfer Bosko's body, linkage to the hunting group, and of his desire to directly or indirectly kill members of the group, with Fidalgo and the FBI closing in, the outcome of his upcoming trial was clear.

"Seems like you don't give a rat's ass about what I just said?" Trish said.

"I don't. It's a Chapter I'd like to forget."

"Then what seems to be bothering you?"

"Nothing."

"Come on, out with it."

Benny volunteered that his niece continued to be a recluse, and that John and Anne were considering moving to San Diego. They had already put their Beach Pond cottage on the market. Trish didn't find that surprising, though felt a change of scenery might not be the solution.

In asking if he patched things up, he let her know that his mother had tried to mend fences at a small family gathering but "there was no warmth between us."

"Sorry to hear." Trish figured that Anne would eventually recognize that if it weren't for her brother, she wouldn't have Julie. About to say something, she blushed seeing Charlotte near with her old college boyfriend. She had invited him to the grand opening, hoping that the Foxwoods casino exec, who oversaw security there among other responsibilities, might have a need for Gotcha Inc. Her real reason for the invite: an excuse to see him. While he told her he had a conflict, she loved being played.

"Trish, I found this good-looking guy asking for you."

Though embarrassed, especially as Clark Winslow leaned in and kissed her, she introduced him as a friend.

"Friends?" Benny said, smirking.

Seeing Trish tongue-tied, Charlotte checked her husband, "Clark, you'll have to excuse him. He's a bit old-fashioned."

"I can see by the duds."

"Touche."

Addressing Benny, Clark asked if he could spare a few minutes to talk about investigatory work at Foxwoods. As Benny led him to a conference room, Trish glowed and Charlotte noticed.

"He seems like a keeper."

"I'm trying not to get my hopes up. Sorry for being so secretive."

Trish peered toward the conference room door hoping that the two hit it off. She hadn't said anything to Charlotte but things were moving along. She had snuck up to Foxwoods a few times but was reluctant yet to make an introduction in Blacksburg, especially to her daughter. With his making the trip, she felt that their relationship had moved up a notch, maybe two.

"Gotcha Inc. wasn't his priority in coming here," Charlotte said to Trish. She had approached Trish about dating, even ran a Jacobi anesthesiologist by her. But Trish wished to distance herself from her divorce.

"Let's dine soon," Charlotte suggested. "Would love to get to know him. Maybe an overnighter at Foxwoods?"

"Sounds like a plan, though are you sure your spouse can break free?"

"You know him only too well. I was just glad we were able to spend three weeks in Portugal. Turned out to be amazing, better than any other vacation for it allowed him to chill and reflect."

Trish, envious of Charlotte's tan, figured the trip not only benefitted Benny but Charlotte too. That was the point of the trip, according to Benny.

"You know what he wanted to do over there," Charlotte continued. "Walk the El Camino, the pilgrimage from Madrid to the coast of Spain."

"Really!"

"Yes, sprung that on us."

"How long does that take?"

"For some, months. Others as little as three weeks."

As Trish digested it, she felt it might do him a world of good. Then again, he'd probably focus less on the pilgrimage and more on the challenge to complete it in record time. "What changed his mind?"

"This. I could see him preoccupied with plans for the business."

Hearing laughter, their eyes landed on Murph entertaining several by the buffet line.

"This is a blessing for him," Trish said.

"My husband wouldn't have started this without him."

With Clark and Benny exiting the conference room, in good spirits, Trish was glad. "Seems like your meeting went well?"

"I educated Clark on roulette…to play number twenty-four."

Trish raised her eyes. "Didn't work for me." As Benny and Clark had spoken in confidence, Trish couldn't probe. "You and Murph must be set to do some major hiring with the space you have here."

They spent a moment casting their eyes around the large open room, with no partitions, and only two occupied desks among several. Even with 30 people chatting and eating, in small groups, the room appeared enormous.

Benny held up crossed fingers. "We may already need to offload work."

"That's impressive," Trish said. With business out of the way, Trish wanted Clark to herself. "Even though your spread looks delicious, I'm going to introduce Clark to Blacksburg cuisine."

"We have it here…straight from Munnos?"

Afraid Clark might agree to stay, Charlotte stepped in. "You guys go off. Trish, I'll bring a dish to Emma."

As Trish and Clark departed, the owner of a warehouse in Blacksburg introduced himself to Benny. Charlotte excused herself. Upon hearing his needs, Benny didn't waste a moment beckoning to Murph.

"Mr. Greaney, meet my partner, Dennis Murphy. He will be only too happy to conquer what needs conquering."

He let them be. For Benny, Greaney's project was signature Murph. While the proposal from Clark Winslow to look into the fleecing of high rollers at Foxwoods sounded appealing and worth pursuing, he was more eager to sink his teeth into finding out what happened to the woman's husband who had vanished in Harlem.

The End

ABOUT THE AUTHOR

Tim Connolly is a retired public relations executive. He has written several Benny Fidalgo detective novels, which he hopes to publish. His first two, *The Painted Turtle* and *Beyond The Beach*, are available on Amazon. Tim resides in Rockland County, New York, with his wife Anne. They have two sons, Daniel and Brian. The highlight of his week is in viewing photos/videos sent by daughter-in-law Kristen and son Brian of granddaughters Quinn and Cora.

ACKNOWLEDGEMENTS

To all who have cheered me on in my fiction writing. Top of the list: my wife and my mom.

To all my readers, especially Cathy LoBosco, Ann Marie Lee, Kate Simpson, and Jim Donnelly. I also have to express my sincere thanks for the kind feedback from my extended family, my childhood friends and the many others I've made along the way, and all those I've worked with in my public relations career. My heartfelt appreciation to the Dominican Sisters of Sparkill, NY for accepting a kid from The Bronx into St. Thomas Aquinas College and giving him the confidence to make his way.

I feel blessed. I wake up each morning, coffee in hand, and embark on a fiction writing journey for three to four hours that takes me…who knows where. As a result, I've written nine books.

Note: If anyone knows an agent who will take me on as a client, your name will move to the top of all future acknowledgement pages.

Other Benny Fidalgo novels by Tim Connolly:

The Painted Turtle

Twelve-year-old Tommy Gorman goes missing. With his mother watching his sister's softball game at the Little League complex, Tommy seeks to find his friend and is lured into the woods by a man holding a turtle. Following the softball game, neither Tommy's frantic mother nor anyone else can find him. Only thing found: a dead painted turtle. Assigned to lead the investigation, Detective Benny Fidalgo quickly gathers that the abduction was pre-planned and fears the worst after a search party discovers the grave of a murdered boy near the Little League grounds. Eager to solve his first major case, Fidalgo errs when he prematurely arrests a suspect who sues the town. Undeterred, he pushes forward…able to do so with the support of two seasoned detectives who believe their new colleague has what it takes to find the missing boy.

Beyond The Beach

After finding out she was pregnant, Deidre Esposito laid out her jewelry and wallet on her dresser and leaped head first from her third-floor dorm window. Ruling out murder, Blacksburg Detective Benny Fidalgo seeks to find out why but his police chief, uninterested in getting behind an obvious suicide, reassigns him to chasing car thieves. Defying the chief, Fidalgo finds himself pitted against Deidre's private eye uncle who is out to find the guy who wronged his niece. Aware that she hadn't been dating, Fidalgo discovers that the young woman had won a campus contest and a trip to a Caribbean resort. Believing it relevant, he travels there and identifies the individual Deidre hooked up with but not before the uncle had already done so. In the end, Fidalgo learns the awful truth…that the college senior took her life to extinguish the devil's lascivious sneer in the nightmare of nightmares.

Made in the USA
Columbia, SC
29 December 2024